For [...]
"[Da[...]
expe[...] sort of good,
solid [...] make a reader a better writer. Fleming takes
pains to demonstrate that this is not just another vampire novel,
this is a *Dark Ages* novel, and does so without lecturing us. There
are few who can do something like that."
—Michael G. William, *RPG.net*

For Dark Ages: Assamite by Stefan Petrucha
"There are quite a few twists and turns and a level of thoughtful-
ness that take this above the average vampire adventure. **Dark
Ages: Assamite** is an imaginative and gripping winner."
—Jim Brock, *Baryon Magazine*

For Dark Ages: Cappadocian by Andrew Bates
"**Dark Ages: Cappadocian** is, more than anything else, that wonderful combination of fascinating and fun. You'll be amazed at how
well the seemingly disparate ends tie together, you'll meet beauti-
fully created characters who all make sense (considering their
individual positions and needs), and you'll love the story Andrew
Bates has brought alive with his talent and humor. **Cappadocian** is
topflight vampire literature ... I can't wait for the next installment
to come out."
—Laurie Edwards, *Culture Dose*

For Dark Ages: Setite by Kathleen Ryan
"The cold, undead world of **Dark Ages: Vampire** has never seemed
so warm and alive, thanks to the storytelling of Kathleen Ryan.
[**Dark Ages: Setite** is] masterfully written ...[and] leaves us crav-
ing more."
—Johann Lionheart, *Dimensions*

For Dark Ages: Lasombra by David Niall Wilson
"Veteran author David Niall Wilson, who has been wowing me for
years with his tales of dark fantasy, [...] delivers a heart-stopping tale
of adventure and intrigue in this particularly vivid installment of the
epic **Dark Ages Clan Novel** series. *Don't miss it!* "
—J.L. Comeau, *Creature Feature*

For Dark Ages: Ravnos by Sarah Roark
"A seductive horror novel that I could not help but find attractive.
The author, Sarah Roark, managed to make the main character,
Zoë, innocent and lethal at the same time. It is a feat not easily
accomplished. ... Excellent!"
—Detra Fitch, *Huntress Book Reviews*

Dark Ages and Vampire Fiction from White Wolf

The Dark Ages Clan Novel Series

Dark Ages: Nosferatu by Gherbod Fleming
Dark Ages: Assamite by Stefan Petrucha
Dark Ages: Cappadocian by Andrew Bates
Dark Ages: Setite by Kathleen Ryan
Dark Ages: Lasombra by David Niall Wilson
Dark Ages: Ravnos by Sarah Roark
Dark Ages: Malkavian by Ellen Porter Kiley
Dark Ages: Brujah by Myranda Kalis (forthcoming)
Dark Ages: Toreador by Janet Trautvetter (forthcoming)

Other Dark Ages Fiction

Dark Tyrants by Justin Achilli & Robert Hatch (editors)
The Erciyes Fragments by C. S. Friedman
To Sift Through Bitter Ashes by David Niall Wilson
To Speak in Lifeless Tongues by David Niall Wilson
To Dream of Dreamers Lost by David Niall Wilson

The Clan Novel Saga

A comprehensive, chronological collection of the fourteen-volume
best-selling Clan Novel Series. Includes all-new material.

Volume 1: The Fall of Atlanta — foreword by Stewart Wieck;
new material by Philippe Boulle
Volume 2: The Eye of Gehenna — foreword by Eric Griffin;
new material by Stefan Petrucha (forthcoming)
Volume 3: Bloody September — foreword by Anna Branscome;
new material by Lucien Soulban (forthcoming)
Volume 4: End Game — foreword by Gherbod Fleming; new
material by Janet Trautvetter (forthcoming)

The Victorian Age Vampire Trilogy

A Morbid Initiation by Philippe Boulle
The Madness of Priests by Philippe Boulle
The Wounded King by Philippe Boulle

Also by Ellen Porter Kiley

"Tiger by the Tail" in **Demon: Lucifer's Shadow**

For all these titles and more, visit www.white-wolf.com/fiction

Ellen Porter Kiley

With additional material by
Kylee Hartman, Myranda Kalis, and David Niall Wilson

Dark ages Malkavian™

AD 1220
Seventh of the Dark Ages Clan Novels

Cover art by John Bolton. Graphic design by Becky Jollensten. Art direction by Richard Thomas. Copyediting by Snigdha Koirala and Jonathan Laden. Special thanks to Sarah Roark, for eleventh-hour editorial assistance.

ISBN 1-58846-831-3
First Edition: October 2003
Printed in Canada

White Wolf Publishing
1554 Litton Drive
Stone Mountain, GA 30083
www.white-wolf.com/fiction

What Has Come Before

It is the year 1220 and France is at war, among the living and the dead. The Fourth Crusade has given way to the Crusade against the Albigensians, pitting French and Toulousain knights and soldiers against one another. Religious ferment and political ambition go hand-in-hand, with each side calling the other heretic and unfaithful.

Camped in the Bière Forest outside of Paris is a motley band of undead pilgrims and their living companions. Many have come from as far as fallen Byzantium under the false assumption that Alexander, the ancient vampire who sits at the head of Paris's Grand Court, would welcome them. He has not, and they have suffered in battles with members of the Holy Inquisition and from internal strife.

Anatole, called a madman by some and a prophet by others, has taken up residence among these pilgrims and taken the young vampire Zoë as his ward. They recently ejected agents of the Cainite Heresy from the camp, but they remain vulnerable to attack and it remains to be seen how long Alexander (or his closest advisor, the Countess Saviarre) will tolerate the presence of vampires in his woods.

And still nothing has been heard of Malachite, the Byzantine vampire who inspired the migration to Paris. He vanished along the road, following portent in his search for the Dracon, an ancient whom he thinks can restore Constantinople to greatness.

N

Rheims

PARIS

Orléans

Tours

Poiters

F R A N C E

Bourdeax

Bayonne

Toulouse

Carcassonne

Prologue:

The Omen

**Samarkand, Empire of Khwarazm
February, AD 1219**

It was the night of the feast of Idu'l-Kabir in the 615th year after the Prophept Muhammad's *hijrah* from Mecca. As in years past on this night, Sultan Karim, elder of the Cainites of great Samarkand, held audience from his throne, a great carved seat of perfumed wood. For centuries, his fingers had lightly traced the graceful designs while he spoke his words of wisdom and command, but no longer. Now his corpse-dead fingers clutched at the armrests, driving splinters of ruined decoration deep into his unfeeling flesh. Before him stood Alam the Prophet. Many called him a madman, but tonight his words were chillingly sane.

"How does the end come?" Karim demanded.

"First, the waters dry up. Stone and metal and wood all hold fast, but flesh and bone give way. Death's riders come on ashen horses to reap all that the children of Seth have sown, and the children of Caine will be cut down like tares amid the wheat." The madman answered in a clear voice, his head unbowed, even though he had never, in hundreds of years in the golden city, stood before the sultan in his court.

Malkavian

Silence filled the hall. Administrators, servants and suppliants all stared at the seer. Some were aghast at his words, others at his temerity to give them voice, and still others made small motions of disbelief with their mouths. Yet none would dare to speak before their sultan did.

I should deny him, Karim thought. *I should have him driven from the city, or staked for the sun. If I do not, the wolves within my walls will be at my throat before any army this prophet has seen could threaten us.* But he did not speak. A sorcerer's curse had done in ten years what the ebb and flow of the centuries had not—he was numb to joy as well as pain, and now he had lost the will to survive.

"How long until our doom falls?" The sultan's voice no longer demanded: the shocked susurrus that arose from the watchers devoured all echoes of his question.

The madman shrugged expansively. "It is already in motion. There will be a sign. A broom star in the heavens, its straws red with blood, will sweep us away." The mention of the evil portent renewed the muttering among the audience.

"And what do you see for yourself, Alam?" the sultan asked. "Will you meet your end here as well?"

"I see myself transfixed as a skeletal rider thunders up on his terrible steed, my head struck from my shoulders, my body falling to ash," the madman answered.

Bemused by the passionless recitation, the sultan pressed on: "And so what will you do?"

"I will be wrong," the prophet replied. He bowed gracelessly, yet politely, and strode to one of the torches braced on the wall of the audience chamber. With great purpose he thrust his hands into the fire, and flames licked greedily up his arms.

As the madman, wreathed in flames, cavorted among his terrified audience, Karim studied the splinters in his hands with a smile. It would not be long now before his torment was at an end.

Part One:

The Woods

Chapter One

Vision and prophecy had been with Anatole as long as he could remember. Even before his death, before he assumed the Curse of Caine, the whispers of angels tickled at his ears, indecipherable murmurings of the Most High. Now, benighted and undead, his ears were sharper and fragments of the holiest songs would waft into his mind when God wished it to be so. He was long past surprise at such fragmentary revelations. He accepted them humbly and patiently.

Tonight, sitting in this windy lodge, staring at the patterns made by burns and knots in a wooden table, a new fragment came to him. An echo of the holy: *the bones of the living will save the dead.*

"It's clear, then. The entire camp must move." Bardas slammed his hand on the table, then glared at each member of the so-called council in turn.

Anatole watched from his least-honored seat at the table's foot. The table continued to rock from Bardas' blow; one leg had all but burned away when the Red Brothers attacked the camp, pulling down the huts that guarded those refugees of less station from the sun and setting fire to this very lodge that sheltered the elders. Anatole let the table rock, fascinated by the sound of wood on stone—so very like the sound of wood grating past breastbone—until Bardas' scowl verged on the apoplectic. Then, with a courteous smile, Anatole leaned forward to stop the motion with his hand. An uncomfortable silence spread over the room, marred only by the heavy breathing of the single mortal present and the quiet crackle of the small fire in the grate, which provided a thin, flickering light.

He hopes to be gainsaid, for once, for another plan of action to be put forward, Anatole thought. *He snatched Malachite's mantle of authority from the dusty ground when the Rock of Constantinople left, but he staggers under its weight. Will any of them take the burden from Bardas' shoulders?*

Helena was gone; even her vaunted marble-like skin, so precious and white, had not saved her from the churchmen's torches, impregnated with frankincense and lit with holy incantations. The smell of the frankincense, and the gritty feel of Helena's ashes, had been impossible to clean from the lodge.

Gallasyn sat to Bardas' left, a piece of lacework pressed primly against his thin nose and mouth so that, when he must inhale to speak, neither smell nor taste could give offense. *He will be no help to Bardas*, Anatole concluded. The Toreador would hang back until he recovered the stature lost when the heretics—his erstwhile allies—had betrayed the camp. *But he may yet come back to the path of the righteous, if he does not trample the seeds of faith as he grasps for temporal power.*

Yousef, so recently promoted to lead the camp's bandit horsemen when their captain Iskender fell to the Red Brothers, sat to Bardas' right. His face was an inscrutable mask at the council table, his dark eyes unconcerned but his spring-like body coiled, as tense in the chair as he was graceful on horseback. Bardas barely knew him, for all that they had crossed the continent within the same dwindling group; but Anatole and his followers spent their nights and days out among the refugees, not closed into the lodge. *The bandits have become more insular since their chieftain's passing. Poor, ill-fated Iskender; he fell into the trap that Zoë's vengeance laid for her. If Bardas pushes them too hard now,* Anatole thought, *the horsemen might pull up their tent stakes and leave us to our own devices.*

Urbien had started the night in his place before Yousef on the right, but the Gangrel had been unable to sit still. He had gone out into the night to find his scouts. *He will lead skirmishers better than anyone present, if the refugee camp is pushed to fight,* Anatole mused, *but I suspect that Baron Feroux, who trained him in*

Constantinople, did not waste many lessons on the fine art of the retreat.

Behind Anatole, Zoë stood to one side and Stephanos to the other. Bardas had been annoyed when Anatole's adopted childe and sunlight-scarred Nosferatu disciple had followed him into the lodge at the start of the meeting, but had chosen not to press the matter. *Lo how the mighty have fallen, that Bardas must offer a chair at council to a madman, and must trust to the loyalty of the Ravnos. But, now that mighty Constantinople has been laid low, his whole world might as well be turned upside down.*

Bardas turned back to the heavily breathing man trying to warm himself by the meager fire. "We're sure this is Gerasimos' man? He doesn't look familiar."

"His name is Nikodemos." Zoë had stepped up to the table with her outburst, but at a look from Anatole she took a step back and calmed her voice. "Gerasimos altered his features for safety, since he had been held prisoner at the abbey. I saw him in this guise before he left, and Gerasimos saw him—briefly—on his return."

Nikodemos nodded. "I know the proper sentry passwords," he offered. "For today it is—"

Bardas waved his recitation off. "When did they leave St.-Denis?"

"Three wains left two nights ago. They were loaded with fat-soaked wood, food and other supplies. The monks and knights had not yet ridden out when I left to bring word, but there was a great bustle of them in the abbey, with farriers brought in for the horses and squires sent running to the smithies. More knights came every day I watched. Twelve of them I counted, some wearing the crusader's cross."

"It will take at least a day for heavily loaded carts to get past Paris, between the weather and the tolls," Gallasyn ventured, his voice muffled under his bit of lace.

Ellen Porter Kiley

"The knights will ride out in time to meet the wagons before they enter the forest," Yousef said. "Alone, the wagons would be easy targets for bandits."

"And how quickly will they be able to press through the forest?" Bardas asked.

Yousef shrugged. "If they bring extra beasts for the carts, and push as fast as they can to cut short any warning we might receive, they could be here tomorrow night."

Someone sucked in a breath—a liquid, mortal noise. Anatole couldn't see who. Yousef continued unflappably. "But not before nightfall, and they know not to come at night, of course. So we can expect them here on the second day."

In the silence that fell as the room's occupants considered their precarious position, there was the sound of approaching hoofbeats, and the jingle of harness outside the lodge door. Anatole, who had not spoken since the council had taken their seats, looked up and spoke softly. "The nights grow darker for us as the moon fattens."

The door thrust open and Urbien stalked into the room, followed closely by his scout. "We should leave now. The whole camp." The words grated roughly across Urbien's tongue. "There are Lupines hunting the forest."

Overwhelmed silence was clearly not the response Urbien had been looking for. Word of these savage beasts had been known to send even the hardiest Cainite running for shelter. Said to be half-man and half-wolf, and to prize Cainite flesh above even human meat, Lupines stalked the deepest woods under the light of the moon.

Urbien hooked a chair with his leg and dragged it to the table, glaring across it at Gallasyn. "There are at least five of them, coming through the forest from the south. It's probably a war party, with that many."

"You've seen them?" Bardas asked of György, the scout, who remained standing behind Urbien.

György nodded. "Saw some. Counted tracks of others." He pulled up a mouthful of blood spittle with a harsh noise, then edged over to spew his disgust and defiance of the creatures onto the fire grate.

"Are you sure they aren't just bold, hungry wolves?" Bardas asked flatly, with no real hope in his voice for a negative answer.

"I survived my first encounter with a 'wolf.'" György wiped his chin with the back of his hand. "It's not a mistake I'd make twice."

"The Red Brothers will come first," Anatole said. Urbien and György, newly come to the discussion, refocused their attention swiftly on Anatole. "The wolves will be too late."

"How do you know this?" Bardas asked. "Do you see this?"

Anatole turned to György. "The Lupines prefer to go to war under the full moon, correct?"

György scratched at the coarse hair behind his ear. "According to legend, and my thankfully few observations."

"They will come at the rise of the full moon in two nights' time. The red monks will come by sunlight that very day to cheat them of their slaughter."

The discussion had been calm even through Urbien's loud arrival, but the gentle tones of Anatole's voice seemed to sap Bardas' reserves of inner quiet. "There will be no slaughter!" The camp leader shoved his chair back and stood in one abrupt motion. "We will leave as soon as the sun sets tomorrow."

"They will pursue us," Yousef objected tersely. "With so many of you on foot, how will we get far enough away by dawn? They can follow us night and day." Anatole did not fail to note the subtle stress the horseman placed on the word *you*. He doubted Bardas had either.

"And where will we be running to?" Gallasyn asked, with an apologetic nod of the head in Bardas' direction.

"The second question is easier than the first," said Anatole, standing. He looked to Bardas for permission to continue.

Bardas gave the Malkavian an unhappy glare, but then nodded his head sharply, giving his assent.

"Yousef, if you would send one of your riders east with Stephanos," Anatole said, indicating the Nosferatu at his side, "he is too injured yet to make the journey on his own, but he knows of a place where we can beg shelter."

"How many nights' ride?" Yousef asked.

"One, for the distance," croaked Stephanos. The crisped skin of his face cracked as he spoke. "Likely two, to find the landmarks and the place itself."

"That is not very far," Yousef said. "The Church has a long arm, and her knights all have horses."

"You yourself said we could not outrun them, Yousef, and you were right," Anatole replied. "We will have to go to ground for a time." He turned to Bardas. "Your plan to leave at sunset tomorrow seems wise. We should all go now and make what preparations we can. Have the belongings of those who died or were destroyed in the last attack spread around the camp, and gather wood to build the fires high as we leave."

"Is there anything else?" Bardas snapped.

"No, those are my only suggestions," Anatole replied, as if oblivious to Bardas' aggrieved tone.

"Then the council is adjourned. Sunset tomorrow, we leave, and anything not packed, or anyone not prepared, we leave behind."

* * *

Anatole and Zoë left the lodge just ahead of the others—Anatole's new seat was the least-honored, the one closest to the door. The others were not lingering, he noted, and of course not. Even the most callous

Cainite could be spurred into a violence of movement when their own destruction threatened. Whether they acted from their own best interests or in those of others mattered not just now, so long as they acted.

"It will only take me a few minutes to have my things together," Zoë said, at his side. It was true, he knew, and it saddened him—not because she had a right to exist in luxury, or even comfort, but because her deft hands could craft such splendid things from beautiful materials. Even in the roughness and filth of the camp, the last fine thing she had—the fabric of a gown long past repair—was transformed in ways that brought joy to the beholders. Here, a glimpse of dark blue satin as the cover of a hand-sewn book; there, in the hands of a mortal child as a dress for a carved wooden doll. Little spots of color that testified to her presence. "And your things…"

Anatole turned with a smile to meet the girl's grin, her gentle jest made nervous by the looming threat. "I have no things."

Zoë ducked her head away from his glance, her grin fading away completely. *She feels this threat personally*, Anatole realized, *and she feels responsible for this renewed assault*. Well she might, for although the girl was blameless in this—the heavens had sent her and her quest for revenge to Anatole when he had needed a mission, a focus, and in the end she had laid aside her vengeance in the service of faith—the Red Brothers would no doubt have a stake prepared just for her, a sword for the white curve of her neck.

"Have you seen Lupines before, Zoë?"

Her head snapped back up, a blood flush building in her cheeks. In her rising panic, she thought Anatole sought to lay blame for the second wave of attackers at her feet as well. "Yes, but… far from here! With the caravan. I didn't…"

Anatole shook his head. "Of course not. But you have seen them, their shape, their movements."

Zoë nodded hesitantly. "It was dark, so I could not see well. And I did not fight, I hid." Pale and blush fought across her face as she remembered the embarrassment and terror of that night.

"The fear will help you remember, Zoë. Could you build a model of one of them, a framework?"

Zoë nodded again, even more hesitantly than before. "I could, but it would take more wire than we have in the whole camp, and thick metal or wood poles… oh." She trailed into silence as Anatole chose a shovel from the row of tools leaning against the side of the lodge.

"The bones of the living will save the dead," Anatole intoned. "Gather your bundle, then find Gerasimos, and be sure that he is well fed. I will have some materials for you to work with by then. You will only have tonight to work, I am afraid, but do the best you can."

* * *

Night had fallen in Bière Forest, but the full moon's light shed its silvery glow over the small clearing that straddled the rough, rutted road. Abbot Gervèse sat with his head in his hands near the forest's edge, beside a makeshift table, a broad wooden plank balanced on two freshly cut tree stumps. The trees themselves fed the bonfire close at hand, their burning sap filling the air with thick, pungent smoke.

Sir Lionel approached, carefully brushing moss and bark from his cross-emblazoned tabard. "We will find them, Abbé. They cannot have left long before we reached that cursed place, and they can only travel by night. We will rise before dawn, and press hard. We should have them before the sun sets."

Gervèse wrenched his head from its resting spot. Sir Lionel deserved the courtesy of a direct and mature response, not the recriminations that would spill forth if he lessened his grip on his passions for even a moment. "We should have come sooner, or more quickly. I should have brought us here sooner."

The abbot had led his fellow Brothers of St. Theodosius and a complement of allies from the military orders into the camp earlier that day while the sun was high. This was the place where the damned had squatted with the living men and women under their thrall. Where Abbot Gervèse and Brother Isidro had been dragged, bundled and roped like slaughtered pigs. Where in front of his slaves and Gervèse himself, the blond vampire had stolen God's grace from Isidro and then murdered him.

The camp had been empty when they arrived. Spindly spirals of smoke still rose from the fire pits. Belongings—clothes, pots, toys, combs—were left lying beside the pale dead swaths of grass where tents had been pitched, or inside the tomb-like huts the hell-spawn had slumbered in to hide from the sun's purifying rays. They were gone, all of them. But they had left a clear trail heading east, deeper into the forest.

Sir Lionel's broad face looked serene, untroubled. Even the dancing light of the bonfire failed to give his features a sinister cast, but instead imparted a glow of ruddy health. "You chose to gather experienced fighting men, in numbers enough to finish the monsters lurking under the forest's branches for good. It will only be a matter of time, now. If we do not catch them while the sun shines tomorrow, the fires will again keep them away at night, and every day we will gain on them."

Tents now dotted the clearing like giant mushrooms—almost every yard that was not claimed by fire was now claimed by brothers' canvas. The force had pushed on as late as they could, but now they would have to leave the road. The dangers of making their way through the boulder- and root-strewn forest with only the moon's light to guide them, in addition to the ever-present danger of an ambush, a nocturnal flanking maneuver, or even the devils simply deciding to turn and fight like animals at bay, were too much for Gervèse to inflict on his men. Once the fires crackled and sang with the thin whistling of wet wood, the rest of the camp was set up in good order.

"Would it be safe to leave the wagons behind?" Gervèse asked. He looked over the busy camp, on the one hand proud of its efficiency and rough-but-efficient protection, but on the other begrudging every extra acorn's weight that might slow their pursuit.

"The trackers may be able to tell us tomorrow. If they are sure that none have split from the group to circle around us, then probably leaving the wagons would be safe. We would make much faster time without them." Nothing in Sir Lionel's voice or carriage gave away his personal opinion on the matter—he had not been asked.

"If we wait for the trackers to make that decision, we will have lost more than an hour waiting for the sun. I am not even certain a clear path can be found through rocks and fallen trees. We will have to leave them here at the road," Gervèse decided. "Those who will stay with the wagons can pack up the camp and save us that time as well."

Sir Lionel nodded his understanding, then moved to spread the word through the camp. In his wake spread muttering, most of it good-natured, some less so.

Gervèse's self-recriminations did not go undisturbed for long. Two knights brought him a strange find from the devils' camp—the only thing left there that spoke to the twisted and hellish nature of all that had happened there. In the warm ashes of one of the camp's fires, they had found a body. It was not human, nor had it crumbled away into dust like the devils sometimes did. In his hurry to follow the trail left by the fleeing hell-spawn—*Cainites*, Isidro had said they were called—Gervèse had ordered this new body to be wrapped in a tarp and tossed into one of the wagons.

Now, the knights brought it to him and placed it on the table. Or half of it, at least—the half with a cruelly pointed muzzle and long arms ending in dagger-clawed hands.

"Our apologies, Abbé," said one of the knights, as both bowed low. "The… body was jarred about in the wagon, and the wrappings came loose. It was held together by very little when we first lifted it."

The knights turned and went back, Gervèse supposed, for the other half. "What in God's name is this thing?" he murmured. He lifted the shoulders of the thing to bring the head into the light, and found it curiously light. One knight alone could have carried it, if they were not being so cautious. The bones felt strangely slick, and in places looked as if they had been pulled and twisted by some monstrous force. The skeleton was only loosely held together, its ligaments rotting away, but little tags of skin and flesh still hung about the tortured joints. "Surely this is a demon from Hell itself. Where else would a creature encounter such torments?"

Isidro's death was still a fresh, open wound; moments like this grabbed at the edges of that wound and worried it until it bled. Isidro would have some idea of what this was, he would have seen it in a book somewhere, or remembered an old tale from his travels. He would know what its presence in the camp meant, or he would guess in his educated way, and his guesses were sound. But instead, Gervèse stood alone in the forest beside the burned and dismembered body of a demon.

The knights approached again, carrying the lower half of the body. They placed it on the table, arranged it as best they could although their disgust at the task showed clearly, then left the abbot to study the creature alone.

"The head looks like a dog's," said Sir Lionel.

Gervèse startled. He had not heard the knight approach over the roar of the fire—*and I am distracted by mourning for Isidro*, Gervèse thought. He snorted laughter, with tears gathering in his eyes. Were Isidro here, he would be distracted from following the Cainites by this creature's body. If they had not killed him, perhaps the monks would have slackened in their chase. If they hadn't killed him, there might be no chase.

"Abbé?"

"I am sorry, Sir Lionel. What was it you said?" Gervèse put aside his mourning for a more appropriate time, and turned back to the body at hand.

"The head looks like a dog's. I have had the misfortune to see many hunting dogs killed, and many bodies of men and animals left unburied on the field. It's the size of a horse's head," Sir Lionel added, "but shaped more like a dog's."

"I will defer to your judgment, good knight, as it has been many years since I spent any time working in the monastery's larder or pens." Gervèse moved down the table to inspect the corpse's feet—one of which was missing. "The foot structure is strange. It would not walk like a man but, again, like a dog?"

Sir Lionel moved around the table, so as not to block his own light. "I believe that is correct. The heel is pulled up, the weight put on the toes."

"Interesting. In the lands of the Pharaohs, there are drawings of creatures with the heads of black dogs, but they walk like men. I have heard tales of wolves that take the shape of men," Gervèse paused, tapping at his temple as he thought. "But I have seen nothing drawn or painted in that style. And if these," he indicated the clawed fingers, "are hands, then this is less like a man than an upright dog. Or wolf," he added.

In the distance, a lone howl sounded. Around the fires, Gervèse could see many men frozen, as the ancient fear of wolf seized their muscles. Sir Lionel stared across the table at him; then the knight's hand went to his sword. Just as quickly, the rest of the camp began to move again, with some laughter and jesting thrown up against the fear and the blackness underneath the trees.

Sir Lionel had not relaxed his grip on his sword's hilt. "I fear that tonight we may learn all that you wish to know, Abbé. Perhaps more."

Gervèse did not doubt for an instant—the knight was not a man with any sort of fancy about him. The abbot turned and walked toward the center of the small camp, singing a hymn of protection. There were those who called the Red Brothers of St. Theodosius black sorcerers in monk's garb, but Gervèse thought that no one in the clearing would begrudge his brothers and him their holy arts tonight. He motioned the other monks to him.

Sir Lionel barked out a call to arms. Many of the knights had at least the time to grab their weapons before a sentry's agonized scream filled the air, and the night dissolved into a whirlwind of fire and prayer, of bloodied claws and fierce yellow eyes.

Chapter Two

"Anatole. Get up, Anatole. We have to leave here quickly. Open your eyes, please. Anatole!"

The pleading voice—Zoë's voice—finally penetrated Anatole's consciousness. He sat straight up; the blanket, snowy dirt and leaf litter that had covered him for the day had already been cleared away. "I dreamed of a burning bush," he said. "As full of dread as Moses was, I fear that I far surpassed him."

Zoë's face wore a worried frown; she had been afraid, he guessed, that he had drifted back into the long sleep from which he had so recently arisen. As he spoke, the frown melted away, and a broad grin took its place. She pointed to something behind Anatole's shoulder. He turned; there, at the head of his resting place, was a holly tree covered with red clusters of berries.

Anatole's answering grin was sheepish. "That's some comfort. I had been dreading the arrival of a pillar of flame. I did not think I could convince anyone to follow it."

Zoë stood, shaking clean the woolen blanket that had covered him. Her humor ebbed away as the mood of the makeshift camp reasserted itself. "So long as it did not lead back west, I think they might. They're scared, Anatole."

Nightfall could not have come quickly enough for the beleaguered refugees. Anatole was the last Cainite to rise; the others had all scrabbled out of their shallow trenches as soon as the sun's orb dipped below the horizon. Now they stood in small clutches around the boulder-strewn forest, whispering, looking back to the west. The dying embers of the fires that the mortals had lit to ward off winter's chill provided some warmth to the brave; others, despite long years of privation since fleeing the ruin of Constantinople, could not bring themselves to stand so near a fire not restrained by hearth or grate, but only by a ring of bare earth between the heat and an inferno of burning trees. Bundles, handcarts and wheelbarrows were close to hand, the few necessities of undying existence shoved into the spaces among the last hoarded treasures of the golden city.

Zoë added the blanket to her bundle, which Anatole picked up as he had the night before, again despite her protests. Zoë would have enough to carry, he knew—someone else's things, or one of the few remaining living children, born to the refugees or stolen from some poor village. The children were frightened of him, except on the rare occasions that he remembered to cut the matted blood from his hair.

"Some of the captives tried to run during the day." Zoë steered him toward one of the piles of glowing coals. Beside it were two bound men, sagging limply against the ropes that tied them back-to-back, and one woman. She was not restrained, but lay weeping weakly by the dying fire. All three showed the marks of teeth at their necks and wrists. "One of them is missing. He slipped away while the riders were running these three down. Urbien said that it was too great a risk to bring these three any further. So we've all…" Zoë turned her face away from the dying, or already dead, men.

"Have you taken your part of their blood, Zoë?" Anatole asked gently.

"I have," she answered, her voice tight.

"Did you take the last drink?" he pressed, but cautiously.

"No." Zoë still could not bring herself to look at the bodies of the two men, still balanced upright.

"Good." Anatole felt keenly the years he had spent slumbering among the roots of the forest, his body and soul pressed into the earth by the great crushing weight of the will of God. For him, the time had been bittersweet: all around him were the voices of angels, and some few blessed times they spoke to him, or spoke to each other in words that he could understand; but he knew at the same time that the world was moving without him, that Zoë, whom he had taken as his charge before Cainite prince and God, was suffering for his absence. She had never been taught by her sire how to hunt for herself, how to feed judiciously and thus keep the Beast from lashing out. *How ironic that she must learn these things from me, who had less time with his sire than she. Still,* he thought, *perhaps in this way my own stumbles and errors when new to the blood earn their redemption.* To kill, though, to still a beating heart with her hunger—for whatever reason, even as punishment for the most terrible crime—that would be too much for her now.

"We will all need their strength," he continued. "Even if we reach our safe place, there will be lean times ahead. And, since even we do not know our destination tonight, there is no way the man who escaped can betray us." Anatole pushed a lock of hair aside from the nearest man's forehead, and lightly touched a spot of sweet-smelling oil. "Gerasimos gave them the *sacramentum exeuntium?*"

Zoë nodded.

"And I was the last to rise, so I am the last to feed."

Zoë nodded again, once, curtly, then left the fireside. Anatole studied the weeping woman. He was sure that, somewhere on her thin frame, there was a scrap of Zoë's dark blue kindness. He did not search her for it.

Anatole knelt in the snow beside the woman, and lifted her gently by the shoulders. She shuddered in his grasp. "Where would you flee to, in this bitter cold?" he asked.

The woman's sobs slowed into pained laughter. "The only direction I knew. Back the way we came. I left myself a trail in the snow."

Ellen Porter Kiley

"And why did you run?" Anatole asked. The woman's skin felt cold even to his hands.

"The red monks were coming. I wanted to be saved," she whispered.

"Do you worship Almighty God? Do you believe in His son, Jesus Christ? Have you felt the breath of the Holy Spirit move across your soul?" Anatole folded back the edge of the woman's headscarf and touched his thumb to the smear of blessed oil left from Gerasimos's rites.

"Yes, Frère! I believe," she gasped. Her eyes fluttered open wide; flakes of snow blew onto them and only slowly began to melt.

"Then you were saved already," he said simply. The woman's eyes closed, and a look of peace settled over her worn face. Anatole fastened his teeth into her neck and drained away the rest of her life.

Anatole laid the woman's body to rest where he had dreamed, at the foot of the holly bush. He cut the ropes that fastened the two men; others came to him and took the bodies to other cold graves where undead flesh had hidden from the sun. These others, his new disciples, had followed the heretic Folcaut; then Folcaut was destroyed—worse, discredited, his faith proved weak when put to the test against the Red Brothers. Now these reformed heretics followed Anatole, but their faith was green and untested. *How long will I have this time? How long do I have to bring them securely into the fold, before I find the road beneath my feet once more?*

His attention fell again on Zoë. *She is so strong,* he thought. When he had slipped into torpid slumber, abandoning her and the camp for years, she had kept faith. She had rejected the Heresy and its seductive lies. So many of her fellows had fallen for Folcaut's honeyed words. They'd been willing, even eager, to believe that Cainite blood was somehow holier than that of mortals. That Caine had not been cursed and tested by God, but inhabited by Him. That Jesus Christ *was* Caine. Zoë had rejected all that for the harder truth that to keep faith with Caine, vampires must look to him for lessons, not benediction. Caine might be a teacher, a father, and even a judge of his people—but never a messiah.

Yousef rode into the camp, thundering through the milling vampires, and breaking Anatole from his reverie. The bandit's horse spat foam and leapt nimbly over or around the now-emptied trenches. "Yes, leave these great festering holes all around. Maybe a knight's horse will break a leg," Yousef called. "It isn't as though we can hide your trail; leave the digging and move!"

Anatole left the gravediggers and went to stand by Yousef's stirrup. "The dead must be laid to rest," he said, "but it will be accomplished quickly."

Other riders pulled up around the camp. Yousef called out to them in the coarse pidgin tongue the bandits used among themselves—a warning, Anatole guessed, about the great festering holes. "You should be far from here, or at least moving," Yousef insisted. "Where's Bardas? Or Urbien? Does anyone actually lead this lot anymore? They wander like unattended sheep."

Anatole shrugged apologetically. "I was late waking. What about the weather? Will there be new snow to cover our trail?"

Yousef made some small disgusted noise; Anatole could not be certain whether it was directed at him, or the sky. "Not a flake," Yousef said. "We've ridden back and forth across the trail, sent riders off into streams, and disguised our numbers as best we can. They'll be wary of an ambush. But there's no hiding this trail. They'll follow it right to us—the only question is how careful they will be."

Yousef's mount snorted foam and bloody mucus; its flanks shuddered. With only that small warning, the horse reared up, dumping the unprepared bandit chief to the forest floor. Yousef cursed, and the horse bolted into a thicket of saplings. The raucous laughter of the other horsemen was cut short as their own mounts began to sidestep and buck. Another rider lost his seat, another horse bolted into the darkness. Fear spread among the refugees; some clutched their bundles and tried to run, others pressed toward the imagined safety of the crowd.

Yousef sprang from the snowy, hard turf to go after his horse with murder in his eyes. Anatole scrambled to bar the way, grabbing at the horseman's arm. "Wait, wait! Listen!"

In the distance, at the edge of hearing, rose a thin canine howl. It was joined by another voice, and another—not the thin cry of a lonely wolf, but the fierce baying of a winter predator.

"Lupines! They've found our trail! They're coming after us!" someone shouted. There were muffled screams, strangled shouts from the refugees; in many, the Beast was close to the surface, displayed by flashes of ivory fang and the rank miasma of blood sweat.

"No!" barked Yousef. "They aren't coming after us. They're too far away." He stepped back from Anatole, who released his hold on the bandit chief's arm. "They've found something else to hunt."

Anatole turned toward the refugees, his arms spread wide in a gesture of benediction. "Brothers and Sisters, children of our Dark Father and children of Seth! Set aside fear. The sound you hear is not our doom. It is the sound the Israelites heard as the sea closed behind them, sweeping away those who dared to threaten harm to the Lord's chosen. The sea that closes behind us is red; red robes, red blood." Anatole walked back to the graveside where he had left his bundle. Lifting it to his shoulder, he turned to the east. "We cannot wait, as Moses did, for the bodies of the Egyptians to wash up on the shore. Exile awaits us once more. Let us go now, rejoicing in God's mercy."

Bardas took the refugees in hand then, and led them through the forest. Yousef looked long and hard at Anatole, before leaving with the other bandits to go after the horses. As the crowd thinned into a wandering line snaking its way through the forest, Zoë rejoined Anatole where he stood, staring at the holly berries, bright red against the dark leaves and white snow.

"I wonder now," Zoë said, "how often is a miracle simply a plan that worked?"

The tone of her voice was teasing, but his was solemn in reply. "Always, Zoë. The question is only: Whose plan?"

* * *

The refugees had walked for hours in the cold darkness. Last night, when they left the spare comforts of their camp behind, fear drove them, keeping their feet moving along the winding path through boulders and trees. Now that the danger was supposedly past and the fear gone, a different mood came to snap at their heels and worry at the backs of their minds. The camp had been rough and uncivilized, being forced to exist there an embarrassment; but the camp was theirs, and it provided more security than they had found anywhere on the long road from Constantinople. There was murmured encouragement to be heard: "Not far now." "They say we'll reach safety before sunrise." But all it had taken was a second night on the road to allow the overwhelming despair of the pilgrimage to Paris to trickle back into their minds, and the encouragements sounded hollow.

The forest floor was everywhere littered with boulders, but as the refugees plodded east, the ground grew rockier, the path more broken. An outcropping of stone half the height of the surrounding trees loomed out of the darkness. Without conscious thought, the refugees in front of the ragged line paused, then milled around in front of the outcropping, unsure of their path, their white faces in the moonlight like the foamy tops of waves broken against unyielding rock. The mortal refugees gathered around those of their number carrying torches, those Cainites who likewise needed the light to see forming a second, uneasy ring around them. The outriders, brought in through whistles and calls, trotted their mounts up the edges of the group, shepherding the last stragglers into the crowd.

"Where do we go from here?" "Is this the place? Where will we sleep?" "How long until dawn?" "Have we come far enough?" The whispered questions increased in frequency and agitation as the crowd cast about at the base of the rock; then the whole night went still as a powerful voice, richly familiar to many of the wanderers, rang out in flawless Greek:

"Children of Constantinople! Children of the Dream!" Atop the outcropping, a hunched and disfigured body shimmered into view. "I have come among you to bring you into my home, to offer you shelter in your time of need." The figure's voice cracked now, and lost its unearthly resonance. "But first, you must forgive me, for it was by my voice you were led astray."

The crowd pulled away from the base of the rock, craning their heads upward for a better view. The crouched figure stepped off the edge of the rock, landing heavily in the cleared space in the center of the crowd. The torchbearers held their flames high, the moon slipped free of a dark bank of cloud; the face of Malachite, Rock of Constantinople, was illuminated in unwavering silver and flickering red.

Vampires crowded forward, eager to touch Malachite's robe, or his hands, even his ravaged face. Many mortals among the refugees, those who had made the long journey from the blessed city, fell to their knees, seized by their old customs of reverence. Malachite stood among the throng for long minutes, embracing travelers, grasping their hands, allowing himself to be seen and felt and heard. Every Cainite

Malkavian

from his golden city, even every mortal who had tasted vitae within its walls, he knew them all by name. When the crowd had satisfied itself that Malachite was truly present among them, he left its embrace, and came to stand before the camp's gathered elders.

Malachite looked around the faces, solemn and frowning. "There are fewer here than I had hoped. And many of your number are missing. Have so many perished?"

Gallasyn took a stumbling step forward, then fell heavily to one knee before Malachite to kiss his hand, which Malachite allowed. There was a light of adoration in Gallasyn's face—a light that those who had joined the pilgrimage since Malachite's departure had never before seen. "Those of the highest station and the most hoarded influence left us to make their own way, or to claim shelter from those indebted to them. Those who were brought to the lowest have been lost. What remains before you are those stranded in the middle, we who were too weak to lay claim to a place of our own, but too faithful and proud to give up."

Malachite laid both hands on Gallasyn's head in a brief blessing, then took his shoulders and raised him up from the ground.

"Urbien. I have no word of your baron and his war, I am afraid. Verpus left my company to return to him long ago, and I have heard nothing more of either of them." Urbien nodded impassively, but respectfully, in reply.

Malachite looked up at Yousef, who still sat his mount. "You also have the look of a Turk. Do you lead this band of cavalry?"

"We are bandits here, thieves in the night, not cavalry." Yousef bowed from his saddle. "But if the Rock of Constantinople wishes to make war, my bandits will take up banners."

"Bardas, have you not returned to your Senate?"

"No, Malachite." Bardas' words sounded squeezed, as if voiced with too little air. "I have taken responsibility for this gathering, and I will stay here among them until a rightful place is made for all of us, as you yourself promised it would be, and Hugh of Clairvaux vouchsafed."

"You lead, then?" Malachite's voice was bland, his question innocent.

Bardas straightened his shoulders and met Malachite's eye. "I do. I took over your authority when you left the pilgrimage at Zara. Your authority, of course, is yours to reclaim at will."

"Of course," Malachite nodded, but said no more. He came at last to Anatole.

"You have returned to the pilgrimage, I see. Tell me, did we move too slowly for your travel-hardened feet?"

"It was not the speed of the pilgrimage but its direction. The Lord called me to serve in the wild places of Dalmatia. The Bogomils are quite strong in the hills there."

"And are they still strong there, after your time among them?"

Anatole shrugged expansively. "I cannot hope to know the full impact of my actions there. I did as I was called to do, no more, and I prayerfully hope no less."

"Indeed, that is all any of us can hope for."

Malachite turned now to address the full gathering. "It lifts my heart to see all of you here, and I grieve for the losses so recently suffered. We will lead you now to a place of refuge." At his words, other misshapen, tortured figures stepped into the light, or shimmered into view at the edge of the crowd. "It is not very far off. The Knights of St. Ladre will lead you in smaller groups on different paths, so that the marks of your passing can be more easily hidden."

As the knights began dividing up the refugees, Malachite turned back to the shabby council. "Spread yourselves among the groups, if you will. The knights, and your own people, will be reassured should they harbor any doubts." After a moment's consideration, he added, "Anatole, will you walk with me?"

"Whenever you wish, Malachite."

Anatole motioned for Zoë, and together they followed Malachite's hulking form deeper into the forest.

* * *

They walked in silence for some time. "What I cannot say to them," Malachite began abruptly, the *langue d'oïl* of Northern France harsh in his mouth, "is that there was no room for them in this safe place of mine, until so many of them were destroyed. And too, that there were those among them that I would not allow to sit on the road outside my door, let alone into a place of secrecy and strength." Malachite stopped walking, and turned to face Anatole and Zoë. "Why does the childe of Gregory Lakeritos follow you, Anatole, in the guise of an empty-handed waif? Would you have me speak so frankly before her?"

Anatole answered in his heavily accented Greek. "I have adopted her as my childe. The Wonder-Maker was one of the many unfortunate pilgrims to fall into the hands of the Church's hunters." Zoë took this opportunity to snatch her bundle from Anatole's shoulder; she clutched it to her chest as she watched Malachite with wide eyes. Anatole chuckled. "It is not she who comes to you empty-handed, Malachite, but I."

"A Wonder-Maker's hands would never be truly empty." Malachite studied the girl's face. "You shouldn't be surprised that I remember you. Your sire Gregory was held in great esteem. I am sorry for your loss—it is a loss to all of us."

"Thank you," Zoë said.

Malachite turned back to his path, continuing along his prior line of thought. "Stephanos has told me much of what happened between you and Folcaut, and of his betrayal of the refugees to the Church's inquisitors. Are the heretics truly purged from among you?"

"I believe so. Those who most strongly favored their blasphemy left the pilgrimage long ago. Many were lost to the Heresy in Adrianople, even though neither Calomena nor her Chosen haunted the streets. I was not the only Cainite to wander off as we crossed Dalmatia, though others did not do so for as noble a purpose. When they crossed into Languedoc, so weary from their trials, I do not doubt that still more souls were lost among the Cathars. Wherever mortal heresy and schism dog the Church, there our own heretics flourish."

"And when they reached Alexander's gates, he refused to admit them to his city."

Anatole nodded. "Desperation feeds the Heresy as well. It is a far easier view of the world to consider yourself a god among men, than a servant of God. Such a blow, to lose Michael's Dream, and then to lose the dream of Paris as well…." Anatole paused there, pacing his steps to bring him even with Malachite. "What of your journey? What drove you away from your own pilgrimage?"

Malachite's ruin of a face remained impassive. "I do not share your gift, Anatole. God does not speak to me; I have no visions. Nor had I ever wanted them. God spoke through the Dream, the Dream spoke to Michael, and Michael spoke to me. That was blessing enough."

They walked on in silence, Malachite stricken by some sadness, Anatole patiently waiting. Zoë tried her best to match their larger strides so that not even her footsteps would be heard.

"When Michael began to drift away from us, and I found I needed guidance, I had to look outside myself. I have been seeking out oracles. That is why I left them at Adrianople, and again at Zara."

Anatole chose his next words with caution. "These oracles, their visions—from whence do they come?"

"I do not know," Malachite replied sharply. "I am not so far lost in my quest that I am unwary; I will not bind the infernal to the service of the Dream."

"These visions then, are they true?"

"They have been accurate, yes. But it seems these visions, for which I pay the price, are more helpful to others than to me."

Anatole heard the sorrow that welled up in Malachite's words. *What price has he had to pay? What price will he yet have to offer up in ransom for Michael's Dream?* "And what is your course now?"

"I await a sign." Malachite said wryly, the sadness hidden deeply away once more. "This is something I have learned about oracles and visions: that their symbolism tends to remain impenetrable until the moment is upon you. When the moment arrives and my sign comes, I will follow it. But until then," he gestured as they came around the side of a particularly large boulder, "I will share this place with you." Malachite sighed. "All of you."

Before them yawned a vast grotto, half again as tall as the boulder from which Malachite had hailed them—sapling trees at the edges of the surrounding clearing did not crest its height. The rock shelf that covered it was more than twice as wide as it was tall, curving down at its edges. When the moon hid and only torches lit the night, it looked like a vast mouth devouring the earth with sharp teeth of rock.

Zoë looked at the cave dubiously. "It's big, but will that shelf keep out the sun?"

"No, it will not," Malachite answered agreeably. "It doesn't need to. There are tunnels that extend back into the ground from the rear wall. The rock lies in layers, some of it relatively easy to dig. We've expanded two chambers since we came here; the knights have removed their belongings to the smaller one, and the refugees will fit into the larger. It will be crowded," he snorted in amusement at his own understatement, "but those who find themselves less than comfortable can dig."

They stood under the massive shelf now. Even from here, the tunnels in the recesses of the grotto were almost impossible to see; the Nosferatu had put some care into camouflaging the entrances with scree and boulders. "The mortals will do well enough, for now, setting up their tents and fires in here, out of the wind," Malachite continued. "They can build huts in the clearing once we're sure the churchmen are no longer combing the forest for the lot of you. Stephanos said that you foresaw no pursuit. Is that true?"

"It is true," Anatole grinned, "but I will not know that it is not correct, perhaps, until the moment is upon us."

Seeing that Malachite was not amused, Zoë interjected, "We heard the Lupines set upon the Red Brothers. Or at least we think we did. It was far off."

"The further away, the better," Malachite said. "That is not a match I'd care to meet the victor of."

"The survivor of," Anatole observed. "Though I fear, in the long run, the holy brothers will prove ever more dangerous."

They stood together under the great stone teeth of the cave's mouth and watched as the knights led the small bands of refugees into its shelter. There was some consternation initially, until the refugees were directed to the tunnels in the rear. Then there was a period of frustration. The tunnels were so tight that it was impossible for two to pass in opposite directions. Zoë ducked behind Anatole's shoulder to hide her amusement at watching Gallasyn lower himself on hands and knees into the tunnel, only to be forced to crawl out backwards as a knight and his charges emerged.

"Will you laugh every time you see him crawl, Zoë?" The words were a rebuke, but Anatole's soft voice was full of humor.

"No, I won't," Zoë admitted. "But I might the first few times." Then she sighed. "I get the feeling I'll be sewing a lot of patches."

"Undoubtedly. Perhaps you had better try the tunnel yourself now, to find a place for us in there."

Zoë nodded, and taking her bundle with her, disappeared down the tunnel's throat.

Anatole waited until Zoë's feet slipped out of view, then turned to Malachite. "This camp cannot last for long either."

"Is it the hunters you fear, among wolves and men?"

"Not only the hunters—though they are no small worry. I fear for our souls, and the souls of the living among us." Anatole turned to watch the mortal refugees put up their spare shelters against the cold. Roaring fires blossomed in the darkness of the grotto. "It is not wise for Cainite and kine to exist so closely, to wed unlife so intricately to these few men and women. The children of Caine have fallen into sin in this way before, with whole cities to dwell in. Will we find it easier than they, or harder, in burrows and tents?"

"The first cities did not fall within the lifespan of a man. Your flock will be strong enough. They will survive."

"Will you lead them? I cannot. I am a prophet. I bring chaos and unrest to the foolish and wicked. I am no fit prince for Cainites, and I am no fit shepherd for the souls of men."

"I will not lead them. Let Bardas keep the authority he has gleaned for himself from the rows that I planted. When my quest calls I will leave again, and again, I will not stop to be sure the camp's affairs are in order." Malachite looked out over the cloth tents, shabby with use, and the back of the cave, crawling with ant-like activity. "This is all that is left of my people. Michael's people. It is their quest too, whether they know it or not."

Anatole turned his piercing gaze on Malachite. "You want something from me."

Malachite nodded curtly. "I need your sight. We have been here for years now, largely in hiding, digging in the dirt like rats. I begin to fear that I have missed my sign, that it came and went in the night while I scurried around under the earth."

"The sight is not something I command, Malachite. I can invite it, but the visions come in God's time, not ours. And even so, we have that advantage over mortal men."

"I understand, but I am tired. I am soul-weary of hunting after oracles. I have more faith in a vision that is sent to you, Anatole, than one that I must wrench from unwilling lips."

"What is the sign you are waiting for?"

Malachite reached inside his robes and drew something from a hidden pocket with great care. He held it out to Anatole, relinquishing it into Anatole's palm with some small, unconscious hesitation.

Anatole stared intently at the fragment of ivory that rested in his hand. On it was painted with exquisite skill the image of Christ ascendant, his face lifted towards heaven, his head haloed in luminous gold. "What is this?"

"It is a fragment of an icon found in the ruins of Constantinople."

"Who is this?" Anatole held the broken piece with the nervousness of a child who has caught a particularly large spider.

"Is it not the face of Christ?" Malachite asked blandly.

"No… and yes. It is meant to be Jesus Christ, I can see that. But something is wrong. What is it that is not right?" Anatole raised the piece of ancient bone, bringing it closer to his eyes. He felt the rough edges, where the rest of the image had broken away. As he brought the icon still closer to his face, searching the surface for meaning, the smell rising up from the white tile seized his nostrils and woke his slumbering Beast.

"Blood!" Anatole wrenched himself away from the icon, holding it out at arm's length. He felt his fangs shudder loose from his jaw. "It reeks of blood… and not mortal blood. Vitae, powerful vitae. Take it! Take it back!"

Malachite snatched the piece from Anatole's hand and held it up to his own nose. "It smells of bone."

Anatole shook his head, his eyes wide and staring. "What Cainite is that, painted as our Lord and Savior?"

"It is the Dracon. It is he whom I seek."

"Did he see himself thus?"

"No! Nor did Michael envision himself an archangel at the front of the heavenly host. Yet he allowed himself to be painted in that fashion, knowing that the artist would otherwise be unable to capture even a fraction of the Patriarch's glory, unable to conceive of such unearthly glory without a guide. That part of the tile fell to fragments; this part survives. It is the Dracon I seek, the Dracon who can restore the Dream."

Anatole could not tear his eyes from the tile in Malachite's hand; it commanded his attention, like a viper's sinuous dance.

"Like your oracles," Anatole said after a while, "I have a price as well." The Malkavian smiled reassuringly as Malachite turned a baleful look at him. "It will not cost you more than the rest of tonight's moonlight." He went to his knees on the hard, rock-strewn ground. "I have not been shriven by a confessor since I left the pilgrimage so long ago. My sins weigh heavily on my soul. Will you hear them for me, Malachite?"

Chapter Three

Abbot Gervèse leaned heavily on his staff as he walked down the row of merchants' stalls, trying to reach the road to the abbey. It was the Lendit Fair and the lands of the great Abbey and Basilica of St. Denis were brimming with activity. The basilica sheltered the tombs of several French kings along with the relics of the St. Denis himself, and the abbey was among the leading religious institutions in Ile de France. Gervèse's own Theodosian Abbey, much more humble, rose in he shadow of its big brother, and it was that mighty church's protection that Gervèse often credited with the allowances made to his Red Brothers and their unorthodox methods in fighting Satan on earth. Come fair time, however, Gervèse and his brothers were expected to help manage the crowds and merchants for the common good.

The sun had already set, but still some stalls were open, most often those belonging to the foreign traders who brought silk, leather and spices from far away lands. Other merchants had covered their goods with tarps, and then pitched small tents for themselves, to spend the night in wine-fueled merriment while guarding their goods until morning. The taverns and cook shops in town did a rousing business, since everyone here had coin in hand. Minstrels and whores roused business as well, for the same reasons. *A perfect hunting ground for the bloodsucking Cainites*, Gervèse thought. *And the abbey gathers in its profits*.

St.-Denis had extended its hospitality to as many important visiting personages as it could possibly fit within the abbey's walls, and a few others were hosted among the Theodosians. That was where Gervèse should be right now, playing the good host among the minor nobles and churchmen, discussing the grave reports from the crusade in the south or, perhaps, hearing rumors of the king's health. Instead, he wandered through the fair grounds after dark as he had every night for the last ten, since the opening of the fair. Every Red Brother who could be spared from other duties did the same, along with several poor knights who had come at Gervèse's request. *Even with the knights, our numbers are too few,* Gervèse thought. *They have been too few since that terrible night under the moon in Bière Forest.* The Red Brothers had recruited as heavily as possible following the tragedy, but the Brothers themselves were spread thin as teachers. And, even with all the theological schools in Paris to search through, finding men with faith, courage and intelligence in the proper measures was still a difficult task.

Perhaps I should reconsider the abbess's offer to send the Red Sisters to help us keep watch, he thought. *But only to watch.* Gervèse winced as he stepped clear of a man carrying two large bundles. The abbot had forgotten his disguise as a common cleric; without his robes and ring, no one would step aside for him. His leg still troubled him even though two years had passed since the bite, but he hadn't needed a cane or a staff for months, until the strain of walking the fair day and night proved too much. *Without the excellent care provided by the Sisters, how many more of us would have died from our wounds?* Gervèse thought. *I would not have the Sisters brought into harm's way if I can avoid it.*

Gervèse finally gained the roadway and turned himself toward the abbey. Even more stalls along the road were still open, as the merchants tried to use their prime location to advantage by luring departing customers into making one last purchase. Gervèse banged his staff on the wooden frame of the first booth he came to. "Stalls are to close at sundown!" he shouted. Even in his plain brown robes, Gervèse's voice rang with an authority earned through hundreds of sermons; the stall's occupant hurriedly began to cover his wares.

Malkavian

The flurry of closing activity traveled up the roadway like a ripple in a stream, as Gervèse continued toward the abbey, banging his staff where necessary to punctuate his exhortations to close up shop. A saddle painter who could not be rid of a drunkenly appreciative customer smiled gratefully at Gervèse, who chivvied the drunk up onto the road and toward home. A spice merchant's wife grabbed the last of her three children by the collar and lifted him into the back of a cart, where the young ones would ride back to Paris surrounded by fragrant packages and bundles. In the booth beyond that, a seller of silks hurriedly finished a transaction with a young girl in a hooded robe, exchanging a few silk ribbons for a small coin. The girl flinched when the merchant blew out his candle.

Gervèse hurried a few steps forward, not bothering to use his staff. Beneath the hood he could glimpse dark hair, and dark eyes. The girl's cloak shifted slightly as she tucked the handful of ribbons into the bodice of her dress. He saw her face—a face that was in every single nightmare he had suffered through in the last two years.

"*Her*," he hissed. Clutching at his staff with both white-knuckled hands, Gervèse moved to follow the hooded girl.

"She is only buying ribbons. Where is the harm in that?"

Gervèse whirled around. Standing there, less than an arm's length from him, was the blond monster who had murdered Isidro. He had sunk his teeth into Isidro's neck, and worn the crimson stains of Isidro's blood like a pilgrim's badge. There was dried blood still in the locks of his hair, and fresh smears on his lips. Gervèse planted his staff firmly before him, then reached for the chain of religious medals tucked into his belt.

Just as his fingers brushed the chain, the creature moved like a striking asp, fastening one hand above and one below Gervèse's on the staff. "Do you truly wish to do this here, Abbé? Which of us will be Jacob, if we are to wrestle?" the thing whispered, his urgent tones pitched for Gervèse's ears alone. "Look around. Would you have all these people learn what hunts the night? Will you destroy their innocence?"

Gervèse listened to the rustle and clatter of the fair all around him. One of the spice merchant's children began to sing in the back of their cart, a lullaby to send her brothers to sleep. His scarred leg pulsed with warm pain, as if the jaws that had savaged him were closing again on his thigh. With a grimace, Gervèse lowered his hand from his belt. "You destroy innocence every time you prey on the living," he snarled. The hooded girl of his nightmares disappeared into the darkness further down the road.

The blond Cainite stepped back, lifting his hands from the staff and raising them in a gesture of appeasement. He spoke again, his voice still quiet. "I do not seek out the innocent. There are more than enough worldly people to feed from."

"How dare you come here? Within sight of the walls of my own abbey!" Gervèse threw his staff to the ground, as if it had been tainted by the creature's mere touch.

"My name is Anatole," he offered with a gentle smile.

While Gervèse stood stunned by this naïve effrontery, Anatole continued. "We came so that Zoë could buy her trinkets. A hundred years of the selling of trinkets has built a most beautiful abbey. Do you not ever worry, though, that its spires reach for heaven in the same manner as the Tower of Babel? Listen to the chatter of tongues around us," he mused, trailing off into silence with his head cocked, listening.

"There is blood on your face," Gervèse grated.

"You walk with a limp," Anatole replied without hesitation. "Have you still not healed the wounds the Lupines inflicted?"

50   Malkavian

"You set those wolf demons on us."

"Your curiosity brought them down on you. Would you rather not know of them?" Anatole questioned. "They are a danger to your flock just as surely as I am."

"Do not play at philosophy with me," Gervèse said. "Do you think you are here to give me some sort of lesson?"

"I would not play at philosophy," Anatole said soberly. "It is a poor plaything, all hooks and barbs. I told you why I came here. Why I *am* here, you are right, may be different." The blond monster considered for a moment. "I do not believe I am here to teach you, but perhaps you are here to learn from me."

A silence fell between them. The cart full of children was gone; the other vendors had covered or packed their things, but the voices of men and women still drifted all around. With an effort, Gervèse broke the silence. "What were they?"

"Wolf demons, as you said. Lupines," Anatole shrugged.

"How can they be destroyed, or stopped? If you truly serve God, and do not merely pretend to do so, you will tell me," Gervèse insisted.

"Do the words of the devil carry weight with you now, Abbé?" Anatole asked with mild reproof. "In any case, I cannot help you; I do not know, myself. Send the knights out to capture one, and experiment on it as they did on me. I do not doubt you will discover all you need to know. You should wear the red robes."

"What? I do."

"Tonight you do not. If you mean to protect these people, wear the red. Every Cainite in France knows by now what the red robes mean." Anatole chuckled to himself. "To us, of course, they mean blood—but ours spilled in the dusty street. There are not enough of you to keep the Cainites away from the fair, but your presence here has kept them very cautious."

"I could keep *you* away from the fair," Gervèse stated flatly.

"You could, Abbé. But would you come at me alone, or would you call to your brothers for aid? If I ran, would you give chase?" Anatole looked out across the expanse of booths and tents. "If you commit to chasing one Cainite, the others will slip in, like wolves when the shepherd leaves his flock. And some will not be content to only feed. They will kill."

"I will not have this." Gervèse whispered hoarsely. "I will not have all these Cainites creeping around in the darkness, drinking the blood of the faithful in front of the very doors of the Church."

"Indeed, in front of the counting room doors. What will you do, Abbé?" Anatole asked. "Will you close Lendit fair? Send home a thousand merchants? Who will explain to the bishops and barons where the fees and taxes have gone? The King himself will want to know what you have done. Will you stand before the throne of France and tell the King about the monsters creeping around in the darkness?"

Gervèse did not answer. There was no answer he could give.

"Abbé," Anatole said softly. "No one has died here tonight. That is your victory. Is it not enough?"

"Now you decide to tempt me with hollow victories. Do you not even have a throne to offer me?" The mocking words were dry in Gervèse's throat.

"You rule here already, Abbé," Anatole replied. "I am not here to tempt you. I think now that I am here, and you are here, because we are done. For a time, at least. He will call us to other things."

"You are right; we are done." Gervèse stooped to pick up his staff; the motion was stiffened with pain. The Cainite knelt swiftly, picked up the staff from where it lay, and proffered it to him. Gervèse took hold of it with some reluctance. "Find the girl. Leave; take her with you."

Anatole nodded, his blond locks matted with blood bobbing obscenely in the waxing moonlight.

Gervèse continued, emboldened. "Do not return here to hunt. Do not return here to seek me out. I will confront you if I find you here again, and any innocents who perish for my doing so will count against your soul, not mine."

"God will weigh my soul, Abbé, not you, and may He have mercy on us both." Anatole made the sign of the cross on his forehead with those words; Gervèse fought down a wave of nausea. "Still, I do not think I will return. We have finished the here and now. I would kiss your ring now, but you are not wearing it. If there will be another time, another place, I will give you the kiss then. Do you know what it is like, Abbé, to look for something unaware of what it is? The choirs of angels rarely sing in the tongues of men. Can you tell me, Abbé, is His will more plain to you, or is the path just as narrow?"

"Go." Gervèse slammed the butt of his staff into the ground.

The thud jolted the blond Cainite violently from his reverie. He stepped back, confused; sharp fangs jutted out among his teeth, drawing blood from his lower lip. The taste of his own blood brought focus back to his eyes. "I think I could have been like you," he whispered, then backed away, melting finally into the darkness.

Gervèse crumpled once more onto his staff. He listened. Insects creaked, owls called their mates. There were the laughing whispers of a man and a woman, the snoring of a man who slept alone. All the sounds were alive. "Done for now," he said to the winking stars, "but not finished."

Leaning heavily on his staff, Father Gervèse made his way back to his abbey full of barons and bishops.

* * *

Ellen Porter Kiley

Ava escaped into the cool night air with little Ernaut on her hip. Inside, her husband had the fires stoked and kept his hammer ringing until well after dark. Both the heat and the noise flooded up the stairs to their living quarters. They would all make do with less sleep until the Lendit fair was over.

It does no good to complain, she thought to herself. *He would not work so hard if his wares were not selling so well, but how can I explain that to Ernaut? He would rather have a few shiny pennies than one well-bitten denier.*

She sat on the horse block with the toddler on her lap. Ernaut played with the ribbons at her throat while she looked up at the stars, letting the ringing in her ears fade. Ava's ears had been so traumatized by the incessant clanging of the hammer that she didn't hear the man approach until he was right at her shoulder; she started in surprise when he spoke.

"Do you see it too, lady?" he asked.

Ava laughed to cover her surprise. "It is kind of you to call a smith's wife a lady," she said, "but I do not see anything." She studied the man's face, to see if she should recognize him, or perhaps even know his name, but her eyes were still unused to the darkness. He was looking up—that she could tell from the inclination of his head. "Are you an astrologer?"

"It is also kind of you to speak so handsomely of a stranger," he answered, "but I have no training in the science of the stars. I do not need it to see that great crimson streak in the sky. It is as long as my hand held up to the sky, a dripping wound in the heavens. Can you not see it?"

It seemed to Ava that the man shivered as he spoke, perhaps in fear, perhaps in delight. Neither interpretation made her comfortable. She pulled Ernaut to her side, away from the man, so that she could stand and go back to the safety of her house. At this interruption, the boy looked up. "I see it, mama!" he piped in his clear little voice, and pointed upward. "There it is, a star with hair, red like Thomas Milner's."

"Yes, yes!" The man erupted with enthusiasm, lurching around behind her to follow the angle of her son's arm thrust up to the sky. "You see it too! The eyes of innocent children, they see so clearly, they see so much." The stranger leaned in to plant a kiss on Ernaut's cheek. "Perhaps you will be the astrologer, eh? But when you have grown, your eyes will be clouded with sin and regret, and then what will you see in the stars? And that is if you survive the doom that bloody star brings."

"Stop that!" Ava pulled away from the strange man, both angry and scared. "He'll not sleep a wink tonight with words like that in his head." Her eyes stole back up to the heavens, seeking in vain for the portent that her son and the stranger could both see. "You do not speak like an innocent, yet you see this thing. How is that?" she demanded of him.

The man began to laugh then, quickly sliding into hysterical hiccoughs of laughter and sobbing. "Innocence! Innocence! The innocent will suffer alongside the damned when the bloody star rules the sky!" He stumbled across the ditch and into the street, howling up at the black sky.

Ava ran down the short path to the door with Ernaut clutched to her chest, darted into the house, then pulled the latch string safely inside. Back in the safety of the glowing fire and clanging metal, she turned her son's face to the light, to see if he was scared or confused. When she saw the dark smear of drying blood on her child's cheek, Ava began to scream.

Chapter Four

Antoine de St. Lys, bishop in the True Church of Caine, walked sedately through the warren of ancient Roman corridors that led from his private chambers to the underground rooms in which he held audience. Behind him, the cleric whose privilege it was to wait on the bishop as evening fell struggled to keep pace, his steps ungainly and his breath raspy. It was a necessary sacrifice the bishop made, to allow this clumsy and mortal attendance. If St. Lys were to open a vein and let his shining blood flow past the man's lips, soon enough the cleric's footsteps would be cushioned by shadows, his manner smoothed and blurred by enfolding darkness. The holy fluid was so powerful that it would also slow the man's aging, stopping his life in the semblance of youth, and the bishop knew all too well that a young and fresh face was no aid to advancement through the Church of Rome's ranks. Thus, he allowed those who served him only infrequent tastes of the glories that awaited them beyond death— enough to feed their faith and still their tongues, but no more. It was for their own good, and for the good of the Church of Caine. St. Lys reminded himself of this every time his attendant stumbled, every time the rank odor of sweat reached his nose.

There, that was the smell he wanted. The smell of dust. Not the dust of a moldering library, but the sort kicked up by industrious men: wood, mortar, stone. Above him and across the *parvis*, out in the open air, the vaulted chambers of the Notre-Dame cathedral rose from the ruins of a squat, ill-favored basilica. St. Lys had first come to Paris not long before the work began, a bright and studious boy, but rough and naïve. Here, in the long shadow cast by the climbing edifice, his eyes had been opened to the truth of the blood and his feet set on the course he still walked tonight. It was hard sometimes, even for the learned and devoted bishop, to separate his love for his Church and for Caine the Messiah from this remarkable place, but it was merely a building. It was only stone on stone and colored glass, material things that shuttered the eyes of mortals from truths their false God did not want them to see. Still, he enjoyed the opportunity to abide nearby while it suited his purposes.

St. Lys entered his audience chamber, gesturing curtly for his panting subordinate to remain outside the door until summoned. Here, where once Roman soldiers had stacked their spears and shields, the bishop pulled the strings of two churches: the false and day-lit Church of Rome (or at least a substantial portion of its apparatus in Paris), and the true and benighted Church of Caine. Those who had not recognized the holiness of the shining blood in a vampire's veins still called the True Church the "Cainite Heresy," but they would one night be brought to heel.

Deep, plush rugs on the floors and vibrant-yet-pious tapestries on the walls effectively muted the room's martial nature. When he settled into his usual chair, another cleric gracefully and quietly placed papers that required the bishop's attention on a nearby table. When the man did not withdraw, St. Lys looked up from the letters before him.

"What is it, Dalfin?"

"There is someone here to see you, Your Excellency."

"I don't remember arranging any meetings for this hour," St. Lys said mildly.

The cleric ducked his head apologetically. "No, Your Excellency, you did not. She came unannounced, and she has been quite insistent."

"Who is here to see me, Dalfin, that you are so out of sorts?"

"A Greek of Malkav's blood. One Sister Takhoui of Constantinople. I am sorry to interrupt your work, Your Excellency, but she is adamant that she must speak with you urgently."

58

St. Lys considered a moment, then carefully gathered the papers into a sheaf and handed that to the cleric. "Bring these to me again when we are done speaking. Remember this: we should not put our trust in the words of the Malkavians, but it is never wise to ignore them. And this particular madwoman is well known for the keenness of her sight. I hope you were gracious to her."

"Always, always when acting in your name, Your Excellency," Dalfin said.

"Good. Escort her in, then remain outside until I call for you."

Dalfin left to do as bid. His steps were silent even when he was reduced to scurrying, St. Lys noted with some satisfaction.

Takhoui swept into the room ahead of the still-flustered Dalfin, who retreated without even crossing the threshold. St. Lys was pleased to see her dressed and accoutered like a wealthy and respectable matron, her rich brown hair nearly as intricately plaited and gilded as an abbot's miter. She had arrived in Paris in a religious fervor, all worldly concerns swept aside by the passion of her conversion to the True Church on the long road from Constantinople. While sackcloth and ashes might befit a wandering missionary or a pilgrim, the bishop had advised, it was unacceptable for a member of his congregation here within the walls of Paris to be so poorly attired. And so, under the wing of Bishop St. Lys, Sister Takhoui and no few others like her had found safe harbor in Paris, while other Greek refugees spent their nights among squalid tents under tree boughs.

Takhoui made a graceful obeisance before the bishop, then kissed the ring on his proffered hand. That done, she held on to St. Lys' palm. "Help an old woman up, if you don't mind. Settling down onto the floor is easy; getting up is harder."

St. Lys helped her rise, allowing only faint amusement to spread across his features. He had no doubt that the woman before him had no trouble standing up from the side of a blood-drained corpse. He led her to a chair. "What brings you to see me this evening, Sister?"

Takhoui clucked, patting her bishop's hand before relinquishing it. "Such a hurry. Still, I came here quickly enough myself when the sun set, and I've no doubt that you have many things to do, important things."

The bishop found the comfort of his own chair and waited, silently, for her to continue.

"There will be fire in the sky, Your Excellency," Sister Takhoui said. "I can see it now as I sleep, flickering at the edges of my closed eyes. Soon enough the world will see it."

"Are you now an astrologer, Sister?" St. Lys leaned forward in his chair, his cool demeanor set aside by his interest and Takhoui's plain confidence.

Takhoui chuckled, an earthy sound. "Not by formal study, no. That's a matter for educated men, theologians and scientists. I would not have thought to bother you, except that I remembered, or I've at least partly remembered, that Aristotle said these fires are not from the material world. They are bits of the spiritual world escaping into the material." She tsked at herself. "So long ago it was, and it's not something I'd ever thought to see. Nor was it so important before, the spiritual or the material, before I saw the truth of the shining blood."

"A comet, then," the bishop mused. "An omen."

"An ill omen," Takhoui confirmed with incongruous cheer. "A portent of doom. The only question is, whose? After all I've seen, walking from Constantinople to Paris on these very feet, I still could only have imagined such a sign likely to hang over the dome of the Hagia Sophia in the nights before the cru-

Malkavian

sade. What could happen now to deserve such a blazon, if the death of my home did not?"

"Indeed. It would herald an event of great significance."

The thoughtful silence did not settle for long. "That is all I have to share," Sister Takhoui announced. "Many things, I am sure, are awaiting Your Excellency's attention." She rose from her chair without assistance, with a slight effort.

"Thank you, Sister. I appreciate your insight. You have been given a great gift. You will be sure to inform me of anything else you foresee in conjunction with this omen." The bishop's gracious smile smoothed over the plain command.

"Of course, Your Excellency. Conjunction, indeed. I will keep my eye on the heavens for you."

Dalfin was waiting outside the door in a state of even greater agitation than before. He retained enough control to bob an approximation of a respectful bow to Sister Takhoui as she departed, then bolted through the door, the sheaf of papers trembling in his hand.

"What is it?" St. Lys asked sharply, annoyed at the graceless interruption of his thoughts. Dalfin held out the letters. There was a new missive atop the stack, on smooth, fine parchment, under the seal of the Archbishop of Nod himself, the highest priest in the True Church of Caine.

* * *

Veronique d'Orleans walked through the streets of Paris's Latin Quarter, where she had chosen to lair upon her arrival in Paris some years ago. The recognized ambassador of the court of Julia Antasia, Prince of Hamburg, she could have claimed a lair on the Ile de la Cité, the heart of Paris and home to many of its high-blooded Cainites. But Veronique had preferred the Quarter, with its press of mortal students, shopkeepers, comfort girls and every other variety of man and woman thought unseemly on the more-noble isle in the Seine. Veronique was not a Cainite who eschewed the company of the living or the low-born. The stewhouses of the quarter were also an excellent source of rumor, including the well-reputed bathhouse she had made her haven.

Tonight, the Quarter was its usual lively self. The streets were filled even at this late hour with busy mortals finishing their day's work, readying tomorrow's, or more fortunately, seeking a bit of pleasure in a few late cups of wine. The living were wrapped in their tiny little worlds, their heads stuck in everyday problems of brick and coin, love and death. They moved aside for Veronique as she glided through their midst, thinking only *there goes a great lady*, and not realizing that death, in fact, walked among them.

Anatole followed in her wake. The sparse crowd jostled and bumped him at every turn, his monk-like robes granting him no immunity or respect. Paris was full of clerics and many deserved no special treatment, especially not ones out so late, who were likely drinking or whoring instead of studying, with clothing stained by spilled wine. Those who brushed against the sword at his side sprang away immediately, but Anatole was already past, forging after the noblewoman who moved with such assurance through the city's rabble. *Tomorrow*, he thought with grim amusement, *perhaps they will give some drunken lout of a priest enough room to move until they are sure he carries no steel.*

Ahead, Anatole glimpsed Veronique as she turned onto a bridge across the Seine. If the sun were up, the bridge would be even more crowded than the streets, but for now it was nearly empty. Most of the shops that lined the edges of the bridge in twos and threes were dark—their keepers were forced by decree to live elsewhere—but here and there a light still gleamed where a long-winded lecturer droned on into the night while his students took advantage of his lamp oil to scribble bawdy poetry. The alcoves that separated the

Malkavian

hunched storefronts and lecture rooms were not empty either, Anatole saw as he passed. In the shadows huddled mortal lovers, entranced by the moonlight on the river, or prostitutes beginning their night's work—it was not always easy to tell the difference.

Veronique's pace had slowed, and Anatole hoped she had tired of her little game. Halfway across the bridge, she slipped into an alcove. It was not unoccupied—mere moments later a roughly dressed man fled the enclosure. Anatole saw the flash of his teeth, smelled the fresh blood. As the panicked Cainite's footsteps receded, Anatole crossed the midpoint of the bridge and stood politely outside the sheltered niche. "Madame? Or do you prefer Mademoiselle? May I join you? It is a beautiful night to sit beside the river."

Veronique looked up from the stone bench where she sat, the body of a young woman draped across her lap. "Anatole. I had not expected to see you."

Anatole accepted the oblique invitation, moving to stand by the rail overlooking the water. "I have been following you for an hour, at least," he noted with mild reproach.

Veronique did not deign to acknowledge the jab. "A beautiful night. That is what she thought, I imagine, when she came to walk along the bridge with him. I wonder if she came because he had a pretty face or pretty coin." She studied the dying young woman in her arms, then dipped her head to catch a thin thread of blood that threatened to spill over the swell of the girl's breast and stain her plain but neat garments.

"Does it matter?" asked Anatole.

"Of course not," Veronique replied, lifting her head from the young woman's throat, where the trickle of blood resumed its slow course. "What matters is that he, whoever he is, was never admitted within the city's walls. He is not permitted to hunt here, so he starves. Then, when he hunts, he kills." She paused, and offered the girl's throat to Anatole.

Anatole knelt beside the women. "You know that I, too, am not permitted within the city's walls." He reached up to the young woman's face and gently closed her staring eyes. "Though I was born here, and died here."

"These things take time, Anatole. You have achieved some standing in the refugee camps, and taken over Folcaut's followers. Now you will have to hold onto them while I find the opportunity to speak on your behalf at court." Veronique's reply was taut with carefully restrained impatience.

Anatole turned the girl's head, studying the ruin of her neck for a moment before leaning in to close her ripped flesh with his own kiss. Her skin was warm and soft, but cooling. Veronique, so close, was hard and cold. He rested his head against the girl's breast, listening to the weak fluttering of her heart. "The time for waiting is over," he said.

"Is it," she said, her voice icy, even imperious.

He leaned back and looked up. Veronique's face was pale and luminous against the dark sky, like a second moon.

"We must act not in decades or centuries, but within their time frame." He touched the young woman in Veronique's arms. "The stars above are shivering in their courses. When I close my eyes, when the dawn comes, I hear trumpets ringing." His voice was touched with ecstasy.

Veronique said nothing, and kept her eyes fixed on Anatole's.

"I must be in Paris," he insisted. "I will come whether or not I am allowed or invited, even if I must climb the walls every night."

"Why?" Veronique asked, a note of genuine confusion in her voice.

"I have been called by God."

"To do what?"

"I don't know," Anatole confessed. "Yet."

The sound of feet pounding up the bridge broke up their intimate tableau. Anatole got to his feet and pulled his sword free while the runner came closer. He could hear, in the distance, the sounds of many people in the street—not plodding tiredly toward home, but running, shouting, screaming and laughing in the dark of night.

The runner stopped on the bridge, looking frantically into the shadowed alcoves, then continued to run along its length. "Madame! Madame Veronique!" he called as he dashed from one to the next, disturbing trysts all along his path.

Veronique, who had laid her burden beside the stone bench, put her hand on Anatole's sword arm. She stepped into the moonlight and gestured silently, angrily, to the man. He ran the remaining short distance in silence, then collapsed on his knees in front of his mistress, clutching at the folds of her *bliaut*. His hands, dotted with blood sweat, left dark crimson marks on the skirt.

"What is it, Sebastien?" she hissed. "And keep your voice down." Anatole listened, but his sword was still in his hand, and his eyes jumped from one end of the bridge to the other.

"I am sorry, Madame. Something came over me. A wonderful thing has happened. A terrible thing! A wonderful, terrible thing."

Veronique laid a hand on Sebastien's head, gently, but heavily. "What is it?"

The Cainite sucked in a deep breath; the unnaturalness of it seemed to calm him slightly. "We were at the market at Les Halles to feed. He came out of the Cimetière des Innocents. He looked like a king, and the mark on his brow blazed like a star!"

Behind Veronique, Anatole turned his sword, clasping it to his chest like a cross, and began to pray.

"Whom did you see?" Veronique pressed.

"Caine. It was Caine!"

Ellen Porter Kiley

In the alcove, on the hard stone of the bridge, the young woman's last breath left her body in a long, rattling sigh.

Chapter Five

Alexander, prince of the Cainites of Paris, and lord of its Grand Court, stood in the cavern of the frigidarium, looking up at the night sky through the opening in the roof. The thick stone walls, designed to keep the day's heat out, also kept out a broad view of the stars.

Although ancient and powerful in the blood, Alexander's antediluvian sire had chosen him as a youth, and he still wore the fair face of a boy not quite on the cusp of manhood. Now, he shook that flawless face and its perfect locks in mild dismay. The view from here would not do. With an exuberance he had not felt in long years, Alexander strode to the nearest wall, squatted and wrapped his arms around a great loose stone—one that had likely fallen from the ceiling long before Alexander had even heard of the city of Paris. The blood in his veins followed the path of his will. Slowly, Alexander lifted the block from the floor and carried it to the center of the room. Behind him scurried Sweyn, now in front of him then behind again—a man more used to upsetting an applecart than keeping it stacked neatly, frantically moving the precious weavings and tapestries that made the old Roman baths more suited to Countess Saviarre's refined tastes.

Alexander dropped the stone block to the floor beneath the opening in the ceiling; the slap and rumble of it shook the whole structure. He vaulted atop his new perch, and again looked to the sky.

"There it is," he said, his voice tense with excitement but his face relaxed, contented. "It's low in the sky. But what a tail on that star, and how red! Soon it will look like the sky is on fire. Or perhaps it will more resemble a great bleeding gash in the heavens."

Sweyn stood stock still, draped with rescued rugs. "Are the heavens truly bleeding? Or afire?"

Ellen Porter Kiley

Alexander shrugged, his eyes still trained upward. "I do not know. But I have seen these before. The fire will go out, or the wound will heal. Saviarre, come out and see it with me. The fire is just starting to kindle."

Saviarre's voice drifted, muted, from beyond the doors to the heated caladarium. "I know what it looks like."

"Of course you do," Alexander replied. "But is that the same as seeing it?"

Saviarre did not answer.

Sweyn began, stiffly, to replace or find new places for the swaths of fabric in his arms. "Milord, if you have seen these stars before, can you tell us what it means?"

"It means there are great—or terrible—events impending. The ultimate success or downfall of a powerful man." Alexander felt the last warmth of the blood he had called on to move the stone wisp away into the cool night air, taking with it some of his bizarre enthusiasm.

"But, who?" Sweyn stammered, made dull-witted by the thought of fire spreading across the dark sky.

Alexander skewered his functionary with a look. "Me, of course. Who else warrants such a display?" He considered aloud, pensively. "Philippe was a great king among the mortals, but his best years are past him. No, there is no one else worthy of such a torch." He shrugged again, his smile returning, then lightly leapt down from the block. "Come, Sweyn, you look like a washerwoman. Let Saviarre and her attendants arrange her cushions. What court business is there to see to this night?"

Sweyn nervously dropped the remaining fabric into a pile. "There are some territorial disputes on the Ile de la Cité to be mediated." He hesitated a moment before continuing. "Milady Countess Saviarre was also to meet with Veronique d'Orleans of Clan Brujah, at her request."

"Saviarre is not available, I do not think. Are you available?" Alexander inquired toward the closed chamber with exaggerated courtesy. "I thought not. I will mediate these disputes myself." He brushed bits of stone and dust from the sleeves and front of his bliaut. "I will also meet with Veronique. Let her know of this change in plans."

Sweyn nodded. Unable to hide his surprise, he dashed off into the darkness on his task.

Alexander crossed the chamber to the caladarium doors. "Saviarre," he said gently, "will you not come out?"

When Saviarre replied, her voice was shaking, uncertain—so unlike the strong woman Alexander had come to know. "I can't. I can't stand to see that thing in the sky, to feel it loom over my head."

Alexander sighed, but closed the heavy doors firmly for her as he turned to go. *She cares so deeply for me,* he thought. It was obvious; she could not stand the thought that the sign in the sky signaled his doom. And perhaps it did, but it would be impossible, unthinkable, to hide from such a grand fate. *It is time to take the city back into my own hands, so that I can seize the opportunity the star will present to me—or drag it down in the flames with me if I fall.*

* * *

Veronique d'Orleans was already waiting when Alexander arrived. He let her wait longer; Veronique was no fledgling who would fall easily into the trap of impatience, but he doubted the wait would improve her temper. More importantly, Alexander wanted the time to reacquaint himself with his surroundings—how long had it been since he had done more than raise a crimson glass in a toast at a banquet or listen with half an ear to the presentation of a childe? The nagging and sordid details that kept the city working smoothly were handled by others, and Saviarre handled the handlers so deftly that his intervention was almost never needed. It had been a pleasant interlude, but now it was time to take back the reins. He would have to be careful when Saviarre recovered that she did not take too much upon herself on his behalf again. She was an accomplished politician and administrator, certainly, but she was also a woman, and it was clear the stress of such important duties had finally taken its toll.

Half the night had passed before Alexander finished his ruminations and poring over of documents. He consented then, finally, to have Veronique admitted to his study. She crossed the threshold and stood before him, dropping into a graceful curtsey. "Milord Prince, thank you for seeing me this evening. May I inquire after the countess?"

Alexander waved this away. "She is merely indisposed. What was to be the purpose of your meeting?"

"Please convey to her both my regrets and good wishes, milord," Veronique replied gracefully. "I was to meet with the countess to discuss the details of my sponsorship of Anatole of Clan Malkavian into the city."

Alexander said nothing for several long moments, but Veronique at least had the civility to seem not to notice. "Anatole. He has only a small notoriety, for one of a clan of madmen. Why would you see him within these walls?"

"I am sure you already know, milord, that he lived his mortal life here, died here, and was Embraced here. I have heard, although perhaps not from the most reliable sources, that Anatole's sire had been granted permission to create a fledgling. It would seem fitting, given all these circumstances, to allow Anatole entrance. After all, without the inconvenient appearance and great numbers of the Greek refugees, would his admittance to the city have been questioned?"

"But there are, in fact, refugees camped outside the gates of Paris. And this madman has some position within the camp, does he not?"

"He does, my lord. A position of respect only, earned when he exposed the treacherous workings of the Heresy, which was preying on the hopelessness of the refugees," Veronique replied, indignation evident in her tone.

"So he has earned the ire of one so-called church. Is he not also pursued by agents of the mortals' church?" Alexander continued thoughtfully.

"We would all be pursued by that church were we discovered. Anatole is one of the few cunning enough to escape their clutches."

Alexander smiled wryly. "I do not wish for any Cainite here to be pursued, or discovered. As you obliquely indicate, it is a danger to all of us." His voice took on a tone of finality. "I am not assured that the Malkavian will be cautious enough for our safety, or would not provoke the churchmen for his own crazed purposes."

"I am willing to guarantee his behavior—or lack of behavior, however you care to define it—on this point," Veronique countered.

For the second time in the short discussion, Alexander was shocked. "You would guarantee a Malkavian's behavior? You would risk the name of your sponsor, Lady Antasia of Hamburg, under whose banner you stand at the Grand Court? Again I must ask: why?"

Veronique laughed. "That is a fair question, milord. It is not a decision I've come to lightly, I can assure you. Have you seen the hair star? Of course, of course you have. It is faint now, a streak of red in the sky like the faint blush of a maid's cheek. But it will be gory-red soon, and all will see it, Cainite and mortal alike. Already the streets are restless. When that bloody star hangs overhead, they will be like tinder waiting for a spark."

"And you think that inviting in the madman will improve the situation?"

"Who knows madness better than a madman?" Veronique answered. "While I do not think he will scrub out the insanity, I think he can channel it. Blunt the more destructive and chaotic aspects of it."

"Why will none of our current Malkavian residents suit this purpose?" Alexander asked.

"None of them have the proper madness, that I'm aware of," Veronique replied. "Anatole seeks redemption: for himself, for Cainites—even the souls of mortals concern him. If Paris goes mad in Anatole's fashion, it is a madness more easily recovered from than most."

"The residents of Constantinople would not think so," Alexander noted wryly.

There was uncomfortable silence for a moment. Veronique broke it in a quiet voice. "At Les Halles the other night, many Cainites young in the blood saw something in the cemetery, or perhaps they all shared a vision, a moment of insight or madness. They believe they saw Caine."

Alexander's reply was likewise quiet, measured. "I had not heard this."

"This was before the hair star appeared in the sky—"

"Call it a comet," Alexander interrupted, in Greek.

Veronique nodded assent. "Before the comet appeared in the sky. When the heavens are doused in blood, then how many visions will there be? And what will they see? Or perhaps even the unthinkable has happened," her voice trailed away to a whisper, "our Dark Father is really here?"

Alexander appeared thoughtful, if unmoved. "Perhaps we could use some redemption—certainly some Cainites of Paris will be less troublesome redeemed than not. Very well. Anatole is free to enter Paris. However, he many only bring three Cainites or mortals under the influence of his blood with him. Additionally, he is not to provoke priests or other agents of the mortal church under any circumstances. I will hold you to your guarantee, Lady Veronique."

"I understand, Milord Prince."

"I will make the arrangements tonight. And you, Veronique—you seem more connected to the rumors and whisperings among the streets than your pleasant dress and manners would allow. I will ask you to convey to me any word of future sightings, or visions."

Veronique curtseyed again. "Of course, milord."

"You may go."

She did, and Alexander sat alone for a while with his thoughts. In his mind's eye, the comet swelled and bled overhead.

Part Two:

The Comet

Chapter Six

Bishop St. Lys stood in the rain, listening to the clop of the horses' hooves as the awaited carriage drew near. He had been waiting for some time; when the rain had started, servants had held an impromptu canvas tent over him to protect his finery and regalia, but he had waved them off as soon as he heard the carriage approach. He would not have the Archbishop of Nod see him bundled up in a blanket like an invalid on their first meeting.

St. Lys had three times met the first Archbishop of Nod, Narses of Venice. Withered and old in body, he had been a master schemer and not a few of the faithful believed that he had maneuvered the Fourth Crusade into sacking Constantinople twenty years before. He had been known to have a longstanding hatred of Michael, the deranged Toreador Methuselah who had founded the vampiric order there. But the aftermath of the so-called Bitter Crusade had not been kind to Narses. Alfonzo, Narses' own childe, had risen to become Prince of Constantinople under the vassalage of the damnable Monçada. That hypocritical bastard wore the trapping of the Church of Rome and presented himself as a defender of the False Church while accumulating power for himself. Worse, Prince Alfonzo had forsaken the True Church of Caine.

Maneuvering in the Crimson Curia, the ruling body of the True Church, had begun almost before the ashes of Constantinople had settled. A previously minor Bulgarian bishop of Tzimisce blood, one Nikita of Sredetz, became the most effective critic of the Archbishop and eventually had Narses stripped of his office. Soon thereafter, another of Narses' childer deposed him as Prince of Venice and called a blood hunt on him. Rumor had it that Narses was now ash, his blood reclaimed by one or the other of his rebellious childer, but St. Lys had no way of confirming that. What he did know was that Nikita of Sredetz was now Archbishop of Nod.

The driver of the carriage brought the horses to a brutal stop in front of the bishop. They rolled their eyes in fear and stomped the puddled ground as instinct warred with training, but they held steady under the heavy hand on the reins. Dalfin leapt down from his perch beside the driver, where he had huddled like a sodden crow.

"The archbishop's entourage fits into one carriage?" St. Lys asked, his face a mask of calm, eyes trained on the carriage door.

"Your Eminence," Dalfin stammered, his usual composure lost somewhere in the rainy streets of Paris, "His Grace is traveling alone."

"Alone?" gasped St. Lys.

The handle of the carriage door began to turn. Dalfin lunged for the handle and opened the door smoothly, salvaging some decorum for the moment.

St. Lys made no attempt to disguise his surprise. The ancient Cainite who stepped out of the carriage would see through any subterfuge, and St. Lys would not risk angering him for a flimsy façade of politeness. "Archbishop Nikita!" he exclaimed in Latin. "Welcome to Paris. I had readied secure lodgings and vitae for at least a dozen, but…"

"All the more for me," said the archbishop firmly, a glint of amusement in his eyes as he came forward to greet St. Lys, heedless of the drizzle or the mud underfoot. "There was no time to wait for this or that member of the Curia or the See to tidy up their affairs before the trip. I travel very quickly alone, as I'm sure you've noticed, Antoine. But it leaves me with such a hunger. You've provisioned for a dozen, and in as little time as I gave you? Very good, that should take the edge off. I do enjoy provincial hospitality."

"You'll not find it lacking, I hope." St. Lys replied. "My assistant, Dalfin here, will see to your comforts. When you are settled, send for me; I am at your call."

"Good." The archbishop started for the shelter of the nearest door while Dalfin scrambled into the carriage for his few, light bundles. He turned on reaching the overhang, and stared dourly out into the rain. "This is not a lark, Bishop St. Lys. But you know that, don't you."

St. Lys nodded, looking up at the starless sky.

They went inside in silence. The driver flicked the reins and the horses bolted off into the rain, glad to be away.

* * *

"You want me to do *what?*"

St. Lys stood shocked in the center of his own audience chamber like a petitioner. Those words had been uttered with absolutely no regard for his listener's esteemed position. He was frozen, waiting for the rebuke, or worse, retribution, that might rightly follow such an outburst. How dare he speak thus to one so favored by the Dark Father?

The archbishop, who had appropriated St. Lys' stately chair, did not seem to notice or mind the lapse. His expression was at once beatific and genial, as though his faith buoyed inexhaustible good humor—an expression St. Lys might expect on the face of one of the preaching friars that infested the countryside like vermin, but which was shocking on a heresiarch holding a crystal goblet of blood to his lips. Narses had been a harsh master for the faith; Nikita seemed jovial in comparison. It was not something St. Lys had expected, nor was he especially comfortable with it.

After an appreciative sip, the archbishop placed the glass on the table atop St. Lys' scattered records and missives. "The end of days is coming. We have seen the signs."

Ellen Porter Kiley

79

St. Lys suddenly and fervently wished his chair were unoccupied. He staggered to the table and leaned on it for support. "The comet. It's that important?"

"You've seen it, then." The archbishop sounded vaguely disappointed, robbed of part of his tale.

"No, I haven't seen it myself. An oracle, one of those converted on the road from Constantinople, foretold its coming." St. Lys gestured at the table where his notes on the conversation were buried. "She said it was an ill omen."

"Ah, an oracle. They can be useful, if managed properly." The archbishop chuckled. "Yes, I dare say the end of the world will be taken ill by many. But it is what I have waited for all these centuries under the stars."

Comprehension flooded St. Lys like a rush of warm blood, tingling in his cheeks, fingers, and toes. Archbishop Nikita spoke again, savoring his words and their impact. "The Third Coming of Caine our Father, who will come to judge all who have tasted the shining blood."

"'And the Children of Seth shall be uplifted or cast down, each according to his deeds and his merits. And those who have been proven unworthy of the shining blood shall be shorn of their glory and thrown into the void,'" St. Lys recited fervently. "But," he paused, confusion battling ecstasy, "why have you come here to Paris, and to me? The comet will be seen all over the world, from Iberia to furthest Persia."

"Of course it will." The archbishop fingered the stem of his goblet, setting bloody gleams of multifaceted light dancing on the wall. "But even endings must have beginnings. And beginnings have places."

St. Lys clung to confusion like a plank in a storm-tossed sea. His shadow, looming and doubtful, crept up the wall to devour the shards of blood-light, stilling their irreverent dance.

"Bishop St. Lys," the Archbishop said sharply, chiding now. "There have been sightings of Caine all over your city. Didn't you know?"

"It's true," St. Lys whispered. "May the Dark Father forgive me, I didn't believe."

"So now do you see why I have asked you to do this?" Archbishop Nikita asked.

"Yes. Yes I do… but no, why me? There are others, here or nearby, far more suited than I." St. Lys rifled through the papers nearby. "Here, Andrew of Normandy, he's a member of the See! Or Bishop de Navarre, here in Paris. Surely—"

"Antoine," the archbishop interrupted. "It is no secret that there are Cainites in our number who use our faith as the means to an end. They see us as a useful tool against the False Church, or an excuse to exercise personal power. But I am not so easily fooled; I can recognize the faithful. The others will answer for their blasphemy soon enough. Let de Navarre play his games. As of now, Paris is your city. The Cainites who dwell here will be saved or damned on your watch."

St. Lys made his decision; faith strengthened his knees and his voice, and the blood-red gleams on the wall began to writhe in elation. "I will save as many souls as I can," he declared. "It is time for the True Church to leave the shadows."

The Archbishop raised his glass in a toast, then drained it and wiped the crimson stain from his lips. "Excellent. How will you begin?"

* * *

A carrot flew past Anatole's ear, the dirt that stuck to it still damp from the early harvest. A basket of new potatoes toppled over, spilling its contents over his boots. The din of small bare feet and of heavier, shod ones chasing after them across the wooden floor above was remarkable.

Carefully picking his way along the tuber-strewn floor, Anatole placed a gently restraining hand on

Crespin's shoulder. "Leave it be. Your cellar is a fine refuge from the sun. We will move what needs to be moved."

Zoë looked up from the large basket of turnips she was tugging with great effort across the floor, blowing at a strand of hair escaped from her kerchief with exaggerated annoyance.

"Brother Anatole, I am sorry," Crespin began. "If I had but known you would have need, I could have arranged far better…."

"You could not have known," Anatole interrupted, "because I did not tell you."

"Not to mention that your vegetables smell much better than the camp," Zoë added.

Overhead, the fleeing child was caught and unceremoniously hauled to bed. Crespin's wife's footsteps were sharp and angry. Crespin took up the shielded candle; the dancing shadows distorted his moue of dismay into a stark grimace. "She doesn't know. I haven't told her anything yet."

"You married a generous Christian woman, Crespin. She allows you to bring two ruffians under the roof where her baby sleeps, at nightfall, without a word of complaint." Anatole waited until Crespin nodded nervously at this assessment. "Ensure our safety through the day tomorrow, and in the evening I will introduce myself and my companion to your wife."

"You…you aren't angry, Brother Anatole?" Crespin ventured.

"Angry? I asked you, and all the others many years ago, to put down roots in Paris. You have a home, work, a wife, a child. You have even," Anatole smiled, "put down roots in your cellar. You have done all that I asked. Now go and reassure your wife."

Crespin took the candle and went up the narrow stairs.

Zoë and Anatole listened for a while as the family continued their interrupted nighttime routine. In the

Malkavian

darkness, Zoë studied Anatole's face. "You're very happy."

"Of course," Anatole grinned. "I'm in Paris. I'm home."

"We've been over the walls more than a few times. Is it so different to be allowed to be here?" Zoë asked.

Anatole considered. "It is different. It's an uncomfortable feeling, to be unwanted in the city I would call home. I suspect you have felt that far more acutely than I."

Zoë nodded, a brief movement of pale skin in the pitch blackness. "But it isn't just the relief of discomfort that makes you grin like a fool, is it?"

"No, no. Can't you feel it, Zoë? After the years of waiting, sleeping, penance—I have a mission again, and my feet are firmly on the path."

Zoë's expression was wry. "My own mission was very angry, Anatole. And in the end, futile."

"Not futile. You saved a man's soul with your forgiveness, and that is a lesson that many will never learn, in fifty years or five hundred. Besides," he elbowed Zoë roguishly, "your mission brought you to me just when I needed you, and I have brought you here."

"And what are we just in time to do here?" Zoë asked.

Anatole frowned thoughtfully, but briefly. "I don't know, precisely. Yet. I'm sure it will be made clear."

"Of course," Zoë murmured.

"But I do know how to begin."

Zoë looked up at Anatole expectantly.

"Once again, I must gather my flock. Come, Zoë." Anatole held out his hand to his childe. "Let me show you the streets of Paris, not merely its alleys and gutters, now that we are citizens."

Zoë took Anatole's hand and preceded him up the stairs. "No more alleys. That seems too much to hope for."

* * *

The evening rain had let up and the skies were clearing. The streets were alive with activity, and Anatole wound his way through the crowds with eyes upturned and his ears attuned to the subtleties of the night. Zoë stayed close beside him, and not long after they departed the root cellar, they were joined by another.

The ruling had been clear: Anatole was allowed entrance to the city, but no more than three childer or followers were allowed to accompany him. Zoë was at his side, as always, and Crespin would count as another. The newcomer—a tall, but somehow insignificant figure who crept along behind Anatole and Zoë—completed his allowed flock.

This last figure was not invisible, but those who saw him forgot him just as quickly. Malachite of Constantinople had spent the last two decades in travel across Anatolia and Europe, and centuries before that unseen in the shadows of Byzantium. To go unnoticed in Paris or to appear as a simple follower of a yellow-haired penitent, was not especially challenging to him. He observed everything as he passed, letting no detail slip, but none took note of his passing, and even Zoë, looking back over her shoulder to watch the Nosferatu candidly, had difficulty in concentrating on his presence.

"Do you feel it?" Anatole asked at last. "It is so rich, so powerful. There is an energy in the air, dancing up the walls and into the stars themselves."

Zoë glanced at him quizzically. Such an outburst, while not unheard of, was unlike the Anatole of late.

"What should we feel?" she asked.

"Great things will come to pass," he answered without lowering his eyes from the stars, "great things that we will be a part of."

They came upon a group gathered in a square. Most of those gathered were mortal, though a few Cainites hung in the shadows. All stared at the sky, as did Anatole.

The three of them slipped closer, blending with the gathered crowd. Whispered voices floated to them on the night breeze. Anatole cocked his head, listening and gathering the snippets of word and thought, sifting through them carefully and weeding out all but those of other Cainites. The mortals were frightened of what was to come, but they had no real direction for their fright or their thoughts. The others, though…

"He's been seen," a voice whispered. "Caine. He's been seen in the city, right here. The hair-star precedes him."

"They say he's come to gather us. Three times risen."

"Right here in Paris."

Anatole frowned. The beatific expression of moments before gave way to a furrowed brow, and before Zoë could move to ask him what he planned, he had slipped into the crowd. She saw him pause between two others—Cainites, she thought, but both dressed in the manner of students. She moved up behind him and sensed Malachite at her heels.

"You have seen him?" Anatole asked. "Dark Caine, you have seen this vision for yourself?"

The other shook his head, irritated, but a little embarrassed, as well. "No, I have heard it said…"

Anatole had turned already to the other's companion. "And you, then, you have seen?"

"We have not seen him," the second stated flatly, "but there are others. Many others. When you hear a thing once, you consider it a rumor; when that rumor echoes from every corner, then something more is at hand."

"Great things are at hand," Anatole intoned, seeming to agree, but Zoë knew that he did not.

And just what had been seen, she wondered, and by whom? Was it a rumor started by the followers of the Heresy? Folcaut, the heretic who had preached among the Greek refugees in years past, had spouted a great deal of doctrine about the "shining blood." Caine was about to return for the third and final time, he had said. Such rumors would benefit the Heresy, Zoë thought; or perhaps they were a few misguided words from someone who wanted to take advantage of the present social and emotional instability in order to find their way to the center of things; or it was simply just wishful thinking.

Anatole turned away from those he'd questioned. "We must act soon," he said softly, addressing those who walked at his heels without turning to look at them. "Things will happen more quickly now. These sightings, or what they believe are sightings, will be taken as powerful signs. There are those who will exploit them to their own ends, and we must be ready with a response."

Anatole stopped and his expression darkened.

"What is it?" Zoë asked, moving to his side quickly. Malachite slipped closer as well, though the Nosferatu did not appear concerned; hidden as he was from recognition, it was difficult to tell what expression he actually wore.

"So many souls," Anatole replied softly. "There is a balance here, a very precarious balance, and all of them," he swept his arm over the crowd surrounding them, "sit perilously on the edge. A push from either side could send them toppling."

"Then we must be first to push," Zoë said firmly, laying a hand on his shoulder. "You must teach them. You must make them see and believe. The comet signals great changes. It is up to us to realize them."

"It is a start," Malachite cut in, "that we have made it within the city walls. Without that, all would surely have been lost. This city crawls with heretics, and they will not stay silent in such a time of prophecy and insanity. It remains only to see in which direction and manner they will strike."

Malkavian

Anatole listened, but his gaze was distant. He turned back toward the two Cainites he'd spoken with earlier, and he saw that another had joined them. All three were leaning in, carrying on an animated discussion, and it was easy to guess what it was they discussed.

"It is not their sin," Anatole whispered. "It's not their need for redemption that concerns them, nor any atonement for the acts they've committed. They wait only for Caine to come and bear them away to eternity."

"Forget them, my friend," Malachite said softly. "Speak your own truth. They are a small group in a large city, and there is yet time."

Anatole nodded, turned into the crowd once more, and began to circulate. He drew a small group, listening to his words, his words of repentance and the imminence of damnation, and soon that group grew. Malachite drew back, preferring to watch from the shadows, while Zoë stayed close to the monk's side, occasionally adding her own words to blend with his.

The group discussing the sighting of Caine had drawn further into the shadows. They listened as well but none smiled, and soon they broke up, each returning to spread the word of this new teacher, and what he had said.

Words spread quickly in darkness.

Chapter Seven

"A bath, Vero?"

"No... not enough time. The night is short—I'll nearly have to run as it is. A pan of warm water, a cloth, and the veil and circlet to hide my hair, if you will. And the green *cotte*, I think."

Girauda hurried off to perform her mistress' command, calling orders as she went. In the room beyond Veronique d'Orleans' sleeping quarters, there was a burst of hurried activity in response to the urgency in her voice. Satisfied, Veronique shrugged into her freshly washed shift and shouted for her secretary. "Thierry!"

Thierry poked his mouse-brown head around the edge of the door to make certain his employer was decently attired before stepping fully into view carrying a small stack of loose parchment sheets and his portable copyist's desk. "Milady?"

"Give me the news." Veronique demanded, irritably brushing the uneven lengths of her hair back over her shoulders. "Quickly."

Thierry set down his desk and stepped briskly aside to avoid the little redheaded maidservant carrying Veronique's wash-water and Girauda, returning with the freshly brushed green *cotte*. As Veronique bathed her face, neck, and arms, he began paraphrasing his parchments. "There was some excitement in the market today—some two-and-twenty men, women, and children all experienced what can only be described as a fit of... well... dancing. Nicolette saw this with her own eyes and swears it true—they danced until they fell, too exhausted to go on. A rumor somewhat less substantiated has it that a woman birthed a child with two heads, four arms, and four legs, and another that the nuns of an abbey outside the city walls are being afflicted by a demon who forces them to speak in tongues and blaspheme most foully against the Lord and—"

"Thierry." Veronique cut him off, sharply. "Unless Christ Himself has joined Caine walking the streets of Paris, you can save *that* sort of news for later. What is the news from our eyes on the isle?"

"Ah. Well." Thierry shuffled through his parchments, the wind clearly knocked out of his sails. "No one has yet had any fortune discovering the identity of Bishop St. Lys' guest, and there are no small number trying. He evidently entered the city traveling with a considerable dispatch and under some effort to avoid being casually observed. Our sources suggest that his arrival was not a surprise to the good bishop—Jean-Battiste de Montrond was contracted to supply viands for at least a dozen on extremely short notice, but evidently only one guest came calling. His men are apparently insusceptible to the lure of both gossip *and* bribery." A sniff. "The Countess Saviarre remains indisposed. She is taking no visitors and, to all appearances, issuing no directives to her underlings. She has not left her apartment in at least two nights."

"Which explains why the announcement of tonight's little event came only a day in advance." Veronique muttered, pulling on her *cotte* and standing still to let her maids handle the laces.

"Yes." Thierry agreed, delicately. "Evidently, there is at least as much confusion and disorder among the servants and minor functionaries of milady's people on the isle as there is here among the people of the Quarter. 'Unrest,' is, I think, the most apt way to describe it."

"The hair—the *comet*—is working its malignancy on everyone." Veronique tucked the last loose strands of hair beneath her veil and set her circlet in place. "Letters?"

Thierry handed her a note, its wax seals unbroken, to his mistress. The seals bore a striking resemblance to those she herself used. "A rider passed through just after noon last, I'm told."

Veronique broke the seals of the court of Hamburg and scanned the letter. On the surface it was a bland report of discussions between German dignitaries, but embedded within was a second, coded message. She smiled slightly. "Sebastien has arrived safely," she said, and turning to her maidservant, "Girauda, you can stop fretting now."

Girauda refused to rise to the bait, but her relief was still clear to those who knew her. Sebastien, Veronique's second as Antasian ambassador to the Grand Court, had never fully recovered from his sighting at Les Halles and she had finally insisted he return to Hamburg to rest in a safer place. Girauda had been half-worried and half-heartbroken since the fair-faced vampire had left. For her part, Veronique was glad her junior was safe. And, if matters came to ahead, it was probably best that he was far away, where blame could not rebound upon him. "Is there anything else pressing?"

"I don't suppose you'd consider stories about two-headed calves pressing? No?" He stepped aside as Veronique swept past him.

"Thank you, Thierry, Girauda." She paused at the door. "Tell Sandrin and Philippe to keep a close watch tonight while I'm out. I have a feeling... " She let the words trail off, then shook herself. "Tell them to roust out anyone who cannot behave and keep yourselves close to home. I dislike the feel in the air tonight."

* * *

Veronique moved quickly through the streets, not quite running but striding as long as her skirts would allow, her thoughts moving even more quickly yet.

The Countess Saviarre was indisposed. It was all she could do not to crow with glee at the recent turn of events. The Countess Saviarre was indisposed, and without her steady hand on the tiller, her delicate manipulations of the Grand Court and its functionaries, the machinery of the city's Cainite government was gradually grinding to a halt for want of the intelligence that guided it. Veronique was entirely willing to give the devil her due—Saviarre had not climbed to her position of dominance in Paris by any common variety of malice or manipulation, nor through any tolerance for those who would stand against her. When she was in full command of her faculties, she wielded her influence deftly, wove the threads of her schemes through the life of the court, and ruled Paris in all but name, the power to do so having been placed in her hands by Alexander himself. She held the absolute trust of her prince—she was, in truth, perhaps the only being in the whole of Christendom whom Alexander trusted as much as himself.

But she had arranged the mechanisms of the city's government to serve her will first, and without her at the center of the web, Paris responded poorly to the hand of the Cainite who ruled it. Veronique wondered if Alexander had even noticed that yet, or if he even would. His insulation from the life and cares of his city and his subjects was even more profound than she had expected. She'd learned that much from their meeting. She doubted that he could shrug off the detachment left by two centuries spent on no affair of politics more strenuous than a banquet or a presentation.

She reached the bridge, and as she started across it, a familiar voice called out to her.

"Lady Veronique!"

She stopped, and looked about; the bridge was still busy with passersby, but she caught sight of a small, young woman waving from the far side, and the glint of her companion's fair hair in the light of a passing torch. She waited for a gap in the steady flow of traffic, and crossed to join Zoë and Anatole where they stood. "A good evening to you both. I suspect we travel in the same direction?"

Zoë dropped a quick curtsey and smiled shyly up at her. "To the isle, for court. Anatole," she gestured at her mentor, who stood motionless at the rail, gazing out over the river at the comet, hanging low in the sky, "thought there might be something worth seeing tonight."

"Anatole is likely correct," Veronique assured her dryly. "Brother?"

It took him a moment to respond to her voice, detaching himself slowly from the magnetic fascination of the rosy, gleaming apparition. Veronique permitted herself a quick glance, taking in the fact that it appeared both brighter and redder than it had before, then turned away quickly. It would snare her quickly if she stared, and even the glance she gave it was enough to stir an even deeper sense of unease within her. She pushed it down and nodded in greeting. "Shall we walk together, Brother Anatole? It's easy to lose one's way, the first few times."

"Lady Veronique." Anatole blinked at her owlishly, then nodded. "That is very kind of you. May I present Michel, another refugee in search of guidance. Michel, Lady Veronique d'Orleans, to whom we all owe a great deal."

Veronique realized she had ignored the thin man standing near them against the railing as part of the crowd. He bowed awkwardly, as if his bones were not accustomed to such motions, and murmured, "Milady."

"Sir," she said, curtseying slightly, and returned her attention to Anatole and Zoë.

Together they continued on, Veronique keeping to one side of the distracted priest and Zoë to the other, the arrangement decided on by glances between the women that their companion completely missed. They walked in silence for a distance, then Anatole murmured, "Do you know who it is that comes among us tonight, Veronique?"

She shook her head. "No. Only that he is a guest of the Bishop St. Lys."

"You have no thoughts on the matter?" Anatole asked, mildly, his expression still somewhat abstracted, his pale eyes still far away.

"Given the misfortunes that have befallen the proponents of the Heresy here in Paris of late?" Veronique replied, dryly. "I hesitate to guess in the absence of hard facts. It seems, though, that without the Countess Saviarre's wholly reliable support at the side of the throne, the Bishop St. Lys' position has become somewhat less stable. It is possible, I suppose, that this visitor has come in an effort to help shore up that position, but that is a fairly substantial risk in and of itself. Alexander possesses little tolerance for—" She cut herself off quickly.

"—for the religious manias of wandering Cainite preachers," Anatole completed for her, a certain wry amusement lurking in his tone and at the corners of his mouth. "I'm well aware of that, Lady Veronique, and you need not spare my feelings. For what it is worth, I believe that you may be correct… which will make tonight's presentation an interesting affair, indeed."

* * *

Alexander closed the door of Saviarre's innermost chamber, quietly, so as not to disturb her unnecessarily. She was finally resting after spending two days and nights completely awake, vibrating with tension, unable to sleep in her fear for him. He had been forced to perform the majority of his duties from her suite of rooms, where he had remained in a mostly vain effort to comfort her; she refused to be parted from him for any length of time, and she was in no fit state to be seen by anyone else. Only now was she succumbing to the inevitable, her anguish peaking and declining, allowing her to close her eyes and rest, if not yet sleep, to bear to let him leave her presence. Her devotion was sincere and touching, even if the near-madness that accompanied its most vigorous expression irritated him. He could hardly blame her for being out of sorts, when the entire city seemed to tremble on the edge of hysteria. And now she was sensible enough to acknowledge that he must go forth and greet the guest of Bishop St. Lys, his superior Archbishop Nikita of Sredetz, a task she was in no fit state to perform. He promised her, before he left, that he would return as quickly as possible.

Privately, Alexander was rather annoyed at the archbishop's timing. The last several years had witnessed a paroxysm of disruptive religious mania among Paris's population, Cainite and human alike. It irked him like an itch he couldn't reach, or a stone in his boot. It was one thing for the weak in mind and soul to mewl after the favor of their insubstantial and powerless gods—properly disciplined, they were easy enough to ignore or twist to one's own purpose if that was what one wanted to do. It was quite another for the weaklings to climb above their place, causing chaos and disorder with their idiotic doctrinal disputes, their delusions of grandeur, their pathetic attempts to claim a position of spiritual superiority. Such follies gave him the urge to dispense with even the appearance of diplomacy and dispose of them all.

In the halls, his purple-liveried guards stood straighter as he passed, something of his darkening mood touching them. He swept into his audience chamber, only barely waiting for the herald to announce him as he mounted the well-padded dais. The gathered courtiers offered an appropriately deep curtsey to their ruler and he allowed them an appropriately lengthy moment to hold it as his gaze swept the room.

There, at the far end—the lunatic priest, "Brother" Anatole de Paris, his ward hiding in his shadow, and another follower who at least had the courtesy to hide his leprous face under another, better-seeming one. They shared a spot of floor close to the doors, next to the Antasian ambassador, Veronique d'Orleans, who was evidently taking her duties as their sponsor quite seriously, indeed. Lord Valerian had been unable to make it back in time for court—he had sent a note from his country estate, expressing his sincere regrets and his intention to return as quickly as possible—and, in Valerian's absence, Bishop de Navarre had oozed closer to the dais to fill in the gap. He looked as sour as if he'd been chewing lemons all night, dark eyes heavy-lidded, immaculately groomed and dressed, with a folded parchment in hand. Alexander forcefully resisted the urge to roll his eyes heavenward. The unctuous little twit no doubt hoped to accost him after court in his continuing effort to disenfranchise the Nosferatu warren resident on Ile de la Cité and have them evicted to a less-desirable neighborhood. It was not a request that Alexander was inclined to answer positively—ever— if for no other reason than principle. De Navarre had whined one too many times. Directly across from him, Dame Mnemach, the matriarch of the Parisian Nosferatu, stood swathed in layers of dark robes, her face concealed behind a mask of blackened bone, flanked by two of her own. It was unusual, but not un-heard of, for the matriarch to travel accompanied; these two were obviously bodyguards, clad in mail and simple rough-spun tunics, though unarmed. Alexander won-dered idly if the Nosferatu in the lunatic priest's company was a spy of Mnemach's or a rival. He de-cided very quickly that he did not care to expend the energy to find out.

"Rise," Alexander commanded, his voice smooth and regal, showing nothing of his thoughts. "Our friends and subjects, be welcome and at peace. We gather this night to give welcome and greetings to a visitor who has traveled far to be in our fair city." He signaled the herald manning the door.

"His Excellency, Bishop Antoine St. Lys!"

St. Lys strode through the doors, clad in the full vestments of his holy office, and Alexander knew immediately that there was something just slightly *off* about him. He projected an aura of calm competence quite artfully, his expression serenely untroubled and his gait smooth as he approached, offering the appropriate courtesies at the appropriate intervals. It was subtle but evident, if one knew what to look for that beneath St. Lys' polished courtly exterior, he was nervous, tense, more so than the circumstances seemed to warrant. Alexander hid his satisfaction only with the greatest difficulty. He very much wanted to smile at St. Lys' discomfiture, but felt it beneath his dignity to do so. When the bishop came within three paces of the dais, he stopped and offered a polite, if shallow, bow. "Your Highness."

"Your Excellency. It pleases us to see you again—your absence from court has been noticed, and missed." Alexander gestured him up.

"Your Highness is too kind." St. Lys rose smoothly. "I have come this evening to offer Your Highness the greetings and felicitations of my superior, Nikita of Sredetz, Archbishop of Nod and leader of the faithful of Caine and the shining blood. And to deliver a proposal from His Grace." The bishop turned, and gestured impatiently to the herald.

"His Grace, the Archbishop of Nod, Nikita of Sredetz!" The herald's announcement sent a flurry of whispers through the assembled court.

The Archbishop of Nod knew how to play a crowd, Alexander admitted somewhat grudgingly to himself. He paused in the doorway long enough for everyone to take in the sight of him—tall and ascetically slender, fine dark hair and pale eyes, and a face that was somewhere between angelic and wholly divine. For although he was of higher rank, his vestments were simpler and less heavily ornamented than those of his subordinate, but they were of the finest quality fabric and construction. He wore only one ring on his long-fingered hand and he moved as though physical grace were a gift granted by God to him alone. It was likely the closest any Parisian had ever come to a dread and terrible Tzimisce, and he clearly intended to make a show of it, gliding down the length of the room without pause or gesture, stopping only at the Bishop St. Lys' shoulder. Once before the prince, he did not bow; instead, he inclined his head, the gesture a regal acknowledgment of one ruler to another, respectful but in no way submissive. Alexander was torn between the desires to rip his arrogant head off and to applaud the pure audacity of it.

In the end, he merely nodded once in acknowledgment. "Your Grace has traveled far to favor our city with your presence. To what do we owe this highest of honors?"

"Your Highness," Archbishop Nikita began. He had a voice to go with the rest of him—smooth and dark—and he spoke Greek perfectly, without a trace of accent to mar the elegance of his words. "I have come to you at the request of my brother, the Bishop St. Lys, in the hour of your city's need, with the earnest desire to bring hope and peace to your realm in its troubled time. Will you hear me, Your Highness?"

The Bishop St. Lys, Alexander couldn't help but notice, looked genuinely shocked for just a moment, before he hid the reaction behind his customary expression of bland superiority.

"We will hear you, Your Grace," the prince said. "Say on."

The archbishop favored him with a smile, a serene and pleasant expression that made the hair on the back of his neck rise. "Brothers and sisters in Caine," the Tzimisce began, addressing the court in the local *langue d'oïl* rather than Latin or Greek. He turned in a swirl of dark robes, spreading his arms as though he wished to reach out and embrace them all. "It is no secret that we

Malkavian

live in troubled, and troubling, times. An omen hangs in the sky, a dark omen of fear and danger, pain and disaster. At every turn, in every place, we feel ourselves threatened and beset as those things which we believed would endure forever crumble around us, leaving only dust and memories. It is the same here as in every domain in Christendom—the bloody eye of wrath and ruin gazes down upon all, and all feel the horror of its power."

The archbishop was *doing* something—something immensely subtle but undeniable in its power, Alexander was certain of it. He could feel the force of it curling around him like a wave breaking around his ankles, tugging at him gently, urging him to surrender himself to it. He did not succumb to it, but neither could he entirely shrug it off, and so he sat and listened.

"What may we do in the face of such things, you ask? What may we do in the face of a calamity from the skies, in the face of disasters without number and dangers untold?" The archbishop paused, and half the court nearly fell over itself leaning forward to catch his next words. "We may *believe*." A second pause, of longer duration, to let them process that statement. "Now is the time, my sisters and my brothers, to yield—not to despair, not to rage nor to hate—but to the sweet call of faith. Now, more than ever, faith is the armor we must all clasp about us, the sword we must take to hand. It is both our protection and our comfort."

He strode the length of the room, pulling nearly every eye with him, willing or not, speaking as he went. "Each of us here has been touched by the divine hand of Caine, Our Dark Father. In all of our veins run His shining legacy. We may wish to deny it, we may wish to reject the destiny that is ours or shirk the finality of His judgment, but, in the end, we are all His children, as we are all siblings in His blood. This is my faith. This is my truth, which I offer unto you freely and without reservation, to give you peace and comfort in these dark nights of fear and danger." His pale gaze swept the room and came to rest on Alexander and he raised a pleading hand. "I beg this favor of you, Your Highness, Alexander, *Princeps Lutetius*. In your realm, as in so many others, the purity of my faith has been poisoned, corrupted by those who would use it for their own venal ends, to seize power over the minds and wills of the needy and the spiritually vulnerable, to enrich themselves on the pain of their brothers and sisters. I beg of you the chance to redress this wrong and cleanse this stain from the immaculate robe of my church."

Something leapt between them in that moment, as the archbishop's pale, intense eyes met his own—a spark, a silent communion. Alexander shuddered inside at the force of the mind contained within that slender frame, the implacability of the will. It took him a moment to form the words that would respond to the request, and not the voiceless understanding that still vibrated within him like the struck string of a harp. "What do you propose, Your Grace?"

"My brother, the Bishop St. Lys, is a man of great eloquence and profound faith. It is my desire that he be granted a forum in which to discuss and expound upon the true and unsullied nature of our faith, to repair the damage done to the opinions of so many of our brothers and sisters in its regard, and to educate our siblings in the particulars of our church. We do not seek to make converts, though we will not turn aside any who wish to walk the path with us, but merely to make clear matters that have become clouded." The Archbishop approached again, and rested one slender hand on St. Lys' shoulder. "This man is both a rock of faith and a learned scholar. I commend him in all ways to Your Highness, and ask only that he be permitted the chance to speak to your people from his heart."

Alexander smiled wryly in response to that. "I cannot see how permitting His Excellency a forum in which to express his views can bring about more harm than has already come to this city from the adherents of this path, Your Grace. But neither do I expect much fellow-feeling to come of it, either. You have chosen," in a tone of supreme irony, "the most inauspicious of times to attempt this revival. I do not, however, see any reason to deny this request."

"I ask for three nights, Your Highness," the Archbishop replied. "Three nights, and a safe place in which all who wish to gather to listen may do so."

"Very well." Alexander rose to pronounce his judgment. "You shall have three nights in which to speak without fear to the Cainites of Paris. In the past, when such gatherings have occurred, they have taken place at the Roman arena across the river in the Latin Quarter, which remains from old Lutetia. This place shall be yours to make ready, and it shall be a place free of worldly violence for the duration of these… lectures, upon pain of final death for those who break the peace. Let us know, Your Grace, when the first of these gatherings shall occur, that all may be edified."

The Archbishop of Nod bowed then, an elegant gesture from the shoulders, his pale eyes bright. "Your Highness, it shall be my most profound pleasure to do so."

Chapter Eight

"There was a time when people came here to be stirred by the words of pretenders," a youthful looking female vampire stole Anatole's gaze to her own sapphire eyes. She stood with another veiled woman who sat on the ledge of one of the amphitheater's seats. Anatole looked away from the girl to search for Zoë, but the girl continued to speak. "They sometimes pretended to be faithful, and at other times came to act the roles of murderers. But they managed to stir this arena with words alone." She spoke with a Sephardic hint to her voice and dressed as one still shy of womanhood. Then again, so did Zoë, and this girl reminded Anatole of his adopted childe. Another veiled woman found her place next to the girl, and took her hand. The girl acknowledged the woman with her eyes and nodded before gazing back to Anatole. Silence passed between them as his mind picked at the meaning of her words. "The fires of catharsis are not easily quelled," she finally said. "Welcome to your Elysium."

"Here you are." Zoë's voice burst from the mass of people milling their way into the arena. Her body followed shortly after. "I got lost in the crowd."

"Next time hold my hand, Zoë," Anatole suggested, his eyes never leaving the two foreign females before him. The girl smiled to Zoë, who nodded in return.

"So," Zoë mused, "it looks as if your mentor tugged you along to witness this spectacle of verbal blasphemy as well."

The girl shrugged. "It gives me time to create." With that, the girl offered a piece of wood to Zoë. "Make something of it," she said. "Make whatever you fancy. It will keep your eyes preoccupied as your ears listen to the words spoken here tonight. But more importantly, it will let you listen, and listen alone."

Zoë reached for the wood but Anatole's voice halted her grasp.

"Don't take it," he advised, his eyes more preoccupied with a third veiled woman, who stood hunched against the arena wall and whom Anatole had not noticed before. She wore a dead-green hooded cloak, and her haggard hand rested against a jagged walking stick. Her eyes, though surrounded by skin veined with wrinkles, dazzled with a familiar agelessness Anatole couldn't quite place.

"It's rare, this wood." The girl shrugged. "I brought it with me from Constantinople."

"Constantinople?" Zoë looked to the girl again. "You are from Constantinople?"

The girl shook her head. "I am from Greece, but I met Malakita in Constantinople."

The woman, Malakita, nodded. "It's just wood, Anatole. Let her have it."

Anatole cocked an eyebrow at this woman who so easily spoke his name. The girl kissed the woman's cheek. "I wish to greet my cousins," she said. "I'm sure you two have things to discuss."

The veiled figure nodded and lifted her stick to dismiss the girl.

"I knew it was you," Zoë said.

Anatole watched the girl. "Not so loud, Zoë. She'll hear you."

"She already knows my disguises, Anatole," the aged woman said. "Lasthenia has hidden with us before."

"A Jew?"

"A Greek. Yet like myself, she also believes in Byzantium's future divinity," Malachite brought a smile to the false face he wore. "She wanted to come so she could witness and reflect upon the foul blasphemy that plagues these lands. And of course it didn't take much to convince the Brujah of this land to help her stay within the city, if only to hear the lectures at this theater."

"And I see that you've changed your veils as well," Anatole whispered. "Why? What of 'Brother Michel'?"

"He will return, my friend." Malachite shrugged his small shoulders. "But for now, no one suspects a withered old woman."

"Anatole," the voice called out and commanded the attention of all three. St. Lys, garbed in a robe of red and white, stood not far from the trio, Archbishop Nikita just behind him. Anatole and Malachite stood still and wordless as both men approached them. Zoë on the other hand, sneered and stepped behind Anatole's right side. St. Lys smiled to her.

"It must be you," he murmured as he stepped before her. He lifted her chin with his hand and studied the fear in her mahogany eyes.

"Yes, it is you. For Brother Anatole would have only refugees as your followers." St. Lys spat his words as if they contained some kind of bitter poison. Zoë braced herself and forced his hand away with the edge of her wrist.

"Get away from me!" she hissed.

"I wouldn't recommend attempting anything, girl." Nikita's bronze voice announced his presence behind St. Lys' left shoulder. Zoë backed from the Archbishop and to Malachite's side. Nikita watched the girl and the veiled Malachite who guarded her small frame. His face remained as placid as ever.

Anatole remained calm, though he found Nikita's voice far more troubling than St. Lys'. Anatole dropped his gaze to the ground and then looked as well to Malachite and Zoë if only to evade the steel blue gaze of the Tzimisce prelate.

"I am surprised to see you here, Anatole," the Bishop St. Lys finally said.

"I'm surprised to receive your personal audience. How did you know whom to look for?"

St. Lys smirked. "I fear you have chosen to be a part of my audience. Not the other way around." His smirk became a smile as he smoothed his cloak with his polished hands. "Despite what you think," he continued, "I invite my opponents to come and hear what I have to say. For different minds bring us to a better understanding of ourselves. It's best to listen to others and learn from them."

Anatole took another opportunity to study Nikita's stance just behind St. Lys' shoulder. His position reminded the Malkavian of a faithful guard or servant, but it seemed more befitting for St. Lys to be the servant guarding Nikita and not the other way around. Nikita didn't so much as move when he noticed Anatole's wandering eyes.

"I somehow guessed you would be here tonight." St. Lys mused as he stole another glance at Zoë. "Child, do not mind the archbishop. He has come simply to introduce my lecture and to listen to its words. He only wishes to keep the peace tonight. We've come to this arena to debate, not to fight."

Zoë scoffed. "Then don't provoke such fights with your own lips, Bishop."

"Zoë!" Anatole snapped through St. Lys' boiling laughter.

"She is just a childe, Anatole," he said. "Her little outcries mean nothing to me."

Anatole fell silent as onlookers noticed the scene around him and the commanding presence of the clergymen. Veronique watched from her place near Lasthenia. Anatole's followers in turn looked to him with questioning eyes.

"Come," St. Lys finally said. "I've reserved a special place for you and your followers tonight. You are after all, special guests."

Anatole's face twisted in confusion.

"I pray you," St. Lys continued as he rested the palm of his hand on Anatole's left shoulder, "bring your men forth and listen closely with wide eyes and open minds," the bishop said as he made for the stage below.

Anatole took Zoë's hand and led his followers along the path, following St. Lys.

Veronique watched them follow the heretics to the middle of the arena. "Unusual," she whispered to Lasthenia. "I've never seen them follow such men so easily."

"Rest here," St. Lys said to Anatole and his flock, and motioned to the seats nearest to the podium. "I will give my presentation momentarily."

Anatole watched as the two men walked to the center of the stage and said nothing, but Zoë couldn't stay silent. "What does he want? Why did he looked at me so?"

Anatole shrugged. "You would think that the bishop wouldn't touch me if he were concerned with keeping the peace," Zoë mused, her voice still trembling with the anxiety with which the two men left her. "You'd think he would consider me as plagued as the lepers," she laughed trying to find humor in the situation. "I'm surprised he didn't fear our disease enough to force us out of this arena."

Anatole smiled at the sheer theatricality of this event. There was something amusing about this particular arena, its gritty floor and weather-beaten walls. Anatole had seen such open classical theaters in his travels. Most were grand, with stages decorated with godlike sculptures and towering arches. Those theaters were, he thought, inspired by a destructive beauty, and within their bowels, actors performed false words edified by the theater built in man's image of heaven, with which they would seduce their audience. This Lutetian arena, however, was no such stage. It was humble and worn down with age. It didn't attempt to hide anything, although Anatole wondered if that was a mask in and of itself.

"…whatever that is."

Zoë's words pulled Anatole's eyes away from where the walls met the mixture of rock and dirt beneath their feet. "What was what?"

"The fiery star, Anatole. They were referring to the fiery star."

Anatole studied Zoë, his face mixed in confusion. "Who?"

Zoë's hand shoved at his shoulder but he kept still. "You weren't listening. Your mind was drifting." She sighed. "Some woman was trying to figure out what her son meant by the 'hairy star' but she must have seen it herself."

Anatole shrugged. "Most can see it now."

"But this woman was blind," Zoë remarked.

"Rumors," Anatole replied as he quirked a brow at Zoë.

Nikita's powerful voice froze the spectators to attention. "We stand together in troubled nights and beneath a troubled sky, my fellow Cainites. For three nights, one of my most esteemed colleagues will tell to you his interpretation, and discuss the meaning of it. I invite you all to listen in these three nights to the learned Bishop Antoine de St. Lys of Clan Lasombra. I pray you find meaning in his words. For they are only words, and you must decide for yourself if they hold any truth."

St. Lys smiled as Nikita paused for a moment.

"You might ask yourselves why we present a lecture to you if we question the truth behind its words. To that I say that it is best to know the words of thinking men, whether they are true or not. For all investigation leads to some knowledge, and we do better to investigate the truth behind questionable beliefs than we do to have no words with which to debate. So listen and watch my brothers and sisters."

Clapping poured softly from somewhere in the audience like a springtime drizzle. Nikita stepped back from the podium and motioned for his bishop to step forth. With that, St. Lys stood and gracefully stepped to the podium.

"Freedom," St. Lys' voice broke from the center of the theater, demanding the attention of all within it. Two guards positioned themselves at either side with torches to shed light upon the speaker. Nikita sat in the back and clasped his firm hands together.

"Freedom is a blessing, and those who are blessed are free," he announced. "For the liberation from need, is a blessing and a privilege."

Anatole thought St. Lys appeared divine enough to know of freedom, his fine ivory robe glistening beneath the torchlight that danced with the shadows on the cloth. He even drew a few gasps from the crowd as he spoke, and the eyes watching him sparkled with a growing curiosity or awe.

Zoë, on the other hand, was more preoccupied with Veronique and the girl who had given her the piece of wood.

"The Greek Jew. Who is she?" Zoë asked curiously.

Anatole's gaze shifted to the girl for a moment, who, like Zoë, was more preoccupied with something in her hands than the speaker before her. "A refugee Brujah who should be paying better attention."

Zoë quirked a brow, but then settled down to pay attention. It would not last, Anatole guessed, but it would do for now.

The vibration of St. Lys' voice interrupted Anatole's thoughts. "Freedom," St. Lys continued, "is also a natural state, and yet a path few can walk with grace or ease." His gaze bore into the crowd.

Anatole watched as well, his own eyes obedient in their luster. They followed St. Lys' every move in such a way that the Malkavian's mind was etched with each word that left the Lasombra's lips.

St. Lys pursed his lips as he lifted his hands. "The path taken by the greater number is simply to believe unquestioningly whatever seductive lies that they were taught, and this is the path of slavery, not freedom. Faith, if by faith one means mere belief, is not of itself liberating. Without truth, it is worthless. Worse than worthless, it is a shackle to the spirit."

Zoë's sigh diminished both the power of the bishop's dramatic pause and the depth of Anatole's focus. He watched her as her left hand carefully guided the blade of a dagger along the piece of wood she held in her right.

"Listen," Anatole suggested again. "It's important to know what the man thinks even if he is wrong."

She furrowed her brows, her forehead crimping in disbelief, but she watched.

St. Lys cleared his throat. "My brothers," he began as he shifted his gaze to Zoë. His voice melted then, as if to endear the following words into the most rigid of hearts. "My sisters." He smiled to the Ravnos, not minding that she ignored it for now. "We Cainites are not slaves," St. Lys insisted. "We are free by nature, and therefore blessed by nature. We are free because we are not entirely bound to the needs this material world imposes on the mortal souls who walk it. We do not need the things mortals need to survive. Mortals must eat food and water that is not pure. We do not need food or water to sate our hunger, nor do the diseases they carry weaken us. Likewise, we do not need clothing to protect us from the chill of winter, and we may wear the finest fabrics even in the coldest of months. Being free of these needs grants us freedom from the impurity they bring." St. Lys paused to study the anxious Ravnos once more. He smirked at her child's play. "We do not even need the sun."

"It kills us," Zoë muttered sarcastically.

"It kills us." St. Lys mocked Zoë's voice as he watched Anatole. A small smile spread across his face before he spoke again. "This is what the simple mindminded would say, those who are like a child without a suitable teacher."

Zoë nudged Anatole angrily. "Respond."

Anatole moved his eyes from the bishop to once again study Zoë's craft as St. Lys spoke on, not waiting for a response. "Food poisons, water drowns and even the sun burns the most cautious of mortals. Yet, mortals must take all of these harms into themselves to survive, whereas we refrain and thereby remain unsullied."

"Light is a blessing," Anatole said at last. His voice elicited a series of gasps from the audience. Yet, he continued. "God said, 'Let there be light!'" The crowd broke in dismayed humming at his abrupt words. "And that light was good. Yet that good destroys us."

"Silence!" Nikita chided. "This is a lecture, not a debate."

"Have respect for the scholar," another shouted through the array of alarmed voices. St. Lys lifted his hands and there was silence.

"Patience, my kinsmen. The Malkavian has a point, and it is a point upon which I will arrive lest more interruptions rob me of the time I rightfully possess for my speech."

The silence once more belonged to the bishop, and he began to fill it. "All we need is that very divine thing which gives life." He paused as a clutter of murmurs sounded in affirmation. "This blood gives life because it is pure, and we are privileged to take of this blood because the blood within us is the purest and may only have what is pure to sustain it. This blood sustains our instinctive desires to better ourselves. It nurtures within us the abilities to grow strong and prove our strengths whether they be beauty, virtue or intelligence. Our perceptions are even stronger, and we notice what those in the dark realm of imperfection do not." St. Lys paused as Anatole wrung his fingers together. Zoë continued carving, her small knife now smoothing a second right angle into the piece of wood.

St. Lys raised his eyes to the sky. The comet hung there, its faint trail melting scarlet over their sequin-white array. "Like that bleeding star," he finally mused. "Many of us have seen it for some time now, yet there are those of mortal blood who fail to observe its effect on the heavens. We've been enlightened because our blood has brought to us the purest of perceptions. It also perfects our physical shells. We do not age, and even time ignores us. We do not scar; our blood heals all but the most blazing of wounds. It is the shining blood, and it is our blood. It allows us to attain everything that will lead us to physical and temporal perfection. For we will not be prepared for the times of divine perfection ahead if we cannot attain near perfection before those times come to pass."

St. Lys allowed another weighted silence to sink into the audience. Anatole shifted his gaze to those who surrounded this man. Nikita sat erect to the left, the palms of his hands rested over the richly dyed fabrics of his thighs. He appeared so calm in his rigid repose that one might think him gentle. He reminded Anatole of the pagan statues he once saw in Constantinople; gentle in appearance but immortally fixed in their blasphemous purpose.

The bishop continued. "Since, as I have explained to you, our bodies and minds attain to a higher purity by virtue of the purity they imbibe; and since that which is purer and higher must be thereby closer to God, and that which is baser and more imperfect just the opposite, then it surely follows that we are not—as some would have it—specially cursed by God, but specially blessed." St. Lys looked pointedly at Anatole. "We are blessed by nature with a resurrection that gives us freedom. Like the Son of God, we too became still and lifeless, only to rise from death. Like Christ and his disciples, we drink the blood that has been passed down from our divine savior, Caine. It is the shining blood, and like Christ, we share its richness with mortals worthy enough to take of it before the Third Caine rips us from our physical prison. For if we are blessed, not cursed, then with blessing also comes duty."

Anatole shifted uneasily and opened his mouth.

"Anatole…" Malachite began.

Anatole ignored the veiled Nosferatu. "We are not Christ figures!" he bellowed. Once more, the audience murmured in unrest.

St. Lys' heavy eyes narrowed in on Anatole and smiled at the peevish interruption. "No," he agreed. "But we are like such a figure. We are brothers and sisters of that figure, and likewise divine, though of course not to the same extent. However, to mere mortals, we are nearly gods who have the ability to kill them or bring them forth into salvation. We must therefore spread the shining blood so others may be set upon the path to divinity and God's salvation."

"Salvation!" Anatole hissed. "You seek to save by enslaving the weaker with your blood. You speak of purity of spirit but garb yourself in material wealth. You claim to hold the key to salvation, but your church worms itself through the Church of Rome, mouthing the words needed to preserve your position. Are these not words of heresy?"

"And dressing in rags and hiding in woods is a surer path to salvation?" St. Lys asked.

Anatole let out a sound of dismay. "How can you people listen to this and not question the blasphemy behind this man's words?"

Again, the crowd stirred.

"Silence," St. Lys shouted. "I did not come here to drag followers in my wake. I am here to interpret what is present before us, and if you find the Madman's wild words more convincing than an appeal to your own higher reason, then by all means join him. But first, look above you! What do you see there in the sky? Is it not the fiery star? Does it not bring with it the reminder of the prophecy?" St. Lys paused to look over his shoulder to Nikita's sitting form. The elder nodded and St. Lys smiled something of understanding. "The blessing is within us, my fellows." He turned his eyes back to the audience while speaking slowly enough to savor the flavor of each word. His face lit with another treacherous smile. "I am not asking you to believe what I believe. I am asking you to look around yourselves and notice what stands around you. Other blessed souls. Other beings of the shining blood. Brothers and sisters perfected in the image the Creator made you in. Perfected to prepare you to receive the blessing that the Third Caine will bestow upon you."

Anatole glanced at Zoë. Her eyes were transfixed on the small bit of wood at her fingertips.

"Now look again to the sky. If you are able, notice that ruby star that bleeds over the heavens. Look and listen to the faintest of voices. They say that the Third Caine is already here. That the year quickly approaches. Time runs out for the immortals to save the worthy. These voices are faint and few now, but so were those who first witnessed the miracles of Christ. But, as Christ's miracles grew, so too grew the voices in volume and in strength. Similar nights approach us now. My brethren, prepare yourselves and prepare the worthy around you. Share your blood now and save them. For soon it will be too late."

"You lie!" Anatole's mind was aflame with anger. "How can you ask us to spread this curse that has ripped us from the breath of life that God gave unto us? We are cursed and we are slaves to this curse." The crowd gasped in astonishment, either at Anatole's defiance or his audacity.

Archbishop Nikita finally stood from his stone throne. "Silence," his voice vibrated over the arena with such a force that the walls seemed to shake. "This is a lecture, not a debate or a place for questions."

"Archbishop Nikita," St. Lys intervened. "I confess myself rather intrigued by these folk who are so bold as to interrupt me before an audience of colleagues." St. Lys turned to Anatole again. "Please, tell me my brother, why do you brand me a liar? What is it in this blessing I describe which inflames such anger that you will publicly defame me? By all means, enlighten us with your views. What exactly is wrong with this blessing we both share?"

Anatole's face creased at the brows as he parted his teeth to speak. "A blessing? You call this so-called freedom a blessing by nature? A liberation from the base needs of physicality? We are liberated from nothing! For Caine's blood creates false attachment to whomever first spills it upon our lips. We can become helpless to that person, and heel to his every call. We become captive, drained of our own pure blood and forced to take in the blood of the dead lest we wish to end our existence. I can't speak for everyone but I remember the pain of that night. I remember being unable to resist that which kept my physical shell but killed my soul and the spirit within it. Now, to keep the tatters of my pain-drenched soul, I must steal the living blood of others. And every time I do, a little more of that soul is chiseled away. It will eventually leave me with nothing more than an unchanging physical shell and a passionless mind that, as if frozen in time, will care no more for the life that moves with it. Even Christ spoke highly of passion, but of passion that allows for change. If we are forever frozen in time, we cannot change. If we cannot change, we are even more dead than the stones of this theater that age with the weather that damages them."

Anatole paused as if to catch his breath. It pained him to realize that such a pause was unnecessary. "If eternity allows us only to accumulate an infinite burden of sin, then it is no blessing. We, unlike Adam before the fall, know of good and evil."

He looked around at the stony silence of the audience, who if only for a moment, found something truly painful in his words. He felt Zoë lean against him. Malachite hung his head for a moment and even the Brujah girl parted her lips and her stoic face took on an expression of sorrow. Anatole sighed. No one could say anything, so he continued to speak.

"Are we not cursed to find nourishment in blood? This very blood that brings life and breath to the men and women God loves? It is this very blood that we steal to nourish our dead bodies. How could this be a blessing when so many bodies die or sicken for each and every one of us to live? How is it a blessing to watch, night after night, the souls of the innocent fade to death in our arms only to leave their bodies to rot? Why is it that we treat them as if they were parasites when it is in fact we who leech the life from them?"

"They are indeed parasites until they have been saved by our shining blood." St. Lys put on an apologetic face as he looked into the arena. "I am sorry to say that not everyone will receive this gift, but our goal should be to save more lives than we destroy. We must numb ourselves, for not everything we feel sorrow for is pitiful. And just as a father must punish his son to make of him a man, so must we the perfected inflict some pain in order to bring about wider salvation. Our method of nourishment teaches us this lesson and I would beg you to heed it."

"And remember also that by your salvation," Anatole answered, "we destroy everything good by nature. We cannot eat or drink the fruit God provided for His beloved man. We are unable to bask in the light the Creator deemed good. It is that good light which is shining, not our blood. And God divided the light from the darkness. So we are those who must, by nature, remain in darkness, separated from the good and the light. Though we are not the darkness, we are slaves to it."

Anatole took in another futile breath as he waited for St. Lys' response. The bishop's silence only allowed Anatole's mind to fume with the thought of the heretic's previous words. "You say to drink only blood is a kind of freedom? It is our nature to crave blood. We need this blood so much that when we can't have it, we lash out and lose the rationality that separates mankind from the lesser animals. We lash out and attack the innocent for their blood. You claim, Bishop St. Lys, that the pain we impose is a lesson to our fellow-man, but how does murder and disease serve any purpose but to reinforce God's own truth that that which is good is in the light? We not only need this blood to survive, but we are slaves to it. When it is denied, we lash out like the drunken fool does for his alcohol. Furthermore, do our beastly natures not cause us pain? Do we not burn when they rage? If such is the case, then how is our beast of a higher order than the lusts of man and woman?"

St. Lys opened his mouth to answer, but Anatole cut him off. "You claim that we do not need the sun when in fact we fear it! We fear that very light that God deemed good. Can't you therefore see that we, by nature, fear what is good? Who is willing to go before the sun this coming morning and stand in its rays? I ask you. If any of you do not fear this, remain here tonight while the rest of us escape into the shadows of our havens."

"I do believe your teachings are filled with hopelessness," St. Lys said. "For if, your words are right, why should we exist at all? Perhaps we should all stay here and let the sun destroy our cursed souls. Might you guide by example, then?"

"We are cursed by nature," Anatole interjected, "but we may also find a salvation and a way out of this curse. We still have souls, and by our nature, they wither. But we also have free will and by that will we can strengthen and save our souls, though that salvation is much harder for us than for our mortal neighbors."

St. Lys spoke calmly, but loudly. "Of course we are not completely perfect at this time, my brother," he said. "How could we be when the perfect world is one of spirituality? Ours is one of material forms that will eventually fade out with time. We could never be perfect while imprisoned in this physical world, and chained to these bodies of flesh and bone. Though more divine than the mortals who dwell around us, we are still bound to our physical forms and likewise bound to some material needs. Yet, these needs are few compared to the needs of those who lack the shining blood. And our physical prison demands a hunger within us. And because we hunger only for blood, our hunger is stronger for it than human hunger which might be satisfied by more than one substance."

Another smile crept across St. Lys' face as his gaze settled upon Anatole. "We are not perfect because we are not pure spirit, this much is true. However there will be a time when we will finally be free of this one last hunger, and the physical pain that drives us to both frenzy and fear. This time is the true time, my brothers and sisters. It is now upon us and as evident as that star which looms over us. Look up and remember my teachings. I am not here to convert, as our brother Anatole suggests, but to warn you of what comes."

"You lie!" Anatole shouted a second time. "You come to trick us into blasphemy. You come to make weak minds out of us. You come to control us." Anatole turned to the crowd. "This man does not seek to save you. He seeks to rape your minds and sap your spirits. My brothers and sisters, we might be cursed by nature but we are not weak."

"Ah, but you are the one who claims that we are cursed, Anatole," St. Lys pointed out. "Not I."

Anatole faced the crowd. "My brothers and sisters, I know my words are covered with despair, but imagine what it will mean if we make our souls strong enough that they do not deteriorate. We will be stronger in the end because our struggle and our penitence are far more painful and difficult to endure. This is why we exist for as long as we do. The curse threatens to

Malkavian

smother our souls with the pain time brings, but it also gives us the time needed to strengthen our souls so they are worthy of salvation."

St. Lys let out a mocking laugh. "We've already been saved," he said. "It is not our souls that are cursed, but our physical existence that imprisons us. Yet, since we've been saved from death we will not decay like those who are fully trapped in the physical. We have been resurrected and when the right time comes, we will be free of our physical existence and the shackles that come with it."

"We are nothing but physical shells," Anatole said, "if we do not try to better our souls and free our thoughts from the pending hunger of the beasts within us. My brothers and sisters, I ask you now to find that strength, for without it we are no more than slaves to our hunger."

The crowd fell silent as all eyes, fired with inspiration, watched Anatole's humble form. St. Lys on the other hand, looked panicked for words.

"I fear that we are not yet perfect," he finally said, "but the broom star heralds the coming of He who will raise us to such perfection."

"But there have been such fiery stars in the past. Why did the end not come then?" Anatole responded quickly. "Even if the end does come, there is no need to fear it if your soul is strong in faith and full of penitence."

"Oh, I assure you Anatole, the end comes. For the Third Caine already walks. There are many stories of such."

"By all means, bishop, show me this Third Caine." Anatole turned to face the audience again. "Who in this auditorium has seen him with his own eyes?"

Archbishop Nikita stood once more, before anyone could respond. "I fear that our time has run short," he began.

"We have questions!" someone responded. "Let the blonde monk speak! His words ring true as well!"

"That man is nothing but a poor beggar with filthy blood and garments to match!" St. Lys shouted in anger.

The Brujah girl, Lasthenia, stood to speak and managed to inspire something of a hush in the boisterous crowd. "I fear I am no theologian," she said, "so I cannot judge the truth of the two speakers. But Bishop St. Lys, if I may be so bold, I wish to have your permission to say something."

St. Lys nodded in approval. "At least you asked."

"Was Jesus not born in a manger among the filth and stench of the lower animals?"

St. Lys once again nodded.

"And you yourself echoed the wisdom of this so-called Christ, who often wandered the streets with the lepers and the prostitutes. It is even said, I believe, that he cared so little of his garments that he often failed to remember his sandals. And those who watched from their lofty balconies claimed that his words were no better than his garments."

"I find it odd," St. Lys said, "that a descendant of the Pharisees would argue for the sake of a supposedly Christ-loving monk."

The girl tilted her head as she held her arms crossed over her own garment. "Then all the more reason to allow you men of Christ to debate among yourselves. For if even a faithless Jew who has no interest in your doctrines desires to hear the nonsense you men spit, how can you deny those who might actually accept your teachings?" She uncrossed her arms to indicate the crowd about her.

Nikita looked to St. Lys, gave a slight, disappointed head-shake and turned to the crowd. "A debate between these two men is what you want?" The crowd murmured with mixed reaction. "Let me call a recess. I will speak to the bishop and we shall decide what will occur in the next two forums."

As people broke into a dozen private discussions, Archbishop Nikita approached St. Lys. They spoke in tones Anatole could not hear over the din.

* * *

"I believe a debate is in order, Bishop."

St. Lys shook his head. "I do not believe this audience will listen to my words, Your Grace, not against this man's deluded passions."

Archbishop Nikita shrugged. "The debate will give you an opportunity to argue dialectically with the madman. He is so moved with passion that he spits out your rational words now. But force him to operate within a highly structured debate, I believe you could pull this crowd back to its senses."

St. Lys nodded as he spoke. "I am thankful to have your advice, Your Grace. I fear I would have failed to finish my lecture had you not stepped in."

Nikita smirked. "Childe," he began. "You didn't finish your lecture tonight. Nikita allowed his eyes to stir over the audience, and then upon the Brujah Jewess who spoke so carefully of her neutrality.

"And I fear," he added, "that I cannot help you beyond the few suggestions I will give you before I depart."

"You're leaving?"

"Have faith, Antoine," Nikita whispered. "You have the wisdom to steer the remaining lectures to your benefit. You are in the right and the truth of the shining blood will prevail. Besides, by the next gathering, this prophecy will have touched these scholars and fear will boil in their minds. They will be hungry for the logic you can impose on the chaos."

St. Lys nodded as he listened.

"Just be sure to finish the lecture series, Bishop. You are our last hope in bringing any kind of salvation to this flock."

"I understand," St. Lys responded.

"If all else fails, use the flawed passion of that Brujah girl."

St. Lys cocked an eyebrow at the comment. "What do you mean?"

Nikita smiled to him, then looked upon the audience and lifted his hands. "My fellow Cainites," he cried out. "As you request, there will be a debate between the penitent Anatole and the Bishop St. Lys. It will however, be a formal debate and it will require the most temperate of souls to keep its structure and monitor its length." With that, Nikita lowered his left hand to gesture to the girl. "Though you claim that you are not a scholar, and even if you have the blood of a Jew, you speak neutral words. You've proven yourself to be as wise as the eldest of sages, though your physical shape speaks otherwise." Nikita smiled slowly as he let the silence pass through them. "I believe you've made an example of yourself. Will you be willing to monitor the structure of a formal dialogue between these two men of God?"

Anatole looked to the Brujah girl who stood firmly before Veronique. She simply nodded. "I would be honored, Archbishop."

"Your name again?"

"Lasthenia."

"Very well." Nikita smiled. "I therefore invite all of you, children of Caine, to bring yourselves to this place for three nights. Bishop St. Lys of Lasombra will debate with the Malkavian Anatole. Lasthenia of the Brujah will draw out the rules and structure of this debate. I wish you all a healthy debate, and with that, this forum is excused."

St. Lys glared at Nikita as the audience began to disperse. "I've seen her speak with the Malkavian," he remarked. "She is not neutral."

"The audience doesn't know that. Also, this audience will look well upon you if you trust one of their own to mediate a debate you wish to win."

"But she is a Jewess."

"Yes, but unless I miss my mark, she is also one of those Brujah who still holds to a hatred of all things Ventrue." The rivalry of these two clans, said to go back as far as the Punic Wars between Rome and Carthage, was much exaggerated, but not altogether unreal. "Alexander is of powerful Ventrue blood and there will be more than a few of his line in the crowd. If you cannot raise the girl's passions in your favor, raise her ire against you. Goad her into breaking the interdicts against violence Alexander imposed. The prince's men will enforce his law and look highly upon you if stand against one who threaten their peace." Nikita shrugged. "This is a last option in case things turn against you, but at least you have a last option."

"It will get her killed," St. Lys replied.

"Such is the fate of all the faithless." Nikita studied the odd girl for a moment before glancing to St. Lys. "Brujah blood is quick to anger. Use that."

St. Lys followed Nikita's gaze to Anatole and his adopted childe as they met quietly with Veronique d'Orleans. Anatole nodded and spoke, but the bishop could not make out his words. The monk placed a hand on his protégée's shoulder. She looked up to him, hungry for guidance.

"Anatole also has a weakness," Nikita finally said, smiling slightly.

"Oh, yes," St. Lys said. "The Ravnos girl."

Chapter Nine

Anatole entered the square nearest Bishop St. Lys' cathedral with a small entourage of the faithful at his heels. Zoë was at his side, as always. Malachite had resumed the disguise of "Michel." He hung back warily, watching the faces in the crowd, listening for the whispered words of those at the fringes— watching their backs. There were others with them now, many others, gathered from the streets and from among those who'd attended the lecture and sided with Anatole. The structure of Notre Dame de Paris—*A true cathedral*, Anatole thought—rose over a row of houses like a witness to his confrontation of the Heresy. He took it as a good sign.

Anatole had taught whenever he could, moving from street to street and spreading his words of faith through the hours of darkness. As they stepped from the street into the square, he heard the sound of hooves clopping on the paving stones. He paused, turning to see who approached.

The monk recognized the Archbishop of Nod's carriage at once, and his shoulders stiffened in surprise. The carriage drew to a halt, and the driver leaped quickly down to hold the door open for his master. Anatole considered moving into the thinning crowds and losing himself, but before the decision was final, Nikita had stepped into the street and up into the square. The Archbishop's gaze fell on Anatole at once, and with a smile that managed to fulfill all the requirements of humor yet deliver none, the highest of heretics started toward him across the square.

"What does he want?" Zoë hissed, fear edging her usually soft, melodic voice. "Why is he here?"

Anatole raised a hand to silence her, and stepped forward, nodding to the archbishop. Anatole's entire frame was tense. This did nothing to ease Zoë's nerves—

she was astute at reading his moods, as much as anyone could be, and this was not a good one.

"Archbishop," Anatole said. His voice was soft, but it carried easily. "A pleasant surprise."

Nikita's pseudo-smile did not waver. He moved with casual grace, every motion a display of power. His gaze was locked on Anatole's, but there was no particular animosity in those aged eyes. He seemed genuinely amused by the meeting, but not actually happy.

"Not waiting for the next debate to spread your wisdom, I see," Nikita commented.

"Salvation is not something to be put off for better times," Anatole replied, biting back the sharpness in his voice. "It is fine to debate doctrine, but it is imperative that the doctrine lead to faith—and to action."

"Granted," Nikita said, his smile widening, if not warming. "It is the set of beliefs, or precepts, you bestow the faith upon that matters most."

Anatole remained silent. He could have retorted, spawning another lengthy debate, here on public ground and unsanctioned, but he was loathe to let it happen. This was not Bishop St. Lys; something in the way Nikita stood, the cast of his eyes above the crowd, the profile of his face turned skyward, watching the stars in the sky, bothered Anatole greatly. He could not escape the feeling that this was a soul shaped by pain greater than most thought possible.

"I wish that I were going to be present when you and the bishop next meet," Nikita said, breaking the silence. "The first debate was intriguing, and I am curious to know what St. Lys will bring to the table with him in the next round."

"I doubt he will bring anything that you are not intimately familiar with," Anatole replied, wondering where the conversation was leading. "I am surprised that you won't be there to support him—he seems very much enamored of your teachings."

Archbishop Nikita eyed the monk for a moment, as if trying to figure out if he'd been insulted or complimented. Finally, he shrugged. "The bishop knows the teachings of the shining blood as well as I. He doesn't need me coddling him. Other work calls to me."

"You are leaving the city, then?" Anatole asked. He was curious, despite his unease. This was important news. St. Lys with Nikita standing in the shadows at his shoulder was one thing, St. Lys by himself another.

"I must pay a visit to our brethren in Germany," Nikita replied. "There are always those in need of direction." He hesitated, then nodded to Anatole, "But, you know that well, I'm sure."

Malachite, who had been listening in the shadows up until this point, stepped a little closer, trying not to be too obvious, but wanting to be certain he heard what passed between the Archbishop and Anatole.

Noticing the movement, Nikita turned toward Malachite. Again, Anatole felt his spine stiffening. Voices clamored just out of reach, and it made it less easy to concentrate .

"Are you of the city," the Archbishop of Nod asked, "or did you follow my friend the monk here on his journey?"

Malachite hesitated to engage this man of reputedly formidable power. Nikita's predecessor had been a powerful vampire indeed, but the Nosferatu did not know the depth of this fiend's power. Only when it became obvious that Anatole would not rescue him from Nikita's expectant gaze, did he at last venture to speak.

"This is a beautiful city, Your Grace," he said as softly as he could manage. "It is not my own city, but it is lovely. I am late of Constantinople."

Nikita nodded. "I might have gathered as much from your accent," he said. "I have seen the beauty of that city myself. It has been a long journey for you."

The Archbishop turned his eyes to the sky once more. "I have journeys of my own ahead. Would that I might find some time to rest, but this comet streaks across the sky like a jagged crack in some holy visage. It draws me to the east."

Malachite started visibly, then regained his composure. The archbishop seemed not to notice, but Anatole was sharper, and stepped closer, speaking up to divert Nikita's attention.

"It is almost poetic," Anatole said. "You will go into the east, following the journey of Caine himself, who was branded by God and forced east into Nod."

Malachite stiffened, as if some unseen hand had slapped him. This time, Nikita noticed. He watched the Nosferatu for a long moment, seemed as though he might speak, then fell to silence once more.

At last he turned back to Anatole.

"An intriguing parallel, perhaps, but not the same thing," he said. "I go where I am called, and where I am needed. There will be a time when Blessed Caine walks among us once more, and matters of debate will become moot. There is no relief in such conversation, only the reopening of old wounds, and the rehashing of thoughts in minds long set upon their separate trails."

"And yet," Anatole replied dryly, "you sanction the debates between St. Lys and myself."

Nikita smiled again, this time with some actual emotion. "The assembled Cainites wished it, so why should it not be so? And there is a certain entertainment in watching the thrust and parry of educated, swift-thinking minds."

Anatole frowned, but he didn't reply. Malachite had pulled away again, and the monk watched his companion step slightly off into the crowd. Something had moved him, , but Anatole could not discern exactly what it might be from the old Nosferatu's features, particularly not while Malachite wore such a thorough disguise.

Anatole glanced at the archbishop again, scanning those wise, confident features for signs, but seeing nothing. What did Nikita see? How much did he know? How much did he believe? The Heresy was rife with those professing deep belief while using rumors of Caine's rising to further their own ends, and manipulate those around them.

The two stood in silence for a moment longer, then Nikita turned to the monk a final time. "Great things are coming," he said. "I will go to find my answers in the east, following the road beneath the comet itself. For now, daylight approaches too swiftly, and I have much to do this night, as I'm sure you do yourself."

Anatole nodded. Without another word, Nikita turned on his heel and strode past his carriage and across the street to where St. Lys was no doubt awaiting his arrival. Anatole wondered briefly if the bishop had been watching from a balcony as the Archbishop of Nod arrived in the square and conversed with the enemy. Even when the archbishop had gone, there remained something about his visit to the square without warning or guard, the way his gaze swept past Anatole and into the crowd as if following others, that grated like rusted iron against the insides of his mind. The images left after Nikita's departure were vague but tinged with blood. Anatole turned to Malachite, but he too was already gone.

Anatole raised his own eyes to the sky, not facing east, but turning in a slow circle. He closed his eyes the better to see. He felt Zoë sidle up to him.

"What do you see?" she whispered.

He opened his eyes.

"Fire," he replied. "I see fire. What I can't see is if that fire is a burning hell of destruction or the purifying flame of redemption."

Anatole and Zoë turned away from the square, and wended their way back through the crowd, listening to the questions and comments of those who followed Anatole's teaching. He spoke to them all at length, eventually making his way to the steps of a tavern, closed for the night, where he leaned on a stone column and spoke until the hours of darkness drew the shadows creeping toward safety, and the glow of the sunrise threatened on the horizon.

* * *

Bishop St. Lys did not generally walk the streets as Anatole did, but there were times when the weight of responsibility was too much, and he needed the opportunity to clear his mind. This was quite impossible when surrounded by sniveling, whining underlings, so for such occasions, he walked alone. This was no easy feat, as it required him to slip out unnoticed from his own quarters. Fortunately, he had discovered several exits that even his secretaries and seneschals knew nothing about. They would only miss him when he was needed, and this could be after several hours. By then, the bishop could be almost anywhere within the city walls. He slipped out of a door well away from the square where the damnable penitent Anatole had gathered his flock, and turned into the first street he came to. The lengthening shadows shielded him from view and he smiled with satisfaction.

Blessed Caine held his fate, but this night was his alone.

Moving quickly, wanting as much distance between himself and those who would eventually worry and seek him, St. Lys moved down darker side-streets, slipping up and down alleys along his way, winding further into the poorer quarters of the city. He passed few others, and those that he did pass took no notice, which was fine with him as he had much to think about. It was the beginning of the night, and the end of the day, and those frequenting the streets at such an hour were either planning the events of the hours to come, or preparing to move indoors to safety, light, and warmth before the night stole it from them forever.

Archbishop Nikita was leaving, and the second debate would be upon him soon. Anatole, for all his madness, was no fool, and had managed to come off well in their first encounter. It was maddening, and adding to that madness was St. Lys' growing conviction in his own words. When Nikita had first spoken of the comet, it had seemed sudden and vague, and the more the portents aligned themselves with the archbishop's words, the more it seemed to St. Lys that he must get his message across. It was a truth too important to risk failure.

He circled back toward the river with its framework of bridges, its waters dark with the city's offal and debris, boats bouncing on the waves. Moving quickly, the bishop crossed one bridge, flitting through the shadows along the stone rails. He broke into the open for a moment on the far side, returning to the Ile de la Cité, the cradle of Paris where he laired and had started his evening's journey. The city stretched out around him on all sides, and he could sense it, just for a moment, as a huge heart, pulsing with the vitae of Caine in huge veins and vessels beneath the streets and along the banks of the river, which flowed past him, as dark as blood itself.

He continued on, gazing at the stone walls surrounding him as he went, sensing those beyond them, the warmth and the blood. Something was in the air, something he could not place, but that drew him inexorably onward. It was late for mortals, but even so, the streets were just too deserted. St. Lys felt isolated, as though an invisible wall had dropped between himself and the rest of the world, as if the streets he walked on were drawn from some deep, inner place; from some other world.

He rounded a corner, entering another street, no different from the last, except that an alley cut off at a sharp angle to one side. He heard voices, loud and clear, slicing through the eerie otherworldly silence. The bishop moved to the head of the alley, glancing down the shadowed strip between tall, stone edifices, and he

Ellen Porter Kiley

saw two figures, struggling beneath a balcony near the rear, which was a dead end.

St. Lys hesitated only a second. He turned into the alley, pressing himself tightly to the right wall and moving through the shadows as if he were one of them, silent as the night wind. Though his hearing was normally clear over long distances, the voices were a muddle of emotion and slurred sound, and he wanted—needed—to know what they said, what they were doing.

He slipped into the rear portico of one of the shops backed by the alley and watched, concentrating, trying to clear whatever it was that fogged his thoughts. There were two young men struggling near the back of the alley. One was slightly taller, apparently older, his wild hair drifting about his face like strands of fine silk. His eyes blazed with indignation and rage, and his hand was raised high above his head, as though he would strike downward at his assailant and cave in his skull.

"You have brought this upon yourself," he cried.

The bishop shook his head. The words were so suddenly clear that it caught him off guard.

"You cannot fault me for what father thinks, or what he does. I am not our father."

"You have wormed your way into his heart," the taller figure barked. "You have wound yourself about his ankles like a fawning cat, rubbing against him and holding your ears up to be scratched. It is a disgrace, and it has turned his face from me."

The two pulled apart, panting, arms at their sides, glaring at one another. St. Lys watched in fascination, not moving, feeling the pulse of the blood beneath their skin, the anger mounting and the hatred palpable in the cool night air.

"Your jealousy is unbecoming," the younger brother said. "I have made a small fortune in the tavern, drawing in the soldiers and the priests alike. I have made our father wealthy feeding viands and wine to Paris. You have brought nothing but the same output from the vineyard that we have known year after year. The same number of wine barrels bear your crest."

"The wine of your tavern is squeezed from the grapes of my toil," the older brother replied sharply. "The vineyard was our father's, and it was his father's before that. It is the grapes that bind our family, the fruit is our treasure. The wine that bears my name is among the finest in the city. That wine, brother, draws the thirsty to your doors."

"It is wine like any other," the younger man scoffed. "Thirsty men will drink what you serve, as long as she who serves them is fair of face and not too fleet of foot, and the bottles do not run dry." His voice softened. "But you have done well with the vineyard, brother, none has said otherwise. It is a blessing that you hold the family's plot of land. Why is that not enough?"

"You know well why it is not," the older man spun away, angrily. "No matter how much I do, it is your tavern that father praises. If I bring in a fine vintage, he says, 'This wine will fill many of our patrons' cups,' and thus he makes it your success. If I bring home a special bottle, he smiles and suggests that we drink it on the patio where the sunlight will show off the deep blue of the silks you buy for mother. No words for me, at all. Nothing but an invitation to come by the tavern I hate so I can admire along with the rest how great my brother is."

"It isn't like that, brother," the younger stepped toward his brother's retreating back. He laid a hand on his brother's shoulder. "We all appreciate what you do for us. If it weren't for the vineyards, what would I serve? You should be happy in the work you do, and in the satisfaction it brings you."

"That is very easy to say when you are the favored son. Your work is not just for your own satisfaction, you work to make my labor insignificant. I only wish I could understand why they support you."

"In time," the younger said, turning away slowly, "you will understand. In time you will find that the work is what matters, the satisfaction with yourself, not the admiration or praise of others, that makes it worth your time and your life. I cannot help you with this. I cannot change the way you think, or the way father thinks."

Footsteps echoed as the younger brother turned toward the mouth of the alley, head down and shaking slowly from side to side. St. Lys could just make out the expression on his face, filled with sadness.

The older brother turned after his brother. His eyes glowed, capturing a glint of moonlight. His expression was wild, and he whispered his response, so low his brother could not possibly have heard him. St Lys, pressed against the stone wall of the alley and shrouded in shadow, heard clearly.

"I can change his mind, *brother*."

The words hung in the air, as if echoing, though spoken far too softly.

The older brother rose, moving swiftly, and from his tunic he drew a wicked dagger, edged on both sides, like a stake of iron. His steps were swift and sure, and he was upon his brother before the sound had fully registered.

The younger brother spun at the last second, very slowly, his eyes wide and his mouth open for a scream of terror. The scream was never born. The dagger glimmered in the moonlight, raised high and driven down with such force that, though the younger brother tried to block the thrust, his arms were slashed aside. The blade drove home, deep in his chest, the blood spurting and his legs giving way beneath him.

The older brother followed his stroke, pressing the blade deeper and slashing it side to side, up, then down, growling with frustrated rage.

St. Lys stepped from the shadows slowly. He watched in fascination as the younger brother struggled,

Malkavian

thrashing wildly in the dirty street, his sibling's taller frame astride him, all its force—all its energy—focused on the blade.

Chapter Ten

Anatole and Zoë received the messenger in the small yard outside the Crespin's cellar, soon after waking the night before the second debate. They recognized the Nosferatu—once he revealed himself—as Stephanos, one of Anatole's acolytes from the refugee camp. He seemed agitated, traveling alone as he was, but he waited quietly for Anatole to speak first.

"What is it?" the monk asked gently. "I thought you were still in the woods with the rest, Stephanos."

"Malachite has sent me," Stephanos replied, "to invite you to follow me to him. He has gone back through the city gates to the others, and he has news. He bid me tell you that he would have come in person, but time now presses in upon him more tightly than any tomb or coffin, or even the burning light of day. He has asked that we leave at once."

Anatole stood silent for a moment, watching the other squirm nervously, awaiting his reply. Doubtless Malachite would be displeased if they turned him down, but there was so much to do—so many to save—and so little time.

"It is that urgent?" he asked at last.

"I fear that it is," Stephanos replied. "He has not stood still for an instant since rising, and there is—something—in his eyes. I cannot describe it." He paused for a second, then added, "Will you come?"

"Of course," Anatole said with a nod.

Zoë, who had watched this exchange in silence, was clearly surprised.

"We must hurry, then," Stephanos said, turning. "I know you will want to return as soon as possible, and the sooner we arrive, the sooner Malachite will speak."

The three set off without further conversation, stepping into the city streets and moving quickly. As fast as they were, it would take time, and time was an enemy that even Anatole feared.

* * *

They met with more of Malachite's followers before they reached his camp, and they were led quickly inward, passing several guards and bypassing threats and traps. Malachite was careful. He would not be taken unaware, and he and his followers had been in this camp for a while before Anatole's arrival.

When they reached the center of the camp, they entered a large tent and found themselves on a stairway carved from the earth and shored up with stone, leading downward. It was the work of many nights, and there was a central chamber beneath, large enough for a good-sized gathering. In the center of the chamber was a squat wooden table, surrounded by rough-hewn seats, some that were logs with planks and branches crossing them, some that were discarded relics of Paris, or other cities along the road. It was not a meeting hall to rival those of Paris or Constantinople, but it would serve.

Malachite was there already, pacing as Stephanos had described. His movements were quick, filled with nervous energy. Anatole stepped around the table and spoke. "Something has happened."

"Many things have happened," Malachite replied, his gaze snapping up to meet the monk's, then holding steady. "Many signs have converged, and I have seen a vision—such a vision as I never thought to see. I cannot judge it—not fully."

Anatole didn't reply. He waited, expecting more. It was not forthcoming immediately.

"I must gather the others," Malachite said, clapping his hands to get the attention of his followers, who hovered at the corners of the room. "Go, bring everyone here. Leave only the outer perimeter guard in place. They will receive my words from those who relieve them."

Everyone except for Malachite, Anatole, and Zoë melted from the room, and there was the soft sound of boots scraping on the stairs. Malachite stood still for a moment, as if concentrating on that sound, then he began to pace again. Anatole saw the distress he wore on his face.

Zoë was less patient, but she held her tongue. She knew that Anatole would not want her to blurt out her questions, and already the sounds of the others returning had become audible, and whispered voices thick with curiosity floated down to them.

Anatole stepped around until he was near the head of the table, and then he sat. Zoë followed his lead, though she would have preferred to stand nearer to the wall, a little back from the crowd, and observe. The rest filed in quickly and silently, and it was only a few moments before a nod from Stephanos, who stood near the door, confirmed that all who were expected were present.

When all were seated, or lining the walls and watching him expectantly, Malachite began to pace once again. He didn't speak at once. His hideously deformed countenance was twisted yet further into a deep frown of concentration. His head was bowed, and as he paced, his silence seeped into the congregation until even the most quiet of whispers had died away, he stopped near the center of the table, his head still bowed, and turned to face them all.

When he raised his face to them, his eyes gleamed. His hands were clasped behind him, and he took just a moment longer to collect his thoughts.

"I have brought you here," he said at last, "to announce that I must leave. I cannot stay here, no matter the cost. I have been called to a mission, a quest, and I will see that quest through to its end. I will bring back the glory that once was, and I will find the one I seek. It is this quest that draws me now." He paused, letting tension build among the assembled Nosferatu and refugees. "I have been gifted with signs. You all know this. You have heard me speak of my travels and my goals. You all know what I seek."

Malachite paused for a moment, glanced over those gathered, then continued. "You also know that times of great change are upon us. The signs are everywhere, and soon the comet will be visible, trailing its fiery hair across the sky, drawing us... where? For myself, I know the answer. I am drawn to the east, and it is to the east I will depart immediately."

Anatole spoke up.

"Why? What have you seen that the rest of us have not seen? What portents have caused this sudden shift? The comet is surely not enough on its own, for it has been in the sky for months, growing more and more visible."

"You were there for the first of it," Malachite answered, watching Anatole carefully. "You had no way to know it, for you have not walked my road, nor have you heard the prophecies I've been granted. Do you recall your conversation with the Archbishop Nikita?"

Anatole nodded in response.

"Do you recall his words?" Malachite asked. "He said, 'This comet streaks across the sky like a jagged crack in some holy visage.'"

Again, Anatole nodded, but his brow was furrowed, and it was obvious that he did not understand the significance of the words, and equally obvious that he did not believe that when he did understand them that he would agree with Malachite's interpretation.

"Remember Anatole, I carry this," Malachite said. He drew forth a darkened image from the folds of his cloak. It was the icon of the Dracon as Christ he had shown Anatole before the latter returned to Paris. There was a deep crack running diagonally across the face.

"When Nikita spoke of the cracked visage," Malachite said, "I felt the words stabbing at me. I felt as if he spoke to me, though he did not seem aware of it at the time. I do not trust the guise he portrayed that night, nor do I understand the depth of sensation his words caused, but I could see this image impressed upon the night sky as he spoke.

"Then," he continued, "there were your words. You spoke of Nod, and of Caine's banishment into the east. Nikita also spoke of the east, as if he felt there would be answers for him there. I don't know if it was his intention, but he passed that certainty on to me. I feel drawn, as I have felt many times on this quest of mine. I must follow that instinct, if I ever hope to achieve my goal." He turned from Anatole and swept those gathered under his gaze. "The Dream must return. There is only one left who might bring this about, one who has the power and the vision. I must find the Dracon, and I believe from the signs that my road leads into the east."

"It is a single random comment," Anatole replied, not arguing but curious.

"It is more," Malachite said quickly. "Much more. When I was at the Temple of Erciyes, I received a prophecy. I've seen portions of it come to pass while others remain mysterious to me. It was your own words that clarified a new passage for me: 'I see with his fiery halo the branded of God fleeing back to the wilderness, and after him the seeker who will awaken and find the truth of the Dream.'"

"You believe that Nikita is the branded of God? He is a chief heretic!"

"I believe," Malachite said, raising a hand to calm the monk, "that Nikita believes he is following in the footsteps of Dark Caine, who is certainly branded."

"But," Anatole settled back, his eyes deep in thought, "if that is so, then Nikita is the seeker. If that is so, where do you fit into this prophecy? You do not seek Caine but the Dracon."

"It is not something I can easily explain," Malachite replied. "You, among all who will hear this, Anatole, should understand. The Oracle of Bones herself delivered this prophecy to me for the purpose of directing my quest. If Nikita follows that same road, then perhaps he has a part to play, as well. I will follow him into the east."

Anatole nodded, still thoughtful, then his gaze rose and he was on his feet, striding toward Malachite with quick, deliberate steps. The Nosferatu held his ground, but he grew taut, a strung wire waiting to be plucked, or to slice.

"That is not all," Anatole stated flatly. "All of this was true last night when we spoke with Nikita, yet it did not drive you from Paris and off into the east. You have been given another sign."

"You see with eyes not of this world," Malachite replied. He smiled, but it was thin and forced. "And you are correct; there is more. There is a powerful sign that I have witnessed, and that I in no way understand. I can't even fully trust what I have seen."

The Nosferatu fell silent, and Anatole stood beside him, hands clasped behind his back, waiting.

"What have you seen?" Anatole asked.

Malachite raised his gaze to meet the monk's eyes.

"I have seen a brother kill a brother. I have seen blood captured in liquid splendor shine like diamonds or a sliver of moonlight. It is possible,

Anatole, that I have seen Dark Caine himself in the streets of this very city."

Anatole grew very still. This was no random sighting. This was no hysterical childe in the streets, crying out of visions in the shadows and dreams woven from fear and ignorance. Anatole knew Malachite. He knew his heart, and his mind, his quest and his obsession. He would gain nothing by making up such a story, and yet, here they stood.

"Tell me," the monk said softly.

Malachite nodded, but he stepped back a pace, and turned to face those gathered before he went on. He took his time, meeting the gaze of each, gauging their reactions to what he had said. There were many who shared his dream, Constantinople restored, the perfect city more beautiful than before with the Dracon at its head. There were those, as well, who were sympathetic to what Anatole taught, the road toward redemption and the deep sorrow of sin. This was not a room friendly to the Heresy, nor a gathering of superstitious sheep awaiting Dark Caine's revival.

"I tried to follow the archbishop when he left you last night," Malachite began. "I wanted to see if he would leave immediately, or if he would lead me to anything that might clarify his words. I needed to know what it was that I felt, to know if what my heart told me as the two of you spoke was a true sign, or if it was just my own mind wanting too badly to be on the road, on the quest.

"I followed him around the places where St. Lys is said to lair, near that square and even before Notre-Dame itself. It was near there that I grew confused. This in itself was odd, because I have been there many times."

"God's power and grace are manifest in that place," Anatole said. "We can all be made uncomfortable by that holy ground."

"I know, my friend, but this was different. It was as if I moved through a fog and when it parted I found myself on one of the bridges leading across the Seine, with the archbishop nowhere in sight. Just before I gave up my search, I saw another moving through the darkness. He was far away, but there was something in the way he moved that was familiar, so I followed, hurrying my steps. He disappeared down an alley, and very slowly I crept to the mouth of that alley behind him.

"It was St. Lys. He hid in the shadows of the alley as his clan is wont to do, but I could see him. At the far end of that alley, two young brothers were arguing. I couldn't make out the words, but St. Lys was transfixed by the scene, so I waited, watching in silence. Moments later, the younger of the two men turned away, and the older sprung at him with a blade, gutting him in the street.

"I believed, up until that point, that our friend the bishop only bided his time until he might feed, enjoying the intrigue and the entertainment of the preceding battle. I was mistaken.

"The killer turned to face the end of the alley, and beckoned to St. Lys, as though he'd seen through the cloak of shadows from the start. The bishop went to him. As he did, the old one grew. Taller. Darker. His wrists poured blood, and not the blood of his fallen brother, it poured from wounds—stigmata—on his wrists and a shining string about his head."

"Caine?" Anatole broke the other's reverie, speaking sharply. "You think you have seen Caine bearing the holy wounds of our Savior? You have gone mad!"

"I do not know what to believe," Malachite replied. "I know what I saw, but it is not I who hears the voices of those unseen. I am the recipient of prophecy, not the voice of it. I tell you only what has happened. Whoever it was, St. Lys went forward to meet him, and fed. He knelt in the dust of the alley, alone, when I turned and fled, making all speed across the bridge and into the city. I spoke to no one, but came here to think."

"How can this be true?" Zoë cried out. "How can it be? And St. Lys? Why him? Why not the archbishop, who seeks so ardently? Or a true Christian?"

Malachite turned away, silent. He had no answers, only questions, it seemed.

Anatole watched the Nosferatu's back for a moment, then bowed his head. He, too, remained silent. This was unexpected—outrageous. It could have been staged, of course. It could have been for St. Lys' benefit, or even for Malachite's. All was not as it seemed, and yet—who was to judge which things were true, and which were false?

Malachite did not turn back to face the gathering, but he spoke once more. "I do not know what is truth. I know the words that have been granted to me, and I know my own road. I will follow Nikita into the east. The comet, high above our heads, will be his fiery halo, or that of Caine himself. If the Dark Father was truly in that alley, perhaps the only events of real importance will happen in Paris. If so, I will miss them. I follow the Dream."

Anatole scanned the crowd. Last year, he had fought a desperate battle for the souls of most of these refugees, prying them away from the heretic Bishop Folcaut. Malachite was undoing all that, and he could already see the effect on some. Gallasyn, who had been Folcaut's main supporter, was wide-eyed. Finally, Anatole nodded very slowly—almost imperceptibly.

"We will see for ourselves soon enough," he said. "The second of the debates is upon us, and if St. Lys has partaken so directly of the shining blood of his faith, he will not keep his good fortune to himself.

Even if it is a fabrication, he will use it. With Nikita's departure, he is on his own. I must prepare for this."

Malachite turned back, stepped closer, then thought better of whatever thought had possessed him. He met Anatole's gaze. "I wish you well, monk. If Caine walks the streets of the city, it will be a dark place indeed for one such as you."

Anatole smiled thinly. "If Caine walks these streets then I welcome him, for he will surely rid us of the heretics who spurns his lessons in his very name. It is they who should fear." He hesitated a moment, then added, "Your own road is a long one, and as likely to end in destruction as in dream. May God and Caine both watch over you."

Without another word, Anatole turned toward the stairs, and walked away. Zoë fell in behind him, glancing over her shoulder in confusion. She nodded at Malachite, but he was too distracted to see.

As the two of them left, the gathering dispersed. The small band of Nosferatu would likely follow their master, but the others were evidently less sure. Anatole guessed the refugees who'd now spent a decade in Bière Forest would stay where they were, content to wait out the events of the next few nights and follow where the comet led them.

As he stepped out onto the road to the city, Anatole stopped and gazed into the stars above them. With a quick shake of his head, he put an arm around Zoë's shoulder and began to walk.

"Come," he said softly. "Our time is too short."

Chapter Eleven

The night air rang hollow with his name. It surrounded Anatole and echoed from the steady mumble of awestruck voices. "Did you see him?" they asked. "Did you see Caine? Will he bring the end?"

Anatole waded through this filth of gossip, his fingers chained through the digits of Zoë's hand. Anatole noticed that the crowd was far thicker than that of the previous forum. Perhaps seven out of every ten vampires in Paris were in attendance and not a small number of others came in from elsewhere in Ile de France. Anatole noted that this number included many from the refugee camp, including the Toreador Gallasyn who now sat openly with other known heretics. Malachite's inflammatory words were already having their effect. The sheriff and scourge of the city were both here, seemingly content to watch and ensure that the edict of non-violence was obeyed. Anatole assumed they'd do their best to shoo out those not authorized to be in the city once the debate was over. Prince Alexander and his consort, the Countess Saviarre, were notable in their continued refusal to attend.

With the bigger crowd came greater fear. Even Zoë was aware of it, and he felt her hand tense in his. Fear would breed in the crowd and bring danger to even the courageous.

The name of Caine continued to move between the lips of the fearing.

"He saved a child with his blood," a young ghoul told her master. "The bishop told me so."

"I also heard that he frequents the underground scriptoriums, but I have yet to see him."

Anatole listened to these stories and noted that a slow smirk rode Zoë's face as she also listened. "How would they even recognize Caine should they see him?" she asked in a whisper.

"Maybe he's watching us now."

Zoë jumped and turned as these words found their way into her ears. Before her stood a girl with a familiar face. She wore a long glossy dress of some dark color that was hard to pick up in the dim torch-lit theater. Zoë finally smiled, discovering the Brujah girl well-cleaned up. "So," she said to Lasthenia. "Have *you* seen him?"

The girl shook her head and her face mirrored Zoë's quizzical expression. "My ghoul, who made this very gown, says that his aunt saw Caine. He claims that the Dark Father arrived to her cottage bearing bread and soup broths." A sarcastic smile smeared its way across her face. "He cooks the finest soups. Manna from Heaven, they say. Or Hell if you would prefer." The girl paused to run two fingers along her cheek. "Yet, he also says that to taste such Manna would cause sudden death, and of course we are unable to stomach such foods. So I've met no one who has tasted his Manna." The girl dipped her hand into a small leather pouch tied to the waist of her garment. "Unless of course, we've all tasted it during the Embrace."

"He cooks, your friends say?" Zoë smiled as if she liked this game. "My friends claim that he also sews the finest dresses, but unfortunately they're so out of fashion no one wears them."

"I made something for you," the Brujah murmured and offered her fist. "I figured that I would see you again." With that, she opened her hand and dropped a shaped piece of wood into Zoë's palm. Zoë studied its rough shape and noted the six points of King David's sigil.

"A symbol of my faith were I to choose one," Lasthenia said. "Not his."

Anatole watched the exchange between the two vampires. To him, they seemed no different than long-lost sisters. Judging by their appearance, such was quite possible.

Malkavian

"You have not left on Malachite's quest," he said to the Brujah. "I thought the news would have come to you, even here."

"How could I pass up the opportunity to adjudicate your dogmatic battles, Brother Anatole?" she said with friendly sarcasm. "Why, I'd rather miss the coming of Caine Himself."

Zoë smiled a little and reached into her own pouch. "Here," she whispered. "I didn't plan on giving it to you, but it's something to remember me by." Zoë paused and handed the girl an intricately carved Greek cross. "In case the end of the world comes tonight," she finished again, her voice mocking terror.

The Zealot girl smiled. "It's beautiful, Zoë."

"Funny to find you both talking together, especially since you claim neutrality," St. Lys glared at Lasthenia as his voice startled the two to his attention. "You've dressed well, Brujah. What's the occasion?"

"I couldn't imagine that you would allow your chair-person to dress in rags when such heavenly topics are being discussed." Lasthenia smiled to the man as she tucked a strand of stray hair behind her ear. "Being the neutral party in this forum, I wish to show as much respect as possible."

"So you are truly impartial?"

The girl shrugged. "I have no reason not to be. I do not believe in prophecies. There have been signs and warnings before, yet here we are now."

St. Lys smirked. "And the rumors of Caine?"

Lasthenia exchanged a glance with Anatole for a moment before she spoke. "Funny that," the girl responded. "My ghouls, my mentor's servant, and my sire's second childe all claim that Caine has been seen. Yet none of them have actually seen him themselves." The girl paused and looked pointedly to St. Lys. "Have you?"

"Foolish childe," St. Lys laughed. "I have seen him. For he killed his brother on the street two nights ago right before my eyes."

"Until I see him myself, I will not waste my time with an irrational fear of uncertain prophecies," she replied. "You are right about one thing. Our time is limited and ultimately we have no control over its course. Yes, one night the end will come, and someday that night will be tomorrow. Should my end come tomorrow, however, I will feel no regret. I used what time I had to accomplish for myself and my soul what I wished to do. I believe it to be wise to allow others to do the same for themselves before their time runs dry."

Anatole studied her, his heart sinking momentarily at the thought that she would not accept the true faith or deity.

St. Lys laughed deeply. "Well said, sage devotee of Seneca. You would make a fine addition to our apostolate if you weren't so wrapped up in your misguided quest. Right now, you take up too much space. It's a shame that suicide is not one of your stoic endeavors."

"You can't kill yourself when you're already dead," Anatole snapped in the Brujah's defense.

St. Lys looked to him as he crossed his arms. "No," he finally said. "I suppose you can't." He glanced down to Zoë, who stood at Anatole's side. With the exception of Lasthenia, the vampires surrounding Anatole were dressed as mendicants, some in visibly soiled rags. "And who would want to end their existence?" St. Lys finally asked. "At least some of us lead blessed existences and await the tomorrow when Caine comes to save us." He shook his head. "Why am I even talking to you down here?"

No one dared to say anything. St. Lys shook his head before he continued. "People like you make my work difficult," he began, his eyes most intent on Anatole. "There are too many bastard childer like you who believe it better to nurture their greedy souls with the shining blood of their sires, rather than share it with the weak." The bishop paused and stepped up to the Brujah girl. His body towered over hers. "His Grace the Archbishop has told me about you. You have no right to call yourself Brujah, let alone a Cainite."

St. Lys paused for a moment as if expecting a response from the girl. She did nothing as he leaned forward to speak at her ear. "You make much work for my brothers and sisters, and they will grow angry at those who inhibit their duty. Ultimately, that will be what cuts your time short."

Stillness lingered about the two of them. The girl's face remained unreadable, but Zoë noticed her fists clench so tightly that she half-expected blood to drip from her fingers. Lasthenia stepped back a little, nodded to the group before her, and made her way to the podium.

"Hmm," St. Lys said as he glanced to Anatole. "I am glad you decided to come tonight, Anatole. The debate is about to begin, and tonight you will be standing beside me, not below me with these refugees."

St. Lys straightened his massive cloak, surveyed the crowd around him and settled his gaze on Zoë. He stepped forward and cupped her cheek in his hand. "The Jewess is a lost cause," he said. "She has turned her back on the whole concept of salvation. But not you, Sister Zoë."

She attempted to look away, but his fingers held her chin forward as he met her eyes. His voice was cool whisper. "There's still hope for you. Promise that you will listen to me tonight instead of whittle as you did. Yes?"

Zoë's brow furrowed and she wanted to slap him as he emphasized the word *listen*.

"Let— go—" Zoë finally managed to say through her gritting teeth.

St. Lys lifted his hands away from her. "As you wish," he lowered his eyes as he stepped back and turned to Anatole. "Are you ready for this lecture?" He asked the Malkavian. He swept his hand down to motion the path to the center of the amphitheater.

Anatole looked to Zoë, who was squirming slightly. "Will you be alright?"

"Don't let him try anything!" Zoë demanded as she looked to Anatole. With that, she leaned close and whispered to him. "He was trying to get into my mind. I've felt it before, and I could feel it this time."

The bishop laughed at the girl's comment. "I've reserved a space for your disciples in front if you're so concerned about their well-being," he said. "I trust that if anything happens, you will see it and have the full awareness and ability to respond."

Anatole frowned as he took Zoë's hand.

Veronique d'Orleans, dressed in a fine surcoat and her hair elaborately tied, seemed a strange addition to this tense knot. When she pushed through Anatole's followers, none challenged her, both because she was taller than any of the men present and because the anger that boiled off her was palpable. It was directed unambiguously at the bishop.

"The time for the debate is here, your *grace*," she said, her steely voice spitting out the honorific like an invective. She quite pointedly put her hand on Zoë's shoulder and waited for the bishop to look away. Once he did, she turned to Anatole. "Do not worry," she said. "I will watch over her. You go on."

* * *

Zoë took a seat by Veronique. Although she would never admit it, she was pleased to have the older woman as a protector.

Cainite and ghoul alike fell quiet as the two speakers stepped before them, joining Lasthenia on the stone stage below. She stepped forward and lifted her hands to gather the attention of the audience.

"Tonight I welcome you to listen to a debate between Brother Anatole of Clan Malkavian, and Bishop

St. Lys of Clan Lasombra. They have come here in light of current events to discuss the true nature of Caine."

Zoë turned around to glance at the crowd. It was an attentive audience, and she marveled that such a small body—no bigger than her own—could draw the eyes and ears of so many people.

"I know," Lasthenia continued softly, "that, because of recent occurrences and rumors, many of us exist in a heightened state of emotion that could easily provoke our desire to lash out at our neighbors." She paused for a moment as she removed a scroll from the roped belt at her waist. "However, tonight we come in peace to listen to these theologians. Of course, even the most gentle of theological arguments can ignite unwanted behavior, which is why I must speak to you of my task and the structure of this lecture. First, as Archbishop Nikita was, I am charged to keep the peace of this debate, at the order of Prince Alexander himself. There are several here, who will move to quell any fighting brew should I not notice it from here." The girl continued to unravel the scrolled parchment as she spoke. "Furthermore, this debate will take a specific form, and I will intervene should either of our debaters step out of line." Lasthenia took in a needless breath and dropped her eyes to the parchment that she now held open with her hands.

"First, each speaker will present his opinion. Though this part of the forum is timed, you both should have ample time to finish your opening statement." Lasthenia extended her arm toward the side of the stage and a ghoul stepped forth holding a large hourglass. "After the opening statement, each speaker will have a chance to respond to their opponent's words if they feel the need. These responses are also limited by time. If neither speaker wishes to offer a formal response, we will move straight to the open debate, during wish you may exchange opinions and arguments as you see fit, provided you obey the following simple etiquette."

Lasthenia paused for a long moment as she studied the speakers, and then the audience who watched them. "There will be no verbal slandering or interruption. If such occurs, I will stop whomever committed the offense, and let the other speaker continue. You will have also broken the laws of this court, and must therefore speak with its leader."

Lasthenia looked to both speakers, who nodded in turn. She then took Nikita's seat from the night before and said, "Then, I believe we should start. This parchment states that Bishop St. Lys should speak first but may I suggest a coin toss for the sake of fairness of all involved?"

"Certainly," St. Lys said with a reptilian smile. He moved to take a coin out of his pocket, but she already had one.

"If it lands with the serpent up," she began, "Brother Anatole speaks first. If the tree is face up, then Bishop St. Lys speaks first." Despite her stature, her voice cut through the air like rain on a windless day.

Eyes rose with the coin as Lasthenia tossed it into the air. It spiraled down in silver flashes before hitting the stone and bouncing once or twice. She brushed a strand of hair from her face as she read the coin.

"The tree," she announced. "Bishop, you shall begin"—she slowly turned the hourglass and rested it on the ground—"now."

St. Lys waited to have the attention of all.

"Many ask why Caine would rebel against his creator if he loved his creator enough to offer his bother as a sacrifice. Yet, being of pure spirit chained to a physical world, it is no wonder that he rebelled against the creator of that world. For though all living things have spiritual souls, it is obvious that their creator wished for them to ignore that which is strongest within them." St. Lys paused for a moment. "Thus this creator was no God of higher good.

"The evidence of this is plain for those who can see it. Eden, God's garden, the Golden Age—whichever you prefer—was a place where all living things lived in harmony and innocence. They knew nothing of pain, suffering and death. In fact, they knew nothing at all and took in anything they pleased. They were gluttonous, these souls of Eden. They were purely physical creatures content to sate their bodies' appetitive desires. They knew no moderation and they could live this way so long as they refrained from tasting the fruit from the Tree of Knowledge."

St. Lys paused long enough to earn subtle reaction from the audience. He smiled.

"For this tree," he continued, "would awaken their minds, their awareness, their emotions, and their souls. Eventually they ventured to taste of this tree, and they were thrown out of Eden. Punished for wishing to know their souls and of other grand things." St. Lys paused. "That is one story. The second follows as such, and hails to us from the ancient philosophers of lands that might not seem so foreign to many of you." St. Lys paused to smile as he studied his audience. As he lifted his hand, it seemed that his body grew brighter in the torchlight as the shadows lifted off his person. Zoë wasn't sure if he looked magnetic or menacing. In the end, she simply listened indifferently.

"There are two realms," St. Lys continued. "One of the physical and one of the spiritual. The physical realm has two levels—the lowest being appetitive and material desires, and the second being belief. The realm of the spirit in contrast, is divided into virtue and understanding, which is the ultimate good. Many a philosopher believes that to attain such a level, one must shed all but the most necessary of appetitive desires. In other words, one must attempt to avoid the material world and live solely in the spirit. For this life is the divine life and closest to the gods. In other words, this is the good life. Yet, for Adam and Eve to have access to this good life, they had to take of the Tree of Knowledge and leave Eden."

Behind the bishop's shoulder, Zoë noticed that Lasthenia smirked briefly.

"Now, my brothers and sisters," St. Lys said with a grand uplifting gesture, "why would a God of any good prefer that man, whom He claims to love most of all, eat nothing from the Tree of Knowledge? Why would He, in other words, deny man access to the good life of true understanding? If a divine life is good, and the creator denies it from us, isn't the creator denying us of a good existence? Does this not sound vile to you?"

People, for fear, watched St. Lys with wide, trembling eyes. Few had a response for the man, but all wanted answers to the questions he asked. Zoë on the other hand, wondered how long it would take him to get to the question at hand, the nature of Caine. She shrugged to herself, sat down, and removed a balled-up piece of cloth from her bag.

"To answer, I must point out that the God of what is good is in no way the same as the creator of this physical prison. God is instead a pure spiritual entity, unlike the Demiurge who created living things so they might serve him. What's more, this Demiurge *fears* us."

St. Lys paused again and the audience stirred in thought.

Zoë turned around again to see the crowd. They were all focused on the bishop, some looking on with wide eyes of disbelief, others wearing the smiles of pride. She knew that sensation, and knew its dangers. *So many people*, she thought, *take his words to heart*.

The heretic bishop continued. "The physical death the Demiurge offers does not deliver you to a spiritual heaven, but to a place of decay where time continues without you. Tell me then, is goodness greed, is it good to horde all secrets to oneself?" St. Lys again paused to allow the crowd to answer, and again smiled when none was forthcoming.

"From here," he continued, "I would like to remind you of stories that have been barely whispered if not completely ignored since the early days of the Hebrew Bible. The Demiurge's priests will not tell you of Sophia, a spiritual entity chained to a physical world. She was both Lilith, who incarnated the higher physicality of belief, and Eve, who was naught but appetite. It was Lilith who gave birth to the spiritual Caine, whereas base Eve gave birth to the physical Abel. The jealous Demiurge despised Lilith and banished her.

"Caine grew up worshiping the Demiurge of course, as I'm sure many of you did. When both Caine and his half-brother Abel came of age, the Demiurge demanded sacrifice. Moreover, as you know, Caine, believing that this Demiurge was fond of the earth and the material fruits within it, then gave him such fruits and grains as gifts. Yet, jealous of Caine's spiritual nature, the Demiurge instead favored the blood sacrifice of his brother, Abel. In this way, Caine understood that he had been lied to, that even the Demiurge knew the higher nature of spirit-carrying blood to purely base foods. Caine then rejected the lies he had been told and in so doing opened himself to truth. He understood that as he was different from his brother, so must there be a True God who was different from, and opposed to, the Demiurge. It was to that True God that Caine made the ultimate blood sacrifice, that of his brother.

"The one True God, in all His glory, therefore blessed Caine, marked him so he would not be killed, set him to walk the Earth, and bring followers away from their physical wants to a life of spiritual enlightenment and rational thought. The True God taught Caine to do this with his shining blood, and Caine indeed sparked a rebellion in his attempt to save the souls of others. Caine then ascended to Heaven to sit by the True God's side. Some of his descendents remained true, but others lapsed in their faith and fell into the snares

Ellen Porter Kiley

of the Demiurge and his priests. In later years, to sound a second clarion call to those who knew the truth, Caine's spirit returned to us in the shape of Jesus Christ."

"You lie!" People gasped as Anatole's voice cracked the air. Lasthenia looked to Anatole and shook her head.

"Let this man finish his lecture," she said. "There is no rush." With that, she looked to St. Lys, who opened his mouth once more to speak.

"This Second Caine came to both create a rebellion and to save us anew with his shining blood. He managed to gather a large following despite the efforts of the Caesars and Pharisees who hated him. These men were so hungry for temporal powers that they even killed the souls of those who did not share their opinion. This is why they crucified the Second Caine, Jesus Christ. Yet, he rose from the dead and did so in full glory, proving his pure, spiritual nature."

Zoë felt lost as she listened to St. Lys tell this story.

"In the end," St. Lys continued, "the Demiurge and his followers fear our shining blood. And I don't blame them." St. Lys smiled slowly, shifting to flattery. "Think of us, my brothers and sisters. Think of what we, who have little need for the material world, can do with our spirits and our spirits alone. Some of us can read our neighbor's thoughts, while others can persuade with will alone, hide from plain sight, create collages of shadows, change the appearance and structure of flesh with fingertips, and heal with the touch of the hand. We can change the Demiurge's creations and even the image he made us in."

St. Lys studied the crowd as he paused to smooth his cloak with his alabaster hands. "I've seen ugly men make maidens swoon, and beautiful women drive the lustful away screaming. I've seen the frail lift monolithic stones, the obese run like the wind and the wounded walk out of battle and continue on for years thereafter. There are even faint rumors that the most ancient of our kind can move mountains, darken the sun and even still the flow of time itself."

Zoë rolled her eyes and adjusted a patch over a small gash on her skirt. Nevertheless, she continued to listen.

"It is rumored that they can do all this without even opening their eyes." St. Lys allowed another silence to separate his rumination. "These are indeed rumors, but given the thousands of years of thought and contemplation these elders have passed, I would not be surprised.

"It is no wonder to me then, that this Demiurge tried to keep us from the Tree of Knowledge in the Garden of Eden. For our souls, now enlightened, are far closer to the True God than the Demiurge will ever be. He of course, realized the powers of an enlightened soul. For even he, with his mind alone, created what we see around us. He created the heavens and the earth from a void. He created air and matter, light and darkness, life and even death. He created this to keep our spirits from their ultimate powers. Remember, Adam and Eve had immortality before they took of the apple. Once they attained insight, wisdom and knowledge, the Demiurge doomed them to mortality so that they would never discover the true powers of their spirit.

"Yet, because of Caine's daring and sacrifice, we have once again been blessed with an ageless and undying existence. And Caine continued his work for the True God. He returned from the spiritual realm to save and enlighten. He spoke against the many false commandments that the Demiurge attempted to impose upon mankind. He then shared his shining blood with the worthy and brought them to enlightened salvation. In his spirit, please continue on, collect your powers over the weak, and lead them to salvation."

With that, St. Lys glanced to Lasthenia. Someone among the audience began clapping, and others followed by example. Soon, the entire amphitheater roared in approval.

"We must continue," Lasthenia finally shouted. She waited for everyone to sit still before glancing toward Anatole. He looked so pale and humble when standing on the same stage as St. Lys. "Start."

Zoë wanted nothing more than to hear Anatole scream out the disgust he clearly felt for St. Lys' heretical words. Not so very long ago, he had faced off again Father Folcaut, one of the bishop's own acolytes and confounded his heretical arguments. *Please*, she begged him silently, *do it again*.

Instead, he seemed to gather his thoughts, and when he spoke, it was with uncharacteristic calm. "I fear I cannot accept Caine to be any kind of messiah or godlike figure above heaven. I believe that there is only one God, who created everything about us. This God did curse Caine, however He is forgiving of nearly every transgression a being can perform. And in the process of seeking that forgiveness, we learn a little more of ourselves.

"Perhaps our Creator wanted Caine to learn from his curse and gain some insight. Perhaps to know too much is something of a curse! Perhaps God wanted us to discover that immortality and the powers of the mind lead to destruction more often than good. Perhaps He wanted us to suffer from this and learn how to use our powers for the best, and rise from the pains only when we had prevailed. For God, like us, must watch His beloved mankind continually die while He continues to exist. Who has not suffered when they watched the last of their mortal relatives die? Children of Caine, God may not have given us the knowledge of good and evil upon our creation, but He did give us the right to choose. Therefore, how can the bishop say that He wished to keep the knowledge from us forever? By choosing knowledge of good and evil, we became closer to our Creator, but such a privilege isn't without its price. We must suffer, and we must know everything, even death. It is true that Caine is exemplary. He is our dark father, progenitor of our race. He is a wanderer, who searches for forgiveness and understanding as we do. He is a tyrannical teacher who will punish those who forsake his lessons. But he is no messiah.

"For Caine's crime we are cursed, and it is we who pay for his sins. For he will never garner sustenance from the soils of the earth, which means he must live off the blood of the living. Yet, to do this, he may kill again. However, he will never be killed and he therefore has until Judgment Day to repent for the atrocities he has committed. Yet he must commit more atrocities to exist."

"Why then, does he refuse to accept non-existence?" St. Lys said.

"I fear you're interrupting, Bishop." Lasthenia studied the man and nodded for Anatole to continue.

"Because the Lord commanded him to be a fugitive and a vagabond upon the earth."

St. Lys laughed. "And how shall he repent if he is simply supposed to be a vagabond upon this earth? Especially when he turned his back on his creator?"

Anatole remained silent. His gaze fixed on Zoë, and she pleaded at him with her eyes. Many of the others in the crowd snickered at him.

"Are you telling us then," St. Lys asked, "that Caine is living, or rather not living, in fear?"

"I suppose that might be an accurate analysis," Anatole concluded. "After all, we should fear the Lord God, should we not?"

"If you wish to fear a despot who causes death because he is afraid that his creations will rise against him, then by all means, cower away." St. Lys spoke smoothly now. His words wrestled more laughs from the audience and he smiled pleasingly to them. "Are we seriously supposed to listen to the madman," St. Lys asked the crowd, "as he tells us to be afraid?"

Ellen Porter Kiley

"Out of order," Lasthenia snapped again. "Brother Anatole, please continue. There will be time for rebuttal later."

Anatole shook his head, his eyes studying the floor for a moment. "I am done with my introduction."

Lasthenia nodded and called a brief recess.

Zoë went to the edge of the stage and Anatole came over. "I keep looking up to see *you*, Anatole," she says, "but all I see is fear." Anatole didn't respond and when the forum resumed, only St. Lys offered to present a formal response.

He began with a passage from the Book of Genesis: "'When Adam took from the Tree of Knowledge, the Creator'—the Demiurge—'said: Behold Adam is become as one of us, knowing good and evil: now, therefore lest perhaps he put forth his hand, and take also of the Tree of Life, and live forever, the lord God sent him out of the paradise of pleasure, to till the earth from which he was taken.'" St. Lys fell quiet again as he drew the attention of the spectators with his mere presence. "This Demiurge even wanted to strip us of the divine. He said, 'My spirit shall not remain in man forever because he is flesh, and his days shall be a hundred and twenty years.'"

The Bishop shook his head. "Fellow Cainites, we have become immortal despite the desires of the creator of this accursed physical world. We are now the powerful spirits he feared, yet my worthy opponent desires for us to bow to this... this despot who made us in his image and then strove to limit us."

Members of the audience stirred with approval.

"Yet here we are now," St. Lys continued, "far stronger than the Demiurge's original creation, and perhaps even beyond his own power. If anything, we should rule over these mortal children of Seth in order to bring them to us. For we have that power, and without our blood, they will not be saved when the end comes." The bishop looked to Lasthenia. "That is all."

162   Malkavian

Once again, the audience cheered for St. Lys' speech.

"Open forum," Lasthenia announced over the cheers. "If you have questions, you may ask them."

"I'm confused," one unsure voice broke from the audience. "Is the end truly coming?"

"Oh yes, it is my fair lady," St. Lys jumped on her answer quickly. "Men and women have spoken of a Caine that walks the streets these very nights. Just look above you at the fiery star."

"But such stars have come and gone in this sky since the time of Aristotle."

"Did any of them bring with them rumors of a walking Caine?"

"Yes!" someone shouted from the back. "This has happened before. And it will happen again."

"Tell me," Anatole said. "I have heard of the rumors that Caine walks this earth myself. Many of us have. But can one person tell me that they've actually seen him in person?"

Silence fell like a rock on the arena.

"Of course!" St. Lys proclaimed. "The other night I saw Caine myself. I saw brother slay brother in the streets about the Demiurge's great fortress, the Cathedral of Notre-Dame. I saw shining blood poor from the wounds of crucifixion. Caine is among us, my friends and the Final Night is nigh!"

The crowd stirred in fear as the bishop continued. "We must prepare ourselves. My fellow Cainites, mark my words. Bring the Children of Seth to your shining blood, and lead them along our path. For we deserve to exercise the inherent powers that the Demiurge attempted to hide from us. We are the true leaders of men!"

The Lasombra's words lacked any kind of logical order, yet the crowd roared in his favor once more. Anatole looked to St. Lys who stood in the glory of the cheering that surrounded him. Zoë watched Anatole with hopeful eyes, praying that he could muster some sort of response. *Tell them that he's just playing to their greed*, she urged silently. *Tell them that a salvation that depends on sating every appetite for power and blood is no salvation at all*. But, when he moved to speak, the crowd rode over his voice in cheering.

Yet, there were members of the audience who didn't cheer. Zoë was glad to see that Veronique was among them. The Brujah diplomat, after a moment, began looking around the amphitheater and Zoë felt tension rolling off her like a wave.

"This is becoming dangerous," she said leaning to Zoë's ear. "Let us get closer to an exit in case it gets worse."

St. Lys continued to spout heresy on the podium, while Zoë, Veronique, and any others not wishing to listen, quietly made their way out of the arena. They waited for the clamor of the crowd to die down, which took almost an hour. From the shelter of a nearby arcade, they watched the debaters leave one by one. First St. Lys, surrounded by a mass of spectators, hanging on his every word. Then, all but alone, Lasthenia and Anatole. Zoë hailed them and they came over.

"He keeps speaking to me," Zoë said, "and when his eyes meet mine, his perverted words make sense. It's almost as if he can bend my beliefs to befit his. I know it's wrong and I don't like it."

Lasthenia nodded. "This is why I gave you the wood."

"He cheats!" Anatole shouted. "He sways an audience with false appearances and cursed powers."

"Did you expect any different?" Veronique asked.

"When Cainites attempt to sway a crowd," Lasthenia said, "I'm not sure using the benefits of the blood can be called cheating."

Anatole looked like he was biting back anger.

"Don't surrender so easily, Anatole," the Brujah girl said. "His logic is flawed. You might have asked the

Bishop how he expected the Hebrew bible to have any relevance to texts written by Greek philosophers thousands of years later and in a far off land, for example."

Anatole refused to answer and the group parted in silence.

Part Three:

The Faithful

Chapter Twelve

The streets were alive with motion. Though the hour was late, the comet hung brilliantly in the sky above them, and all who witnessed it felt they should be alert. None wanted to be caught sleeping with that brilliant flame-haired prophet painted across the heavens. What if the fire rained down and destroyed the world? What if the last trumpet blew and those left in their beds, sleeping through such a sign, were condemned to eternal punishment?

And for those of the darkened night there was Caine. Would he come? Had he come already? Had he truly been seen, or did every shadowy figure seem to be that dark lord because they wanted it so desperately? Some for ascension, others for a guide to their own repentance, still others dreaming of a single taste of that original shining blood.

Every priest and teacher walked the streets, or strode through his temple with parchments and leather-bound tomes held high, the rafters vibrating with prophecy and threats, beseeching cries and damning pronouncements. Everyone seemed to know what the comet meant, and yet, there was a frantic undertone to their words. There was a not-quite-stable quality to the speeches and the speakers, the sermons and the priests, the lectures and the would-be philosophers.

St. Lys' temple was awash with activity. His followers wound in and out the doors, up and down the halls, talking excitedly among themselves about the second debate, and the strength of His Excellency's arguments. His passion had infected them all, and such passion, in the light of recent events, was like the deadly sword of Damocles, restrained only by the weakest of threads.

In the cellar of Crespin's house, where they had again passed the daylight, Anatole and Zoë conferred quietly. They were in no hurry to make their way into the streets. The debate had not gone well, and the mood in the street was unpredictable. Throughout the daylight hours, things progressed much as they always did, but as the moon rose, drawing them from their dreams, they could hear distant shouting and the muted echoes of high-pitched screams.

"We should be careful," Zoë proclaimed solemnly. "We have to reach them, yes, but we have to avoid conflict. They number too many, and we aren't equipped for major confrontation. The important thing is to keep you safe until the third debate."

"I don't know that a third debate will make a difference," Anatole replied, stepping toward the stairs leading upward to the stone path and the street beyond. "St. Lys has their ear, and it will be no easy thing to sway them, even with the truth. He tells them what they want to hear, and to believe. I tell them that they have sinned, and that their pride will strike them down."

There was a knock and a soft voice called down. Anatole replied, and moments later a pair of young Cainites appeared. One was dark haired, his companion fair. Both wore troubled, brooding expressions. They were among the faithful, those who had either entered the city secretly from the camp in Bière Forest, or who had come to believe Anatole's words through the debates or his time on the streets. Their numbers were not large, but they were devout.

"Something is happening near the heretic temple," the fair one said. His name was Pascal, and he spoke in quiet, measured tones. "There is rioting."

"It is to be expected," Anatole replied, turning away to mask his expression.

Zoë caught it, and, just for that moment, she didn't recognize him at all. His eyes were very wide, intense, and his lips were curled into something so alien that he appeared to be another person entirely. Then his

Malkavian

back was to her, and he took a step. Turning, he was himself again, and with a shiver that ran through her entire frame, Zoë relaxed.

"We must go out, and we must teach," Anatole spoke firmly. "We cannot shirk our responsibility out of fear, and we cannot back down simply because they outnumber us or because they are passionate in their beliefs. Now, more than any other time, we must be strong. We must be among skeptics to correctly answer their questions, or truly this city will fall to heresy, and there will be no place in the streets, or beneath them, for the faithful."

Zoë frowned. She turned to their visitors. "The guard is set? Who is watching?"

"We have been watching the streets and the alleys as best we can since the sun released us," Pascal stated with conviction. "We watch, but there are too many roads, and too few to do the work."

Zoë's frown deepened.

"It doesn't matter," Anatole said, turning away again. "Soon we will be in the streets, and we will watch together. Tell the others to prepare, we will be out shortly."

The two turned and disappeared up the stairs so silently that if Zoë hadn't known they were there, she might have missed their movements entirely. She shook her head to clear her thoughts, then turned away herself, approaching her weapons in preparation.

* * *

In an alley behind St. Lys' temple, a fire burned low. Standing sullenly around it, a group of men huddled for warmth and light. In the shadows beyond them, another group huddled, and in the center of that second, darker group, an old woman hunched low to the ground. In one hand she held a walking staff, carved and polished to a deep lustrous sheen. In the dim light it seemed carved of solid ebony.

Ellen Porter Kiley

Sister Takhoui was in her element. She moved around the circle, fixing first one of her faithful, then the next, with a deep, penetrating gaze. They watched her in fascination, entranced by her words, and the mincing, intricate motion of her aged frame.

Her hair, piled high, was circled by a single woven strand of silver grey, like a circlet across her brow. Her eyes danced, and her lips never stopped moving, her words never ceased their play of sound and thought. It was a sermon and a spell, a binding placed around the necks of those already bound.

The others by the fire were hers as well. They were stout men, and they believed. Though it meant their very souls, they believed: Caine had been seen walking these very streets, and far above was his sign blazing across the heavens.

Takhoui read the signs. She saw things that they could not see, knew things they would never have known, but by her grace, and the power of her words. She spoke to them of Caine, of his return and the shining blood, like a fountain, redeeming them—setting them free. Though she held the cane, her steps had become very near to a dance, and the motion called to each of them to join, to match her motion and her zeal.

"He has spoken to us through his bishop," she crooned. "St. Lys has seen, and he knows. He knows more than he will say, and he has spoken truly. The comet is with us, even now, and it will not be long before blessed Caine steps among us and places us on the scale of his judgment."

She hesitated, then continued. "When that happens, brothers, sisters, where will you fall?"

A slender Toreador stepped from the crowd. This was Gallasyn, who had once been a follower of Anatole's, hiding in the Bière Forest. He asked with eyes wide, "But Sister, what can we do? What can we offer?"

"We must go to the monk," Takhoui said. "We must stop him, his lies and his ranting. Without his interference, St. Lys can spread the word more quickly and completely. None will be lost, not if we get to them in time. Not if we remove the one thing that stands between them and their own salvation. They must not be blind to Caine's glory, but embrace it."

"Anatole." The name was spoken, though it was impossible to tell from where it had sprung. "Anatole is the one."

"Ah, yes, my chicks," Takhoui crooned. "He is the one. He is the voice of unreason, the mad monk with the mouth of a preacher and the heart of the doomed."

By the fire, there was a clatter of metal, and the sound of at least one sword being drawn. Standing about inactive was too much. The comet reminded them moment by moment of the darkness to come. None wanted a their faith questioned at this, the final hour.

"Come," Takhoui shouted, her voice suddenly shrill and loud. "Come with me now. We will go swiftly and silently and we will take them from their doorstep before they know we are upon them!"

There was a mutter of approval that grew quickly to a roar. Those circled about her spun away, joining with the ranks of those around the fire who seemed greatly relieved by the prospect of action, no matter the cost.

They moved from the alley together, roughly centered around Takhoui, but without organization. They surged into the streets, and despite her earlier warning to move quietly, they called out to one another, and to those they passed. Scuffles broke out, but each time, Takhoui quickly stifled them. There was no time. She needed their anger and their momentum to carry through.

It did not take long to draw near the street where Anatole was known to be staying. He had tried to keep this place a secret, but the eyes of the faithful were everywhere now, and Anatole, preacher of the Demiurge, could hide in the root cellar of his ghoul no longer. And that ghoul, Crespin, had once joined the congregation of the True Church as a Judas among apostles. A spy for Anatole. Justice was at hand.

Takhoui danced among the mob. Her eyes glittered and her cane whirled, and there was no longer even a pretense of fragility in her stride. There was strength, terrible, focused energy seeping out of her, infecting those who followed. They would have swept her onto their shoulders and borne her along, but she would not have allowed it. She needed their motion, the patterns of their pounding feet, cursing voices, and feral cries to drown out other voices, and to keep the images of the impending violence from distracting from her resolve .

Anatole would never suspect. Not so soon. Not from her. He might realize there was trouble ahead, but there remained one debate, and it might not occur to him to keep his guard up so far before the event even if he had done poorly in the last. It might work, although she knew that he was no childe. Takhoui was familiar with the monk's reputation. Though she often claimed to be of more noble blood, she knew him—and he her.

So they raced through the streets, gathering strength as they went, calling one to another, some drawn in simply by the sheer momentum of the group, not even certain to where they ran, or why. A cart was overturned in the street, and as the owner, a squat merchant screeched in protest, running into the street to stop them, he was struck down. Then he was grabbed, hauled into the center of the mob, and Takhoui caught the bright warm scent of fresh blood as he became a part of the heat, the fuel that drove them onward.

Off to one side there was the scraping of blade on scabbard, then she heard the music of dancing blades. Her hand dropped to the hilt of the ancient, wicked dagger at her side, and her eyes grew momentarily brighter. She closed them, but her sight did not dim. In that moment, she saw Anatole clearly, his own eyes gazing at her with calm, level strength. She screamed, wanting to break that calm, to run a crack through the smooth, ivory surface of his face, but the image faded until it was nothing but the eyes, and then it was gone. The mob rushed on.

* * *

Anatole had his foot on the lower step leading to the door above when Pascal burst in once more, eyes wide.

"They are coming!" he hissed.

"Who is coming?" Zoë asked from behind Anatole, "and how many?"

"We weren't able to see for certain," Pascal replied. "They are moving too quickly, straight down the center of the street. There are at least several dozen."

"Quickly, wake Crespin and his wife! Get them to safety," Anatole said, climbing the steps and through the door so swiftly it was difficult to believe he had been standing there at all. "Zoë, come with me."

Zoë cursed under her breath and followed. As she came through the door, she could hear loud voices, the clang of metal, and the pounding of booted feet on stone, but no one was yet in sight.

"Come on," Anatole said. She couldn't see him immediately, his voice seemed to float by her ear, and then she saw a hand dangling, and understood. She spun and put her foot to the side of the wall and was lifted up, falling flat on the surface of the roof and waiting.

It was a low structure, and the roof was anything but steady. Zoë pressed flat into the slate and remained motionless. The voices were very near, some of them calling out for Anatole to appear, others over-turning barrels and hurling tools and plants across the small yard. It wouldn't take much to incite them to torch the place.

"Where is the monk?" a brawny mortal cried. He held an ax over his head, brandishing it at the front of the root cellar as if he could summon Anatole from the air. "Bring him forth!"

"Yes!" came the cry. "Blessed Caine calls us, and we have come."

Zoë chanced a slow turn of her head. She managed to catch Anatole's gaze, just for a second. He was staring down into the darkness through a crack between two slate shingles. He was taut, like a cat ready to pounce, and Zoë found herself shivering slightly. There was a sensation of poorly concealed power simmering just below the surface, ready to explode. She wondered, not for the first time, what he heard when his gaze was so distant , and whose voices they were.

The cries from below grew louder, and suddenly a short, older woman in brown pilgrim's robes leaped forward. She brandished a cane, but there was no weakness in her legs, and her balance was superb. Her eyes were bright with madness, and Zoë's mind froze.

"Takhoui," she said softly.

The old Malkavian was speaking to the foremost of her followers, a group of armed men. They engaged in hasty consultation, and after the men took several glances over their shoulders to gauge e their chances of ignoring Sister Takhoui's orders and fleeing, they resolved to enter the cellar. Anatole did not stir, letting them enter the stairway and begin to move downward.

Takhoui slipped along close behind the men, and the rest of those who followed crowded in behind. They were barely controlled, not ready to stand and watch, but to burn, break, and kill. They had come here with a purpose, and they would not be dissuaded.

"What are you doing down there, my chicks?" she called. "What have you seen? Where have they gone?"

At first there was no answer, then one of the mercenaries returned to the street.

"There is no one here," he announced sourly. "We have missed them."

Takhoui stared at him for a moment, then she stiffened. Her head cocked to one side and she began to turn in a slow circle, her head thrown back. All those who had been near her backed away, some slowly, others frantically. The cane was still held tightly in her hand, and if she began to spin, or convulse, they knew the damage she could wreak.

None knew better than Zoë, and she was about to speak, to warn Anatole, when he moved. With a cry, the monk leaped nimbly to his feet, dancing along the edge of the low roof. All around them, the faithful were doing the same, and Zoë saw that, while the mob had been gathering below, others had circled around behind, keeping to the rooftops in silence, waiting for Anatole's sign. She had been so concerned with following Anatole to the roof, and so shocked by Takhoui's presence, that she had not noticed them herself.

Anatole leaped, and like a dark wave, his followers did the same, falling on the mob from all sides. Takhoui had glanced up just as Anatole cried out, as though she'd seen the move seconds before it took place. It did not matter. Anatole was on the ground before she had fully recovered from her premonition but she swung her cane in a vicious arc that nearly caught him.

The monk never glanced back at her. He was among her followers, diving first one way, then the other, his sword drawn. The cries of the mob no longer mentioned his name or the comet, but were all of pain, fear, and the sudden realization that rather than catching anyone by surprise, they had themselves been caught. The fighting was vicious. Dagger in hand, Zoë leaped behind Anatole, but by the time she dove in, half the crowd had escaped through a gap left by Anatole's followers toward the streets beyond.

Anatole signaled to disregard those that had already fled, ed, but those who remained found themselves trapped in a tight circle with Sister Takhoui in the center. She no longer danced. She gripped the cane with both hands glaring at Anatole, her eyes filled with a fire so bright none would meet her gaze. None but Anatole himself.

The outer ring, of Anatole's followers closed in slowly on those within who turned so that their backs were together and Takhoui was tucked in the center. "Stop!" Anatole cried. The force of his voice carried easily through the small square.

All motion stopped. In that instant, Anatole stood straight and clear-eyed, and gazed through both circles of men and Cainites into the mad-bright eyes of Sister Takhoui. They held that stare, the two of them—mad monk and mad sister—for so long that it seemed to Zoë that they must be transferring the stories of their lives across some hidden beam of light.

"So," Sister Takhoui said, her voice dripping sarcasm, "it seems I have underestimated you, Anatole. I expected to find you rushing about the streets, urging every dark brother of Caine to kneel in the street and whine for forgiveness from a god who has turned his back on them."

"And yet you came." Anatole replied. "You came, and you brought swords, fire, anger and followers at the risk of their deaths in order to silence me."

He stopped for a moment, gathering his thoughts, then asked, "Why do you fear me so? St. Lys would seem to have the upper hand even without such a display, so why now? Why me?"

"I have seen what I have seen," she snarled and held his gaze for several long moments.

"What will we do with them now?" Zoë asked, stepping up beside him. "Surely they will be punished for this. They tried to kill you and me. Shall we take them before the prince?"

"Maybe," Pascal called out softly, "we should kill them now, and then ask the prince—or the Bishop St. Lys—for forgiveness." He pressed forward again, and several others joined him. Takhoui stood her ground, but her followers shifted first one way, then the other, nervous as colts. They were ready to bolt, or to fight if it came to it.

Anatole shook his head. He turned his gaze to the sky and stared long and hard at the comet, apparently stationary, but moving—he knew—so swiftly. The time they would have with it as a sign was limited, and the good he could do was bound to its presence, for better or worse.

"We will let them go," he said at last. "We will kill no more this night. I will pray for their forgiveness, and we will send them back to whence they came."

"No!" Zoë spoke before she had the chance to consider his reaction. She had been staring at Takhoui, and memories much better left buried were rising to the surface of her mind. "No, you can't just let her go. You don't know…"

Anatole turned then, and grabbed her arm. She fell silent, meeting his gaze with a scowl.

"We will kill no more this night," he repeated.

Zoë met his gaze for a moment, then turned around and walked away, entering the root cellar without a backward glance.

* * *

Once Zoë was out of sight, Anatole turned back to face the heretical Takhoui.

"I do not think I would have let you off so easily, brother," she said. Anatole was keenly aware that she was watching him carefully, gauging his words, the truth of the safety he promised, and the reasoning behind it.

"You would have killed me," Anatole replied simply. "I know this. I know of a time, though, when you would have worried for our sins."

"The nights are short," Takhoui replied. "Blessed Caine will be among us soon, and the judgment will be swift. I know my reward, monk, do you know your own? Or do you truly seek no reward, but only that you might serve God and find your way back to his weak, ridiculous realm where all is good and proper and the blood is too sacred to drink?"

Anatole smiled and simply stepped back. A minute later, Sister Takhoui and her last followers took the opportunity to flee.

Anatole found Pascal in the crowd. "Crespin and his wife?" the monk asked.

"Safe," Pascal said. "The mob only came from the one direction. Perhaps Lady Veronique could take in the woman for the duration."

Anatole had a fleeting image of Crespin's good wife's reaction to finding safety in a bathhouse, and marveled again at the strange roads God had mapped out for them. He nodded to Pascal and then headed back toward the root cellar. Pascal made as if to follow, but Anatole waved him off. "See to the arrangements," he whispered.

He stepped back into the cellar softly. By the time he made it all the way down, the others had fully dispersed from above and the street was as empty as it had been. Now, standing at the base of the stairs, the silence was so complete that it would have been very easy to believe that none of the events of the evening had taken place, except that he could still see Takhoui's eyes gazing at him. He heard her words, ringing in his ears. He heard the echo of his own final question, ringing unanswered, and he wondered if he was the only one who had noticed that. If she had seen what she claimed to have seen, she would have said so. If Takhoui had a vision, she would share it, reveling in the attention it would bring and proclaiming it to any who would listen. She was mad, and she changed her allegiance with the speed of lightning, but when her mind was set, she was a vicious enemy indeed. She believed as she said she did, but she did not *know* what the comet would mean in the end.

Zoë was standing against the far wall with her back to him, and Anatole closed the distance quickly, stopping just short of laying his hand on her shoulder. She was tight, tense like a drawn bowstring, and he did not want to set her off before he had the chance to speak.

"Is she gone, then?" Zoë asked. Her voice was cold, shivering with barely suppressed anger. "Have you sent her on her way so she can place an ambush for you or me? Why not just kneel and let her take your head? It would be less interesting, of course, but much quicker, and more final."

Anatole didn't reply. He stood, watching her, waiting for her to get to her point, as he knew she would.

Zoë spun. Her eyes flashed with anger. "You should not have let her go, Anatole. You should have destroyed her while you had the chance. You don't know. You haven't seen what she is, what she can do. She will not spare you, given that same chance. She will strike you down and sprinkle what remains of you on the altar of Caine without a thought."

"Doubtless you are right on that point," Anatole nodded, his features grave. "Takhoui believes very deeply in what she preaches. She believes in herself, as well—in her vision. It is frustrating to her that she cannot see what will come. She cannot pierce the veil surrounding the comet any more than I am able to pierce her own walls of secrecy. It is a hard thing to have the sight, and to realize that it is only a fleeting, partial vision. It is incomplete, and so, in the end, there is only faith."

"Her faith is not yours," Zoë hissed.

"Not so long ago," Anatole replied, "she believed as I do. It could come to her again. Not all voices are easy to comprehend, and not all visions are clear. Takhoui is confused."

"She is not confused!" Zoë cried out, barely restraining herself from striking out at him, then backing off a step. "I have seen her, Anatole. I have seen her on the road, that evil tongue slipping and sliding between the minds of others, twisting thoughts and hearts first one way, then the other, and always with her dagger poised at their backs."

"She frightens you," Anatole said softly. "I understand that."

"You don't," Zoë said, turning away again. "You don't understand, or she would not be walking away freely to slip up on us the next time we pass the wrong alley."

Anatole said nothing, certain his adopted childe had more to say.

"She stopped me once on the road," Zoë went on. Her voice dropped, and her tone grew flat and distant, as if she were no longer really talking to Anatole, but reciting a litany. Her shoulders drew in, and her arms were wrapped around herself in a manner that seemed to indicate she needed comfort, but could only seek it in herself.

"It was horrible. Her followers surrounded us on our horses, and we were made to listen to her preach. She was reaching into my mind—I'm certain of it. She brought out such… pain. She would have kept me, made me into one of her servants, following her visions blindly, had we not threatened to ride them down, and been granted our release."

"She can be very intense," Anatole cut in. "As I myself can be."

Zoë spun to him again, eyes flashing, though this time the anger was different. It seemed to draw her back from whatever dark reverie had absorbed her.

"She is nothing like you, Anatole. Nothing. You want redemption, for yourself—for us all. She wants nothing unless it is for herself, and you have left her free to regroup and come after you again. Surely you don't believe she'll just walk away after being humiliated in that way, and leave you alone? You must know she will come after you again, or at the very least, she will do what she can to get others to do the job for her. Next time she will not be so disorganized, nor her party so weak."

"My fight is not against Takhoui," Anatole said softly. "She believes as she will believe, and I cannot force her to change that. I could have destroyed her, yes, but it would have served nothing, and it would be that much more on my conscience. In all the time since my Embrace, I have sinned. I will not willingly add to that simply to remove a possible danger from my trail. And she is among St. Lys' followers. Were I to destroy her, we would face darker and more dangerous conflict with the bishop himself."

"You will not fight for what you believe, then?" she asked. She spoke with bitter anger. "You will allow her to attack you in your own quarters, to attempt to kill you for your beliefs, and your answer is to free her and forgive her, and go on as if nothing has happened?"

Anatole remained silent.

"I wonder if they aren't right," Zoë said, biting her lip as if her own thoughts frightened her. "I wonder if we are chasing a foolish mortal's God, and letting the heritage of our own blood, our own world, fall away from us. Perhaps her sight is truer than we believed. St. Lys certainly believes that it is, and most of the city is falling in line with what he believes."

"What do you believe?" Anatole asked. His voice remained calm, but there was a sudden edge to it that had not been there a moment before. His patience was slipping, and the soft expression he'd worn when he re-entered the cellar had melted away. "What do *you* believe, Zoë? Whose vision do you believe is truth?"

"I…"

He cut her off. "I understand that Takhoui is my enemy. I understand that she would kill me, and that there are dozens of others in and around St. Lys' temple that would perform that act with equal zeal. I understand that it is very easy to see their side, to believe that the dark urges that rush through your being, the hunger that parches your throat and drags you to the feeding again and again is a natural thing—that it is blessed, not a curse but a wonder. Why not say that to sin is our nature, and so, let us all be natural? Why not say that the death of others is our right? Why not justify every dark act of our existence with the image of Caine, risen to lead us once again, his blood shining like the stars and cleansing us of our sin?"

Zoë started to speak, but he held up his hand, and she bit her lip in frustration.

"If I am to stand among others and proclaim my faith, it must be a true faith. It cannot be a partial belief in something that is useful to me and bits and pieces of other things as well. It must be complete, and it is not my place to end Takhoui's existence. There is a time and a place for every deed we might perform.

"She has been turned away from truth. Should I slay her for that, or pray to bring her back into the fold? Should I proclaim myself judge and executioner, or should I do, as our Lord has done, and forgive? Which is the road of strength?"

Zoë's eyes were still blazing.

"She has killed others," she whispered. "She will kill again. She might kill an innocent, or the soul you would have next saved. She would do so with a great sneer and that horrible, cackling laugh. She will smile sweetly in public, and she will return in the dark to feed on those her vision directs her to destroy, and that is her nature. I have seen it—I have felt it—and were it not for a moment of luck, I might have been a part of it. She seems very calm most of the time but it is a very thin veil over her madness and you eventually understand that even that veil is stained.

"And she has gotten away with it. She is getting away with it now. No matter how many she hurts, how many she tramples underfoot in the name of whatever cause she is currently championing, she slips away and leaves others to suffer."

Her expression left no doubt to Anatole that she counted herself among those suffering, and this time he did not hesitate to lay his hand on her shoulder as he spoke.

"The time may come," he said, "when your words will come back to haunt me, but I think—I hope—that we will soon be beyond that. Takhoui is only a small chip from a large wheel. She might cause us to wobble, but she cannot bring about the fall. We will soon meet St. Lys again, and things will change. Some will crumble, others will rise up. As much despair as she might cause, we cannot afford to divert our energy, or our thoughts, from what is most important."

"Do you see more clearly than she, then?" Zoë asked, her voice lowered. "Do you see your truth, the end of these nights to come? Do you know how this last debate will end?"

"You know my sight is not a thing I control, but more a thing that controls me," Anatole replied. "I cannot call up a vision, and though there are times when, if I concentrate, I can see the outlines of images, the hints of things beyond my senses, or our time, it is never certain. That is why—"

She cut him off. "That is why we have faith. Yes, I know that. There are times when I wonder if there is more to faith than just the word itself. I see your strength, and I wonder where it is based. Do you know things I do not? Do you truly believe, or do you appear to believe because you wish others to follow you? When I look at my own faith, it seems such a frail thing, assaulted on all sides by the thoughts, minds, and condemnation of others, like Takhoui and St. Lys. Their faith seems stronger. Their anger, their strength greater than my own. Where I feel doubt , they seem to burn with the fever of their convictions."

She turned to Anatole , and he saw the pain and confusion in her eyes.

"Anatole, where do you get the strength?"

He closed his eyes, then opened them once again, and they were bright with conviction and intensity. "I have not seen everything," he replied. "I would not want to see everything before it occurs—that would be a curse, and I would be robbed of the miracles that remain in the world. It is because of those miracles I have seen, and those that I sense, that I am strong.

"There are rooms beyond counting in the heart and house of God, Zoë. Each is different, and to each a different path must lead, but it is there, and it is the answer. Come, we must go out now, and do what we can. The comet will be waning soon. I, for one, do not wish to miss the ending of this, whatever it might be."

He turned and mounted the stairs once more. Zoë followed, her head down, thinking. They exited to the streets and walked in silence. It bore down on them like the suffocating weight of a great dark shroud.

Chapter Thirteen

Veronique d'Orleans was now forced to remind herself on a nightly basis that she did *not* believe in omens. There were coincidences, and unpleasant chains of events, and consequences for every action, no matter how small, but there were no such things as omens. She told herself this upon waking and upon retiring for the day because, in the cruel way that it had, the world was attempting to prove her wrong on a regular basis. Thierry, her excitable secretary, was firmly and thoroughly convinced that every strange and unnatural thing his spies had reported in the last three months all made sense now as signs of impending disaster for the city. Veronique was forced to regularly resist the urge to throttle him; her temper was hot and sharp and easily roused, and it was requiring more self-control than she liked just for the sake of basic civility.

Thierry was, perhaps sensibly, not in the haven when Veronique rose to find a note summoning her to court, to answer for the behavior of her "ward," Brother Anatole de Paris. A sharp pain started behind her eyes, and she began contemplating the possibility of omens existing after all.

* * *

Minor court was in session but it was not obvious. Normally, minor court was only sparsely attended by those seeking to petition the senior ministers of the Grand Court. Tonight, it seemed like half the Cainites in the city had turned up to watch the show, exchange lurid innuendo, and attempt to take advantage of the situation. They were loitering in the courtyard outside the main entrance, attended by a small army of servants, conversing in groups, calling greetings to one another, and generally behaving with a notable lack of decorum. Veronique was met as she entered by Sir

Olivier, Prince Alexander's younger childe, who looked more harried than she had ever seen him, clad for court and surrounded by a cloud of servants, hangers-on, and lesser minions as he moved through the halls of his sire's haven. The look of relief that washed across his face when he saw her was almost comical.

"Lady Veronique, thank Heaven you've arrived safely!" Olivier announced in a tone that easily rose above the babble surrounding him. He managed to shrug off most of the social parasites around him with the minimum use of his elbows, and came down the steps to catch her hands in his own. "Are you well, milady? Injured? Distressed?"

Veronique hadn't encountered a single thing that could have injured or distressed her during her walk to the prince's haven but could tell, from the rather desperate looking Olivier, that that likely wasn't the appropriate thing to say. "I am well enough, milord, all things considered. It's kind of you to ask after me."

"Excellent. You wouldn't believe some of the stories we've been hearing of late...." He tucked her hand into the crook of his arm and guided her up the stairs, minions scattering before them, except one obviously well-favored ghoul. "Renaud, please tell the herald that Lady Veronique is here in response to His Highness' request. Thank you, lad."

"Dare I ask what's gotten into *you* tonight?" Veronique asked in an undertone, casting a glance at him out of the corner of her eyes; he was always pale, but tonight he looked strained around the edges.

"My illustrious sire," Olivier murmured in the same undertone, "is in a rock-chewing foul mood. Do I even need to tell you why?"

Veronique pretended to grimace for Olivier's edification, but let the expression go quickly.

"I see you understand. The lectures have become debates, due in no small part to the behavior of your friend, whose actions you stood surety for. I'm assuming," Oliver's tone was wry, "that you didn't put the idea of baiting St. Lys into his head yourself and that this development displeases you in some way."

"It doesn't *please* me, I assure you." Veronique replied sourly. "Or, rather, the disorder that's arisen from it doesn't please me. I will not shed any tears of lamentation and dismay for the discomfiture of the Bishop St. Lys, and I am relatively certain that you and His Highness do not, either."

"Perhaps, but I dare say that the bishop's performance at the most recent gathering—and your monk's lack thereof—was hardly discomfiting to the heretics. And even had Anatole had the upper hand, there is a fine line between the pleasure of watching the bishop's arrogance being deflated and the foul taste left behind by repeated breaches of the prince's interdicts, milady."

They stopped at the door of the receiving chamber, where the herald waited to announce Veronique to the assembled court. Oliver continued, "My advice to you is, keep the priest away from the last lecture if you cannot be certain of what he'll do there—and how certain could any of us be in that situation? Stake him and keep him locked in a trunk somewhere for a week or two."

"I shall take that under advisement, Sir Olivier," Veronique replied dryly, and stepped up to the door.

* * *

A half-dozen petitioners preceded Veronique in their order of importance and she took her place among the rest of the courtiers to listen and wait. Or, to be more precise, to pretend to listen and to wait; the pain that had started behind her eyes when she received Prince Alexander's summons was sharpening in intensity as the night wore on, making it difficult to concentrate and even more difficult to retain her grip on her temper. And she was not, she noticed, the only one experiencing that difficulty. There was a distinct undercurrent of resentment circulating through the room, clearly evident in the flashes of the Beast in the eyes of the spectators, the bared fangs that no amount of will could apparently force back. Alexander himself was feeling it, or else causing it—his humor was visibly foul, and he was making no pretense of concealing it. The Cainites closest to the dais were constantly circulating in and out the several side doors in an effort to keep their composure; Alexander's aggravation was like a hair-shirt, persistently irritating the humors of his subjects.

Veronique rubbed her temples and tried not to let it affect her. It would not help her case to come before the prince unable to keep herself calm enough to speak. She stared fixedly at the wall directly across from her and tried to vacate her mind until she felt the pressure in her head begin to ease, the lashings of the Beast beginning to subside, breathing deeply, evenly, and unnecessarily. After a moment, she felt herself under control enough to actually pay attention to the proceedings. Most of the petitioners were Cainite residents of the neighboring community and their grievances revolved around outrages to the dignity of their chattels and property. And she couldn't, in all honesty, argue with the justice of their claims, given the unrest that had followed the second lecture.

"Lady Veronique d'Orleans, envoy of Prince Julia Antasia, approach and be recognized."

Veronique stepped out of the gathering and into the cleared aisle that led to the dais, approaching with the precise degree of courtesy demanded, ending in a deep curtsey three paces from Alexander's seat. He let her hold it long enough to underscore the point of her submission.

"You may rise, Lady Veronique."

She did so, straightening to her full height, which put them at eye level—she was very careful not to meet his dark eyes. "Your Highness is most gracious. How may I be of service this night?"

"You may explain to me, Lady Veronique, how it is that the series of lectures I agreed to host somehow transformed into a series of debates between the Bishop St. Lys and your ward, the priest Anatole de Paris." Alexander, when he was in a foul mood, rarely wasted time dancing around the source of his annoyance and this was no exception.

Veronique paused for a moment to gather some wit under the weight of Alexander's barely restrained wrath pressing upon her like a fire-hot hand. "Milord Prince, I do not know what you have been told about this—"

"I have been told," Alexander responded blandly, "that the lunatic priest belonging to *you* engaged the lunatic priest belonging to the Archbishop of Nod in a shouting match at the first lecture and precipitated another confrontation at the second. Are these reports accurate, Lady Veronique?"

The pain behind her eyes was coming back with renewed force, hot and sharp, and she had to resist the urge to massage her temples again. "In essence, Milord Prince. But in Brother Anatole's defense, I will say that there was provocation on both sides, and that the Archbishop Nikita did ratify the change in format to the series of debates. He also recruited Lady Lasthenia to ensure a certain decorum."

"I was unaware, Lady Veronique," the prince said coolly, "that the archbishop had been made an agent of this court, empowered to ratify anything at all. Much less your diminutive clanmate."

Veronique chose not to argue that point. "Brother Anatole," she said, "like many others, has been strongly affected by the anxiety that is afflicting the rest of the city. I am not entirely certain that he is wholly responsible for all of his actions."

"But you, milady, *are* responsible for those actions, whether *he* is or not." The prince's voice drilled into her skull like a red-hot iron spike. "I am very close to forbidding *Brother* Anatole from attending the final lecture, Lady Veronique. I distrust his ability to control himself and I have yet to see any appreciable evidence of *your* ability to control him."

"Milord Prince, I am not certain that either you or I could successfully prevent him from attending, but by force. He is extraordinarily stubborn and dedicated to his calling." Veronique paused to work more moisture into her mouth. "I would suggest, milord—"

"Milord." The voice was soft, papery-dry, but it cut across Veronique's without effort. "Do not listen to this viper's lies, I beg you. She plots against you— she is the true omen of your demise. Do not listen—cast her from your breast before she strikes."

The Countess Saviarre had entered unnoticed through the door behind Alexander's dais and approached on unsteady legs. She wore a rusty-stained white shift and little else; her feet were bare and her hair undressed, hanging in lank strands down her back. Her dark eyes were wild with a welter of emotions and her pale cheeks torn; the blood under her fingernails was staining the ivory skin of her hands. Veronique recoiled, appalled to find her fangs lengthening in her jaw as the blood-scent reached her. Prince Alexander rose, moving to intercept his consort as she staggered a step closer. He caught her close and guided her to the dais despite her struggles.

Behind them, the entire room was silent, shocked, and Veronique was stunned along with them, unable to speak or act. She had known that Saviarre was somehow afflicted by the presence of the comet, by the same fear that gripped the city, but she had no idea how profound the woman's collapse actually was. It rattled her to see it with her own eyes, even if in principle, she loathed Saviarre.

Prince Alexander gathered Saviarre close against his body and murmured to her as a parent would to a feverish child and slowly she relaxed , resting her head against his chest, her eyes squeezing shut. After a long moment, Alexander raised his head and growled, "Court is dismissed. Out. *All of you—Out!*"

Chapter Fourteen

At the third forum, St. Lys didn't ask the crowd for his attention. He simply stepped at the podium and all eyes fell upon him. To them, he appeared majestic, his white vestments illuminated by the flames of the torches that seemed to chase every shadow to the back. Some shadows lingered however, and they only worked to accent the stable look in the man's eyes. His mere presence could sand the voices among the audience to a hushed silence.

Zoë and Veronique however, had their eyes instead on Anatole and Lasthenia who sat behind him, as if guarding his back. The two nights since minor court had gone very much as they had both feared they might, with increasing madness on the streets and more and more of the city falling in line with the bishop's ways. Alexander had made no appearances since dismissing court. The city was a ship with no rudder and too many sails.

"Excuse me," Lasthenia's dry voice rained over the audience as it attempted to draw lingering eyes from St. Lys. "I fear that I am the only person keeping the prince's peace on this night, so I do ask for your cooperation in remaining calm." Lasthenia drew a scroll from her side and read it out with her modest and watery voice. Though obviously trying to keep her calm demeanor, her voice skirted along the edge of uneasiness. "Tonight's debate shall discuss the obligations of the faithful." She looked to the audience. "I admit to you, I have little to no faith in anything these nights. I will remain the neutral party."

Once again, the Brujah tossed the coin. Once again, Anatole was the serpent. Once again, St. Lys began the debate.

Zoë watched the stirring from the arena as the woman announced the terms and conditions, which were stated in the very same manner as in the previous lecture. Zoë's eyes rested Anatole, who seemed to cower in the presence of Bishop St. Lys. She murmured a prayer to him.

Lasthenia gripped the hourglass. "I have one other thing to mention," she said. "After the last forum, someone requested that you both refrain from using the powers of our blood to manipulate the audience." Lasthenia looked to Anatole, and then to the bishop. "Of course this is something I cannot enforce, so instead call this a test of honor." Lasthenia sat and gazed St. Lys once more. "Bishop, please take your place." She flipped the hourglass with both hands. "Start."

"My brothers and sisters, I apologize in advance if my lecture here tonight rings more of a sermon than of a scholarly dissertation. I still promise to you that I have not come to preach."

Zoë felt the uneasiness of the audience as he spoke. Their fear was so thick that it would be difficult to evoke anything else in them. Would that serve him or Anatole? Again, she whispered a prayer for her mentor.

"Instead, I stand in front of you," St. Lys continued, "to stress the urgency of what quickly approaches and what must be done before these things come to pass." St. Lys paused, inviting reflection. "My brothers and sisters, time is indeed running out, and we all have a duty.

"Though we are immortal, we cannot continue to pretend that our immortality gives us plenty of time to prepare for the hereafter. These are grievous and pressing hours indeed. For the true time draws near and we have evidence of this. There are even more voices now attesting to Caine's awesome presence. All can now see clearly the burning red hair star that hangs over us. The fear swells too as that star brightens, and people are becoming wild and unguarded. They want to flee the inevitable. But I ask you, brothers and sisters: do not flee; do not waste your remaining hours in fear of what shall pass."

"Why am I here listening to you then," Zoë murmured under her breath. She crossed her arms and smirked as she watched the bishop. She thought of those times he'd touched her face. She sighed uselessly, and yanked a pair of ratted breeches from her bag along with a needle, string, and a few patches of fabric. She began to sew as the bishop continued to talk.

"Channel that fear," he said, "and use it to spur yourself to perform your duties, for only this way can you earn true immortality. There is no reason to fear the end of this physical prison if you are faithful and dutiful. By being such, you can liberate yourself from the shackles and pains of this material world, and fulfill your awesome potential in the world of the spiritual.

"Your duty requires that you be selfless, and that you be sympathetic to those who have not been saved by the shining blood of Caine. Think of them, my brothers and sisters. Unlike you, they are utterly damned because they have not the shining blood that flows through our veins. It is this blood which allows us to detach ourselves from this physical world. Our mortal cousins, however, must cling on to this material world. When it ends with them in it, their souls will crumble to nothingness."

St. Lys paused to take in the sea of eyes that so diligently watched him as he preached. They remained fixated, so obedient in their attention that they seemed to forget that he was not speaking. Zoë wondered if they would sit there and watch him in silence forever. She looked up from her sewing and saw a grin creep slowly across his face. For an instant, she saw herself as the bishop must see her: a child of thieves who paid more attention to the forms and shapes she sewed on a pair of pants than to the divine pictures he articulated. To him, she was probably a wretch to be pitied, one who could not see the importance of her own divinity. It was a seductive image and she forced her gaze back down to shake it off.

The bishop slowly ran his hand over the smooth fabric on his chest before speaking again. "Of course not every soul will be capable of withstanding the trials of immortality. Not every soul will choose the path of divinity and we cannot force them to come to us. Likewise, it is not possible to force our shining blood down their throats. Instead, we should expose what we have to offer and let them come willingly. Those who choose to come forth are indeed worthy of this divinity.

"It is more difficult however, to tell if those who do not choose to taste the shining blood are still worthy of its glory. It is easy to think that if their souls held within them any sense of divine rationality, they would indeed come forth, accept the blood and worship the glory from which it came. But, should even the lowest of minds taste the shining blood, they are enlightened and have the opportunity to preserve their souls for all eternity. This is of course salvation of the most miraculous kind, and those who spread that miracle are also spreading the divinity of Caine and bettering their own paths."

St. Lys paused again, and Zoë again looked up. The bishop was gazing at Lasthenia, who did nothing but stare out into the audience with her most neutral gaze. He smirked, and Zoë felt the scorn in it like the stab of a knife.

"After all," he said as he peeled his eyes off the Brujah, "our nearest neighbor could be an unenlightened soul. If they attempt to prevent your divine work, you must throw off their yolk with all your strength. For by preventing you from following your duty, they are infringing upon the free will that belongs to all higher souls. Such behavior is deserving of punishment." He paused for a moment to adjust his stance. "If they do nothing other than refuse to come forth and take of the shining blood, then judge them not and let Caine do the judging when he deems it necessary. Yet, love them as neighbors and continue to enlighten them to your divine work. For it is important to follow the example Caine set, by loving your neighbors, educating them, and welcoming their service to Caine's divine teachings. For even a worthy soul will not be saved if she does not know what path to walk or how to walk it."

St. Lys lifted his hands and the shadows cast his form along the higher walls of the amphitheater. "So I ask you my brothers and sisters, spread my words to all, bring forth the shining blood and share it with those who come forth by their own choice. The unworthy will weed themselves out, but do not follow them. For you are the blood of the shining, and therefore the strong minds trembling to break free from this physical shackles that the Demiurge above forced upon us. Share your blood with one another, for we are all siblings. Spread the blood to worthy mortals, for they deserve to be saved if they choose to come forth. And most important, listen to the wisdom of the blood, and keep heart of Caine's teaching and proclamations, for his is the way of the True God. The Demiurge is a despot, a creator of material things that will wither and fade with time." The shadows shifted again to create around the bishop a sort of luminescence. "We have escaped that withering, and it is now our obligation to save those who have not been kissed with our blessed lips." St. Lys paused and looked to Lasthenia. "Thus concludes my opening statement."

The Brujah girl nodded once, and looked to the hourglass. "It was short," she remarked. "You have more time if you wish to use it."

"Not all speeches are long, girl," St. Lys chided. "For the strongest messages are often said in one or two words," St. Lys grinned at her as his eyes bore into her own. "Believe me," he announced, "it's the truth that matters."

She smiled less than half-heartedly. "Yes and truth is something very few can proclaim. If you can do so, I praise you a thousand fold."

* * *

Anatole listened carefully to this exchange. He wondered if the pomp in St. Lys' eyes and the skepticism in the Brujah's strong voice would make for a more interesting debate. Her steel blue gaze steered upon his own angelic face and her face warmed with a smile despite the shadows St. Lys forced upon her— if only for a moment. For a moment, he thought he saw an angel in the pools of blue that made her eyes. For a moment, he felt confident.

"Anatole are you ready?" she asked as she rested her hands on the hourglass. He dipped his chin to his chest in a deep nod. Lasthenia's hands flipped the hourglass once more. "Start."

Anatole let the silence pass for a moment, his eyes facing the inquiring crowd before him. "In the books," he began with hesitation, "there are many commandments from Genesis through Revelations. Many have to do with what we can and can not eat, how we handle our slaves, children and wives, how we treat our eldest and how we teach our youngest. But," Anatole took in a sturdy breath, "the one commandment our Christ wishes for us to heed is, 'Love thy neighbor.'" He looked to the audience of Cainites, who stared back as if hit by lightning.

"I fear that it is difficult to truly love your neighbor if you are constantly feeding from his blood. That is of course part of our curse. We, unlike most, cannot receive penitence if we simply attempt to love our neighbors. For our curse alone hinders much of our free will, and this is one example." Anatole paused to study Zoë, Veronique, Pascal, Crespin, Stephanos, and those others whom he counted as friends. Zoë's eyes lit with hope as her hands clasped together over the wounded garment. Anatole nodded to her, his mind reflecting on their own debate in Crespin's root cellar. He began to speak. "Therefore, we have no choice but to repent for the grievous transgressions we commit merely by existing. We must perform this duty if we wish our cursed souls to remain truly immortal. Yet, other duties may be accepted with the duty of penitence. For instance, we should not despair for being cursed. For despair only leads to hopelessness, and hopelessness only creates excuses for sin." Anatole smiled at this logic.

Zoë looked up once again from her stitching, and smiled as well. It heartened him to see her eyes became attentive once more.

"Yes," he continued, "our nature imposes upon us more obligations than the average mortal man who has to do nothing more than love his neighbor. Yes, it is a sort of curse." Anatole allowed silence to pass before he continued. "However, it is also a test of faithfulness to our God. For most tests bring with them a struggle, and with that struggle comes pain. Yet, to atone for our evil, we must both endure and acknowledge suffering. Our curse bleeds with pain, yet many of us deny its presence and become numb to its affect on our souls. Should we choose to acknowledge such pain we can repent for our curse by wielding it to cleanse our souls of the foulness that chafes us from within. Though our Heavenly Father is stern, He is not without forgiveness. In His forgiveness, there is still promise for the cursed. In His forgiveness, we may find a salvation of sorts. Yet, in order to earn His forgiveness, we must take responsibility for ourselves and do what is necessary to atone for our sins. Because he is cursed, it is doubly important that the faithful Cainite atone for his sins. Yet, because of how we must exist, God has given us a need to sin and He has given us an eternity to do so. This presents somewhat of a paradox, does it not? It might seem that we are constantly running in circles. To persist forever, we must steal blood from the living. Therefore, we steal life to 'live' forever, only to repent and 'live' again." Anatole paused for a moment and twisted his hands together. "Pardon my word choice here. By *live* I mean exist. This is no way to live."

He fell silent again to study the audience. Their eyes watched him in skeptical disarray. He felt them judge him as a low-blood, a humble soul, or a lunatic. In the end, he knew it didn't matter. For they were as badly off as he was.

He continued: "In addition to the obligations we have to the Heavenly Father, we also have obligations to Caine as revealed in his traditions. Though Caine sinned, he learned from his wrongdoing. One needs to simply recall Caine's traditions to see this. In these commandments, he directs us to treat our brothers, sisters servants, and sires with dignity. Though we are cursed and deserve punishment, he asks us not to lash out at each other, for only the Heavenly Father can judge us. We are to respect each other, protect our servants, and refrain from acting as false gods before mortals, the descendants of Seth. These traditions are of course for our protection and our sanity, for we cannot expect our kind to maintain control over our nature if we constantly attack each other."

Anatole paused to pass a slow look at St. Lys as he cleared his voice. "Bishop St. Lys says that our time runs short. I happen to agree with him here. Unlike him, however, I believe that though we are undying, and though we have plenty of time to repent, we must keep following a road of penitence. For we never know when the final death might strike us, and our souls. We owe it to ourselves, and to our one true Creator to be sure that we are forever in His mercy. We are responsible for our own souls— not some preacher, not time, not God. If we wish to be saved from this curse, we must walk the path of penitence and continue to cleanse our plagued souls."

Anatole noticed the eyes of his followers. They for some reason struggled to find him. They were also oddly dim to his eyes. He then passed a glance to his opponent wondering if he was playing some trickery from the stage. In the end, it didn't matter. In the end, they were both cursed. Anatole looked out to his audience and shook his mind off this thought.

"What do we owe to others beyond the respect that Caine commands of us? The question remains. Are we responsible for our neighbors' souls? Should we preach to them and tell them how to believe? What is right for them?" Anatole shrugged. "While I do believe that we should teach the word and duties of God, I also believe that we do not save ourselves by saving others. We save ourselves by taking responsibility for ourselves. We can preach all we want, but words of salvation are dead if their speaker does not work to save himself. So I ask you tonight, to be responsible and follow this duty as best you can. Ask for penitence and save your own souls, for you are the only ones who can."

Anatole sighed and paused, his eyes finding Lasthenia. She sat in the shadows despite the fact that there was a torch next to her chair. Anatole couldn't make out her face, but he imagined it was still quiet and expressionless. He imagined her eyes in his mind, and finally realized that there was an angel dancing in her pupils, and another in her voice as she spoke. "We will pause here for the remainder of this turn, and then take another turn." She said as she stood. "Feel free to discuss among yourselves."

Low hums of consternation simmered over the crowd as theologians, politicians, philosophers, and rhetoricians of the Cainite blood stirred their thoughts together. Anatole watched St. Lys carefully as he jumped into the arena and approached Zoë.

"What does he want from her?" Lasthenia stood behind Anatole but her lips were still. Anatole studied Zoë's odd stillness, and St. Lys' finger on her chin. Their eyes were locked. "Watch. Watch him meet her eyes," the angel said again. "He's going to speak." Just then, Lasthenia jumped into the audience and intercepted the locked gaze.

"Excuse me, honorable bishop. But I pray a word with this girl."

St. Lys cocked an eyebrow at Lasthenia's sudden arrival. "Very well," he spat.

Anatole watched the keeper as she spoke softly with Zoë. He could read nothing on her face, but he was thankful that she didn't keep a straining eye contact with Zoë's own eyes. Zoë nodded to her and made her way to Anatole.

"Anatole," she asked. "Are you doing alright?"

Anatole nodded as he watched her feet shuffle at the dirt below. "How did I do?" he asked.

"Good, though I'm having difficulty seeing your face." Zoë looked worried for a moment but then she smiled. "Never mind that," she murmured as she took his chilled hand. "But strengthen yourself and be more direct in your words. You have a strong foundation beneath your words. These people are not scholars from Byzantium. They want a show, not a debate." Zoë shook her head as she studied Anatole's face. "I know you can put a show on for them that will actually be worth performing, and truthful too."

Zoë's faith broke Anatole's lips into a smile.

"Lasthenia," she whispered now. "She believes in penitence but not in Christ. She says that this Bishop St. Lys is a farce and a sophist. He's mixing texts up all over the place."

Anatole cocked an eyebrow. *More angels?* he wondered. "She isn't supposed to be stating her opinion."

"It's not her opinion, Anatole," Zoë responded. "It's fact; or at least that's what she claims. But you shouldn't give in." Anatole sighed feeling calmer within his thoughts and words now. He watched St. Lys who leered at Zoë. She ignored him and continued to speak. "These people," she whispered, "are under some sort of trance . How else could they sit still and listen to this heresy?"

Anatole nodded in agreement, as he took her hand with his own. "Zoë, I admire the tests of will you have endured. I believe that one day you will have a soul that will surpass mine both in strength and faithfulness."

Zoë shrugged. "Right now you are the stronger of us. Go and make something of your strength."

Anatole nodded and went back to the podium. He stood there once again in hidden anxiety. The audience stirred up greater unrest than on nights before. They were a torn mass of Cainites. Some preferred the ways of St. Lys, however those who hated him did so with an anger that threatened to burst the arena in flames of frenzy. Anatole feared that even the slightest offense would ignite these fumes.

"Are we ready to resume?" Lasthenia asked anxiously. "To those in the audience who wish to partake in the forthcoming debate, I must ask that you first give the speakers their chance to speak. Please do not lose yourself in the passion of your words. If you interrupt your colleague, I will ask that you allow him to continue."

The crowd settled around them. Anatole watched Zoë nervously as she dipped back into the sea of people. She clasped her hands together and lifted them to him, her eyes shining with hope and faith.

Lasthenia resumed her seat in the middle of both speakers and studied St. Lys with her eyes. "You may start, Bishop."

"My esteemed colleague," St. Lys said to Anatole as he took the podium once more. "I fear that though we are responsible for our own souls, the social obligations of the faithful should not be ignored. For we live in a social world, and among others who will try to control or restrain us from knowing what is good and what is bad. There are other lesser Demiurges out there, and they prey on the hapless only to create a following and lead them falsely. Therefore, our shining blood obligates us to be true to its call. We must spread the word of Caine, and we must not stop for any reason." St. Lys stopped his words and glanced pointedly to Anatole. He smiled. "If you know the truth, as you claim, how can you then deny that your social obligation is to save others?"

The bishop fell silent as Lasthenia looked to Anatole. She nodded once and motioned him to speak.

"Social obligation?" Anatole chuckled. "I find it rather interesting that I am reminding you of Caine's traditions and commandments, many of which are social. For I would hope that one who sees Caine as messianic would at least know the commandments he gave to us in the early nights. For

Caine commanded, 'Thou shalt not reveal yourselves as gods to the Children of Seth.' Yet, you also claim that our duty is to teach these children that Caine is the messiah and that those of his blood are above the creator of the world. I am afraid that by doing this, we are also claiming that we are gods. Furthermore, by spreading our so-called shining blood, you expose our identity and therefore break, once again, the traditions of Caine. Therefore, by declaring that it is our duty to spread this shining blood, you are also suggesting that it is our duty to go against the commandments of Caine who is your god. In other words, you are telling us to go against God." Anatole paused in satisfaction at this line of thought. He thought he had this Bishop against the wall, and for the first time he relaxed.

St. Lys raised an eyebrow as he smoothed his hand over his face. "Maybe your god." He paused and let the silence distill the fact that he was avoiding Anatole's question. "A false god," he finally murmured.

"The scripture says that there is only one true God, and He is the creator of all things," Anatole responded.

St. Lys grinned. "I first must remind you that much gets lost in translation. I never suggested that we tell these Children of Seth that we are gods. Yes, we are chosen and must lead the flock to adore us, but I do not advise telling anyone of our true powers. For, they might strike against us either because they fear our power or envy our superiority."

"Yet, by bringing them to your following you are indeed giving them knowledge of our secrets," Anatole said, his words ushering St. Lys back to the question of social obligation.

"Is there a specific commandment against such besides the ones these courts have made? For their laws are commonly perversions of what Caine truly meant." St. Lys shook his head in frustration. "Furthermore, most who come to us do not know of our awesome power before they drink of the shining blood. Yet, by drinking our blood, do they not become worthy of discovering the truth of our existence? Similarly, we Embrace, which certainly exposes our nature to the Children of Seth. If we are to take Caine's traditions so literally, such Embracing would be forbidden as well."

"Maybe it is," Anatole cut in with words that dodged interruption. "After all, our existence is a curse. Would Caine, now enlightened, wish us to spread such?"

"Such concepts amuse me, dear Anatole. We are blessed and we must share such blessings with those who have not been touched by it. Why should we hide this blessing from those who must already know of it when they come and ask us for salvation?"

"As you say, dear Bishop," Anatole grinned. "Social obligation. The traditions exist for our own protection. Those who know of us might seek to kill us either because we are cursed or because they fear our power. Furthermore, if this blessing turns out to be a curse, we must not tempt those who seek the power of this curse to walk with us. To do so is inhumane and polluting to the innocent world. If anything, we must steer clear from meddling with Seth's children. To them, ignorance of our nature is indeed bliss and we actually protect their innocent souls by keeping our true selves from their mind's eye."

Anatole looked out to the audience. Zoë's face faintly glowed in a torch-light she must have at one point lit for herself. She smiled, her laughing eyes shimmering. He nodded to her and looked back to St. Lys. "Similarly," he continued, "we must be careful with the minds of our own brothers and sisters. To infringe upon their beliefs, damage their domains and break their laws is indeed a good way to provoke the frenzy we work so hard to control. This is in part why we should respect our own laws and the laws of the lands we visit.. It therefore seems that these laws and traditions are kept for good reason, and if you truly care about social obligation, you'd be best to heed to them. For in breaching these commandments and traditions, we risk harming ourselves and thus diminishing the salvation we must seek. I fear that to break them would release chaos among our societies."

"Chaos, dear sir," St. Lys picked up as if nothing happened, "is physical as is our current existence. For the spiritual world is one of forms, order and rationality. There is no room for chaos in such a world. It means nothing to our souls and does no damage to us." He laughed for a moment as he looked over the audience he had in his thrall. "My brothers and sisters, Caine of course meant well by his commandments. Yet, Caine himself is purely spiritual, and so are those addressed in the Commandments. Yet, in these nights, many wrongdoers of our kind have become hopelessly immersed in the physical world. They seek to control and they pervert the holy words of Caine with slurs, and twists of translation, and wordplay. In Caine's name, they promote traditions that work only to benefit their own courts and the powerful that dwell within them. In many cases, these traditions also hinder us from performing our sacred duties. These perverted traditions are walls erected by princes desiring temporal power. We have every right to tear them down."

Anatole shook his head. "Are you claiming that you would risk the protection and existence of your brothers and sisters?"

St. Lys shrugged. "We are powerful and have the ability to rule over those who need ruling whether they be Cainite or not. Yet, we lose nothing if we act in rage, for our spiritual god understands what kind of suffering exists within the souls of the physical. Because we are physical, we are prone to hunger, lust, sorrow, and fear. If we happen to indulge, we are excused because we still exist physically."

Anatole laughed. "So you praise the divine life of the intellect, yet fail to tame the worldly passions that exist within you. In other words, you reap the benefits of both the mind and the Beast. To me, you create the true formula for despotic rule."

Anatole paused for a moment. St. Lys did nothing but smile.

"You may call it that if you wish. I call it divinity."

"Regardless, we risk the lives of those within our society if we fail to take note of the true traditions. Let me also remind you that there are many mortals out there willing to kill us because we are damned." Anatole shook his head in confusion. Deep in thought, he brushed a strand of dust-glazed blonde hair from his face. "I do not understand Bishop," he continued. "You claim that you want to bring those among your society to salvation, and then you claim that the men and women of the shining blood will be saved when a true time comes and the Third Caine brings them from this physical realm." Anatole adjusted himself. "And yet," a weighted medley stole his voice as he said, "you claim that you do not mind exposing yourself and your society to mortals who would hunt you down and threaten your followers. How does this prove your duty to society?"

St. Lys grinned. "These hunters walk a blind road. They would be best to join us."

"But they wouldn't join you. They believe in God the Creator and they keep close to His teachings."

"To his lies," St. Lys snapped.

"That's your opinion," Anatole responded plainly. "Should we begin to feed the living our blood, we would create an army that might one day overthrow our own existence."

"So be it," St. Lys spat. "We need not fear this vile physical world that your false god created. We are above it so let us rule it with our armies. You are foolish to be so ignorant. Caine will save us first. For you, I fear I cannot say the same!"

"Please refrain from personal attacks!" Lasthenia shouted. "It is better to exercise some caution," she suggested more quietly.

St. Lys ignored her. "How does it hurt us if we fulfill our powers, and extend our hands to those who must be saved? Does it not do good to bless mortality with the gift of immortality?"

The crowd bustled in movement and agreement. From the shuffling group, Zoë shouted, "Anatole say something!"

"We cannot just walk into the courts and kingdoms of others, break their traditions, and reek havoc among their people," he said.

"You insolent fool!" St. Lys interrupted.

"You're out of line, Bishop," Lasthenia stated once again. She looked to Anatole.

"We do not want to populate the world with this curse," the monk started calmly. "Likewise, we do not waltz into other courts and tell them how to rule their citizens."

"It's no curse, it's a blessing!" someone shouted from the audience.

"Let him finish!" Zoë responded.

"It's a *curse!*" Anatole insisted, his mind angry at the delusions before him. "It is a part of us, and a part of our existence. If we take responsibility and repent for it, God will save us from ourselves. To spread such a curse is wrong. We must…"

"This Malkavian is redundant!" one voice shouted as the crowd began to buzz in protest. Some laughed at the comment but Lasthenia rose her voice above them.

"This will not be a debate without order!" She looked to Anatole. "Let this Malkavian speak."

"This Malkavian blasphemes!" St. Lys shouted

With that, the crowd roared with boos and hisses.

"Please," Anatole called to them. "We must remain temperate and refrain from judgment."

The crowd laughed again. "You're the only one being judged tonight!" another shouted.

"Silence!" Lasthenia commanded. No one listened.

"We must not stop at spreading the shining blood," St. Lys declared. "The faithful must spread the word and destroy the unfaithful forces who stand in the way." St. Lys glared at Anatole and then Zoë as many among the crowd shouted in approval.

"We must not threaten the pure existence of others!" Anatole responded. "For we must give everyone all the time needed to repent before the Creator."

"Creator be damned!" St. Lys shouted. "We are the ones who have the power and we can only seek salvation through action, not mere prayer and selfish thought. We must bring the willing to salvation! It is our right and we have the power to save the souls of others!" The crowd cheered and a peel of thunder cracked the sky.

"Your salvation is blasphemy and seeks nothing more than to subdue the innocent into slavery with the bonds of blood!" Anatole shouted.

"You fool!" St. Lys laughed. "You said yourself that we protect our servants. This is a way of protecting them."

"You're out of line," Lasthenia stated in vain once again.

"We must not serve but lead. We must stop these forces that deter us and stand up against those who make us into servants. And we must stop them now!" St. Lys stepped off the podium and glared at Zoë as thunder from above shook the auditorium. St. Lys snatched the Ravnos girl from the audience.

"Who wants to see the blood of the unfaithful spill!"

"You're out of line!" Lasthenia shouted again. She looked to Zoë's fear-shaken face, and reached for St. Lys' shoulder.

St. Lys sneered and yanked the diminutive Brujah high by her throat. She coughed out as rain began to splash her face and drench her clothing. She didn't fight, but instead closed her eyes as her thoughts took her elsewhere.

"You're out of line, little wench! You Semitic harlot who lies by promising neutrality." St. Lys gazed over the crowd as he unsheathed a dagger from the back of his cloak. "Did you know that this whore claims to be neutral when in fact she speaks to that Malkavian during our recesses? I've seen her twice with him and his thrall, speaking as if she were wise. Yet, she claims herself that she is no scholar. She is a betrayer."

The crowd laughed.

"Shall I drain her here! You tell me my brothers and sisters! She has influenced this so-called peaceful debate into a mess of shouting and chaos. She is also of foul blood. She is a supporter of those Pharisees who crucified our Caine! For they were the workers of the Demiurge and their descendants must be cleansed in blood. Similarly she stands here tonight, keeping the same rules that prevent us, the true faith of Caine, from carrying out our noble quest."

Someone screamed and another snarled. A third cried out for mercy.

"Our god Caine would not approve of such massacre," the woman said.

"The wench is right," a fourth responded to the woman.

"She is a guest of the court and of the nobility that protects it!" someone else shouted.

"That nobility does not protect this court. Court be damned. This woman is not worthy of Caine's blood and she will be the first to face the final punishment of death." St. Lys dragged his blade along the girl's neck and allowed her blood to spill forth. It fountained out into the crowd as Anatole looked frantically for Zoë.

"They are down there. The unfaithful. The Jews, the refugees, the law-keepers. Grab one and make yourself a medicine of blood!"

"Anatole!" Zoë screamed as she watched St. Lys bury his fangs into Lasthenia's neck.

Anatole reached for Zoë's hand as a woman pulled at her hair. He yanked her to the podium.

"Silence!" Veronique d'Orleans shouted from one of the higher seats in the arena, her voice cutting through the pounding rain. "Release her. This arena is under the prince's interdict . No weapons were to enter. You make a fool of yourself in front of Alexander's court."

St. Lys froze and dropped Lasthenia's motionless body. He kept still.

"Everyone remain calm!" Veronique shouted again, this time bringing some of the raging voices to a simmer.

"Dear Bishop," Anatole said as he stepped closer to the bishop's left shoulder, "why do you spawn such chaos? This frenzy is a foolish thing to seek."

St. Lys smiled as he wiped his face free of the falling rain. "You are the only fool here tonight!" he said as he turned on him.

Anatole did not recoil. The bishop slammed him to the ground and he could feel the knife and tendrils of solidified shadow pressing at him. Anatole knew well that such Lasombra shadow-manipulation could be deadly but still he did not fight back. Perhaps martyrdom was to be his fate.

Zoë shrieked.

"The sky is bleeding!" another frantically shouted.

Anatole looked upward, past the bishop. He saw nothing but crystal rain.

"The sky is bleeding! The end has come!"

"It's an illusion," Anatole heard another respond through the cries of the panicking. The waves of bodies began to crash; some attacking others, some running from the door and some falling beneath the feet of the fleeing.

With a smile, St. Lys forgot about Anatole and raised his face to the sky.

Zoë looked to Anatole. "Come with me!"

Chapter Fifteen

A riot. Veronique had never, in the whole of her existence, been closer to a riot than her sire's description of what it was like to be in the midst of one sometime before the fall of Rome. She wasn't at all pleased to find herself exceptionally close to one *now*.

The crowd surged around her with a sound like the sea meeting the shore, a muted roar of dozens of voices all speaking at once, most shouting, some weeping or singing. The thunderheads that had appeared with terrible speed as the bishop called for increasing violence cast a flickering light and pounding rain on the whole affair. But, for some damnable reason, the hell-spawned comet could still be seen, fat and terrible in the sky.

From her vantage point, Veronique could see clusters of people splitting off from the main bulk of the gathering, already giving vent to the violence St. Lys' words had unleashed. They were seizing torches and prying up paving stones from the square beyond the arena to use as impromptu weapons. Veronique swore with feeling and looked around, trying to catch a glimpse of Anatole or Zoë amid the throng. The Malkavian she couldn't find, but she caught a glimpse of Zoë's pale, worried face as she tried to force her way through the crowd.

"Zoë!" Veronique shouted, trying to make herself heard over the noise of the crowd. The girl obviously didn't hear her, and continued trying to make her way against the flow of traffic.

Veronique swore with even greater feeling and scrambled down from her vantage point, where she'd retreated after her confrontation with St. Lys, heartily wishing for a pair of hose and some heavy boots. Sodden by the rain, her skirts hampered her ability to move quickly, to her fang-bared irritation, and the unpredictable motion of the gathering crowds did not help her efforts, either. The mood she sensed was dangerous, hovering on the edge of an outright explosion, waiting only for something to set off the violence that the bishop's sermon had primed. She wanted very much to hold Zoë, find Anatole, and get them both out of harm's way before they became the focal point of the rage scenting the air.

She did not have the opportunity to do so.

Somewhere close by, a woman screamed. Veronique froze; she didn't recognize the voice, but that hardly mattered. It seemed for an instant as though the entire crowd paused—she could almost *feel* the wholesale shift of focus, a sharpening in the atmosphere, a change in the air like the electrically charged moment between lightning and a clap of thunder. Veronique's senses sharpened to their furthest extent and, in that instant, she heard the woman inhale a troubled, sobbing breath, and let out another anguished, ululating shriek. Blood. She smelled blood, and close on the heels of it, fire and smoke. In the instant, the angry, confused, frightened crowd became an angry, confused, and frightened mob. A roar ensued, and the mob lurched forward, as if directed by a malign will.

For the third time that evening, Veronique used the sort of language that would have earned her a cool lecture from her sire about the importance of being well-spoken at all times. She began forcing her way through the mêlée , making liberal use of knees and elbows to drive others out of her way, working her way toward the place she had last seen Zoë. She didn't even dare call the girl's name for fear of attracting unfriendly attention to her.

Someone caught Veronique from behind as she came up against the tailback of people trying to cram themselves through the arena's nearest, narrow exit passage, gripping her arm tightly and trying to pull her away. She snarled and threw the restraining hand off without looking to see whom it belonged to, and began seriously considering physically heaving people aside. The restraining hands came back, more forcefully this time, catching hold of her shoulder long enough for an arm to snake itself around her waist, pulling her hard against a tall body and dragging her physically back. Her first impulse was to kick and struggle, and so she did, driving an elbow into her attacker's stomach with considerable force—an effort that elicited a grunt of involuntarily expelled air, but otherwise had no effect. She was just about to bring her foot down with force enough to break a few of the bones in his lower leg, when a voice penetrated the fear and urgency driving her.

"Veronique, it's me! Stop fighting, damn you!"

She threw a startled look over her shoulder and, even in the sickly light of the comet, she made out Sir Olivier's face, concealed in the depths of his cowl. His ghoul, Renaud, stood at his shoulder, anxiously covering his back. Obediently, she ceased struggling, and let him draw her out of the press to huddle together against the low wall of the arena.

"Olivier, what in God's name are *you* doing here?" Veronique demanded in a fierce whisper, leaning close enough to be heard. "Have you any conception of how *dangerous*—how foolhardy—"

"Yes, I know exactly how dangerous and foolhardy it is," Olivier replied, apparently choosing to ignore her amputation of his honorifics, "I was at the second lecture, too. I'm certain you realize we have to get out of here, quickly, before that mob," he nodded in the direction of the mass unable to reach the exit, "comes back this way and decides to vent itself on anything they find?"

"The idea had crossed my mind, yes," Veronique assured him, tersely. "But Zoë and Anatole are still out there and I cannot—"

"You most assuredly can," Olivier replied evenly. "I saw the Ravnos girl catch up with him—she may even have him under cover by now. And, in any case, they can take care of themselves, milady."

Veronique opened her mouth to argue the point, realized the futility of it before she finished drawing the breath to do so, and simply nodded. "The wall is low in the rear—we could probably climb the seats and let ourselves down without too much danger… if we move quickly."

"Sensible—a woman after my own heart." He took her arm firmly in hand. "Stay close, and please don't kick me again, that wasn't very pleasant."

***

They made it over the wall with only minimal difficulties, the majority of which arose from Veronique's rain-soaked skirts, which she finally ripped to strips in a fit of irritation as they climbed. The streets beyond the arena were something more of an adventure, as they were being roamed by bands of fear-and-fury crazed mortals and Cainites alike, who had no particular fear of attacking anything that looked a likely target on which they could vent their fury. Olivier and Renaud were unarmed, as per the laws that had governed the lectures in the first place, and Veronique had no particular desire to engage in a street brawl with a rioting street mob armed with fire. They navigated between dark alcoves and narrow alleyways, heading for the bridges that joined the Latin Quarter to Ile de la Cité, with a brief stop at Veronique's haven to warn her people to stay inside and be prepared to defend the house if necessary. The woman, Anatole's man Pascal confided to her, was safe, thank heavens. Then they were off again.

Behind them, Veronique could hear mounting sounds of violence—screams of pain and rage, demented laughter—and the air was beginning to thicken with smoke and the stench of spilt and burning blood. It took all of her strength not to turn around and run back toward it. Something inside her, something fierce and hot that pounded at her temples like rushing blood, wanted to be back there, ravening and rending with all the rest. It hardly helped to know that Olivier was feeling it too; twice she caught him looking back in the direction they had come with such naked, hungry longing on his face that it made the blood freeze around her heart. She took his arm and pulled him as he had taken hers, and between them, they managed to keep each other focused and sane until they reached the river and the bridges that traversed it.

The traffic crossing was light, but gradually increased as the unrest swelled out into the Quarter, a wave of madness and violence that lapped at their heels. As they reached the isle, Veronique let Olivier take the lead, his hand tight on her wrist. "Hurry, Veronique—we need to reach my sire—tell him what's happened before anyone else gets to him—"

Her stomach lurched. *Before any of St. Lys' cronies get to him first.* She heard it clearly in Olivier's tone; while there was no particular love lost between Oliver and Anatole, she doubted that the prince's childe really wanted to see the priest staked out to meet the sunrise.

* * *

They did not reach the prince's haven first—they didn't even reach the reception hall first. As with minor court only a few nights previously, the halls were milling with courtiers, but the atmosphere was entirely different. No small number of the assembled Cainites and their servants had wild-eyed looks of fear and outrage about them; a few bore obvious signs of having endured violence. Olivier didn't give her the time necessary to take in more than a few quick glances. He led her rapidly through the halls, barking commands to guardsmen as he passed—ordering up extra guards on the entrances to the prince's haven, diverting some men to the bridges to report on activity there, summoning his own household guard to add to the force already deployed. Within moments, he had the place humming with well-ordered activity. Renaud was sent to fetch his armor and sword as soon as they came in the front entrance.

Veronique was, almost in spite of herself, impressed. She also wasn't permitted too long to enjoy that unfamiliar sensation. Olivier strode past the herald gawping at the doors of the reception hall, not even pausing long enough for them to be properly announced, pulling her with him. A half-dozen bloodied, angry, and frightened Cainites already occupied the side galleries in the room, being tended to by a small herd of the prince's household servants, all of whom looked as disturbed as those they were attending. Veronique recognized faces she had seen in the seats during the debate.

Alexander was on his throne and he was clearly, visibly displeased. His barely restrained fury leapt the length of the room to slap her, making her stride falter and nearly forcing her to her knees here in the middle of the room. Olivier stopped long enough to steady her.

"Milord sire," Olivier said, with what Veronique was prepared to describe as genuinely preternatural calm, "I fear that Lady Veronique and I bear news of the most dire nature to impart."

"Obviously," Alexander replied, an expression of the deepest possible distaste marring his handsome features.

Olivier chose to interpret that remark as permission to approach and speak. He strode forward, pulling Veronique with him. Together, they sank to their knees before the dais, pressed down by the not inconsiderable combined force of Alexander's fury and his will. "Milord sire, I attended this evening's lecture… "

"An activity I seem to recall specifically forbidding you to engage in, Sir Olivier," Alexander's tone was cold and smooth, like black ice. "We shall discuss your disobedience and its consequences later. Continue."

Olivier winced a bit, but did as he was told. "It seemed for a time that this evening's gathering would be more peaceable than the previous lectures—"

"Which you were also forbidden to attend. You disappoint me, Olivier."

Alexander's icy glare would have likely quelled a lesser Cainite; Veronique felt herself quite thoroughly intimidated and she wasn't even the object of that look. Then Alexander transferred his attention to her and she received the impression, more clearly than shouted words, that the Prince of Paris thought her a bad influence on his younger childe. If the situation were not so dire, she might have laughed hysterically on the spot. She was saved from fatally embarrassing herself by Olivier mustering the strength to continue.

"The Bishop St. Lys spoke for some length, almost unchallenged but then… " Olivier swallowed with some difficulty, "But then he… began taunting the priest, Brother Anatole de Paris. Deliberately baiting him, attempting to draw him into a confrontation. It was most disturbing to watch."

Alexander's eyes were still on her; Veronique could feel it, though she didn't dare to meet them, and kept her own gaze fixed firmly on the floor.

"Is this true, Lady Veronique? Did the Bishop St. Lys initiate this evening's little… fiasco?"

She knew he could pry any answer he liked out of her and was entirely angry enough to do so; she addressed her reply to the floor at his feet. "It is as Sir Olivier has said it, Your Highness—the Bishop provoked the confrontation."

"And next I suppose you will tell me that your virtuous and righteous *Brother* Anatole had no choice but to respond in defense of his own faith." The sarcasm in Alexander's tone was heavy enough to crush human skulls. "Do not bother. I have heard variations of this tale from everyone who has come before me tonight—even de Navarre says that St. Lys precipitated it, against the urgings of his own people. *Priests!* Fools and madmen every one them!"

Alexander came to his feet in a swirl of heavy court clothing, his motions agitated, his voice edged with rage. "I am of a mind to order them both put down like rabid dogs—like the demented vermin that they are. They have *both* deliberately broken the peace, *both* deliberately defiled the traditions of the Grand Court to further their little doctrinal feuds, *both* shed blood that *I declared to be sacrosanct!*" His voice rang off the walls, silencing every whisper. "I have had *enough*. Let it be known that *neither* the lap-dogs of the Cainite Heresy *nor* the carpenter's wolf-clad sheep retain any favor in my eyes. I rescind my leniency towards Brother Anatole de Paris—he is stripped of his right to dwell within the walls of my city, he may spend no more than a single night here lest I claim the head he owes me for his disobedience!" The full force of the prince's outrage settled on Veronique's shoulders, battering her like a club. "*You* will inform him of this, Lady Veronique, and I suggest you be grateful that you are not joining him in that cesspool in the forest."

"Yes, Milord Prince," Veronique whispered, shakily.

"As for the Bishop St. Lys," Alexander's voice sank to a hiss of pure venom, "The good bishop has abused my tolerance for the last time. What he began tonight, let him finish at the morrow's dawn. Bishop Antoine de St. Lys is anathema, in breach of the Traditions of Caine and the laws of this city, and his existence is forfeit for his presumptuousness. Sir Olivier, gather your men, and join my lord sheriff in the hunt. I want the heretic's head on a platter before me."

Chapter Sixteen

The arena was awash with sound. Voices rose, some in screams, others in exhortation, all to a backdrop of clashing blades and running, scuffling feet. The rain ended as quickly as it had come and with every moment, the comet seemed to take up more of the sky. The light was as close to day as many of the undead had seen in decades. The ground was still wet and muddy though, and in the mud was a growing amount of spilled blood.

A pocket of St. Lys' followers had taken a small ledge near the gates, and they had spread themselves out, one group protecting the ledge as the others cried out to those around them, beseeching them to listen—to take heed of Caine's coming. In the insanity of the moment, personal preservation seemed to have been forgotten.

"The broom-star fills the sky!" they cried. "The moment of judgment is upon us! Do not deny yourselves the strength and beauty of the shining blood. Accept his gift, and prepare yourselves."

Some fought to break through and silence the speakers; some were s followers of Anatole; others were loyal to Alexander, and in the absence of the prince's own men had become makeshift sheriffs. All was a chaos of color and sound, and as soon as one pocket of dispute was quelled, another arose.

The comet hung high in the sky, following its eastward trek, oblivious to the tumult in the city and the expectations of the faithful. None watched its passing. None acknowledged its presence. The focus, so recently outward to the heavens with expectations of Caine or some other miracle awaiting them, had turned inward. Men and Cainites alike fought for their own beliefs, or out of frustration, or because there was no way out of the arena without fighting. None of those who still attempted to preach could be discerned over the tumult, but still they screamed to the night in voices growing hoarse and frantic as the darkness slid silently across the city on its trek toward dawn.

The sound of approaching horses echoed on the streets outside the arena. None paid them any mind, but moments later, knights wearing the purple livery of Prince Alexander and a goodly number of pikemen similarly garbed broke through the gates, slashing their way right and left through the crowd, then turning toward the pocket of St. Lys' followers still on their small ledge. These newcomers were not unruly faithful, but seasoned warriors, and it took very little time for them to hack their way through the crowd.

As the tide turned rapidly, and it became obvious that this new group would retain control, whether granted to them or seized, the fighting slowed. The cries became quieter and quieter, and then, at last, they stopped.

Sir Olivier rode forward a few paces from the knights and the rest of his own men. "Where is St. Lys?" he demanded.

He was approaching the front line of what remained of Bishop St. Lys' followers, who were backing toward the short wall upon which the more vocal among them preached.

"Bring forth the bishop. Milord Prince Alexander has declared him anathema for his violations of the peace of this place and the laws of Grand Court. Bring him forth!" Sir Olivier ordered.

"The Bishop does not answer to Alexander," a portly Cainite pronounced, stepping forward haughtily. "Blessed Caine will appear, and— "

He got no further. Sir Olivier moved like a dark blur, drawing his blade, wheeling his mount in a semi-circle and whipping the blade through the air. The speaker stood for a moment, gaping at Olivier, then his head parted cleanly from his shoulders, rolled off to one side, and bounced a single time before his body, with no further impulses to control it, jerked in a circle and toppled.

The sword was sheathed, and Olivier turned once more to those by the wall.

"Bring forth St. Lys," the swordsman called out, "or you will all meet the same end. To a man."

There was a roar of dismay from the crowd, and St. Lys' men leaped from the wall. They darted for the gates with wild cries and screams of anger, terror, and righteousness. Olivier and the knights leaped to prevent the escape, but many broke through and were out in the streets before they could be stopped. Though most were easily rounded up and controlled, there was no sign of St. Lys.

Outside the arena, in an alley to one side, Anatole stood. Zoë was at his side, but their followers dispersed to the shadows and streets. The riot had been swift and violent, and many had been drawn into the fray, but when Anatole saw that St. Lys would escape, he disentangled himself from his followers, grabbed Zoë by the arm and steered her out through the gates before it was too late. There was nothing to gain by confronting Alexander's guards, and in any case, the bishop could not be allowed to slip into the shadows unnoticed.

"They won't hold me blameless in this," Anatole said softly. "We have very little time. We must find St. Lys and the others, and we must see this through to its end."

Zoë nodded. The two remained close to the wall of the alley until the first wave of knights had stormed back into the streets, passing them in all directions as they spread out in search of St. Lys. When they had passed, Anatole slipped back into the street and Zoë followed.

"Where will we find them?" she asked. Something in the surety of the monk's steps told her that they *would* find those they sought. She didn't question this.

"For St. Lys, it has come down to this night," Anatole said. He crossed the main street and slipped into another back alley, keeping close to the wall and moving low and fast. "He believes in the vision he has been granted. He believes he has already tasted directly of the shining blood, and that Caine will come this night to raise him up and reclaim the world. He will go where he believes this most likely to happen. He will go where his very presence proves his faith."

Anatole did not name the place, but continued on in silence, leaving Zoë to ponder his words as she followed. The alleys swallowed them quickly, and soon the sounds of the street and the arena were left far behind.

* * *

The Cathedral of Notre Dame de Paris soared above the streets of the Ile de la Cité, incomplete but magnificent and glorious: man's attempt to represent the glory of his God in the stone and symmetry of the mortal mind. Ascendancy through art, some would say. St. Lys thought of none of this as he stood, gazing up at the huge, towering structure, it's highest steeple puncturing the sky.

The cathedral is a fortress, armed only with the belief in the supreme creator of the Earth, the creator of all that is mortal and heavy, dull and dead like clay. The God of men. St. Lys burned with the desire to cast it down. He wanted to offer it as a sacrifice, to drive the spirit of the Demiurge from its walls and stand on the highest parapets, the light of the comet brilliant around him, the blood shining in his veins as he surveyed the world—Caine's world—freed from the weight of sin and pain. And time. So much time had passed, so many years, and lives had passed before him, behind him, and away. So many doubts were passing into the truth as though dragged into a maelstrom.

Sister Takhoui swayed at his side, chanting something under her breath, or praying her own prayers, rocking back and forth to the rhythm. She gripped her cane in both hands, leaning her weight on it, not for support, but to balance her motion. She knew where they would go, and why, and she was preparing herself. Draining her doubt through the wood and into the cursed earth, emptying herself in preparation for Caine's arrival.

There were also present two of St. Lys' most faithful, but as he stared into the night sky, the comet visible only in broken bits and pieces through the tips of the great cathedral's spires, he might have been alone. The last of his kind, the last of any kind, walking the final road of existence. Word had come of the Bishop de Navarre's betrayal—his condemnation of St. Lys as a madman and defiler of the faith! Navarre had wanted St. Lys' place of favor ever since the Archbishop had arrived and this was his opportunity. It mattered not; when Caine returned, all would be made right.

The huge doors, three portals with images carved in intricate, detailed relief at their peaks, beckoned. St. Lys lowered his eyes from the comet and found himself staring into the eyes of Christ, carved above the center portal, surrounded by his four closest believers. The bishop let his gaze fall on each in turn, momentarily resting on the image of Peter. It seemed in that frozen bit of time that Anatole's eyes had stared back from the stone, not in condemnation, but in pity. Then the image was stone once again, and the cold, unyielding surface reflected only the reddish light of the comet.

Without hesitation, St. Lys climbed the stairway leading into the cathedral. The others fell in behind him, each lost in his or her own thoughts, dreams, and fears. It was not such a long climb, but it might have been an eternity, for the flood of images that drenched their minds. Already, just in mounting the steps and moving in close beneath the carved images, the discomfort had begun. It rose up from the surface of the Earth, and pressed in from the very air surrounding them.

They were a long way from the arena now. The crowds that had surged about them swelling with ardor ,had been left behind. The moment was an individual test in which gatherings and followers meant nothing. Their individual faith would carry them through until they were grasped by Caine's dark hands or consumed. *In the end,* St. Lys mused, *it always came down to this.* What mattered was the strength carried within one's own heart and mind. The body, its discomforts and the boundaries it presented were trials, the weakness of daylight and places such as this were no more than light irritants in the face of the glory that was offered. To be worthy, that was what mattered. To reach the end of the road and become something more.

He reached the top step and reached out to the great doors. They were closed, but not locked. The incomplete temple was guarded by daylight, and few would risk being caught on the grounds by night. It was a holy place, a sacred ground. Men held it in reverence for its beauty, and those of the night—the damned feared it as a temple of their enemy. The power that consumed them if they dared to gaze into a sunlit sky, or consumed them from within if they refused to live by the blood.

The doors were too large for a man to open, but St. Lys was not a man, he was Caine's chosen, and he had the strength. He pressed, and the door swung inward, just enough. He slipped through the crack and into the huge cathedral like the shadow of some huge bird, flitting momentarily over a wall, or street, as it passed the face of the moon.

Sister Takhoui followed, and the others slipped in behind. The square at their backs was empty and silent.

* * *

For much of the rest of the night, the sound of Alexander's knights and his men searching the streets and alleys could be heard. Those who had wandered the streets waiting for the comet to show its miracle, had become fugitives, hiding and waiting out the storm of Alexander's wrath. None had seen St. Lys in his passing, and even Anatole's followers had taken to higher or lower ground, waiting. Their leader was missing, the city was in turmoil, and without allowing to be taken in or questioned, it was difficult to understand why Alexander's men ransacked the city.

The debate had grown out of hand, that was certain, and the comet, ushering in all the panic and madness, still beckoned. All of the questions remained, and rumors floated more quickly and more intensely than on any day since the comet's arrival. Caine had arrived. The city was under siege. St. Lys had been martyred and the monk, Anatole had disappeared.

Without success in their quest, Alexander's bands had succeeded in clearing the streets, and quelling the madness that had been pouring out in all directions for so many nights. There were small skirmishes, tiny pockets of resistance, but they were futile. Olivier and his men were prepared, well-armed, and mounted. No serious resistance was possible on such short notice.

St. Lys, however, was not to be found. Olivier sent messengers to report their lack of success, and plunged through the streets. It seemed likely that the bishop had taken the high road, finding the quickest exit from the city and escaping to the roads beyond. Most of his followers would have denied this bitterly, and Olivier himself did not believe it, because he'd witnessed the fanatic gleam in the bishop's eyes as he last spoke; but with no evidence to the contrary, the search slowed and eventually ground to a halt.

Anatole was no more in evidence than his adversary, and this led to further speculations, but with no facts upon which to base them, even the speculations fell to whispers soon enough. The two were not as important as the sensation that something immense was taking place. The night was charged with it. The prince had restored order in the streets, but there was still a sense of the miraculous in the air, and now they waited for it. Some huddled in alleys, others watched the streets from basements and cellars, and still others braved the taverns that were still open and plying their trade to a brisk traffic. None knew what might be coming, but there was not one among them that believed nothing would.

Through this, Anatole and Zoë made their way swiftly and silently. It was not long before Zoë sensed their destination, and not much longer after that when the massive spires of Notre Dame rose before them as they crossed a bridge from the Quarter to the Ile de la Cité. The comet's red heart hung between the spires, as if it had been strung there, a banner of welcome—or of warning.

Zoë tensed at the thought of the place. She felt the pressure of her own sin, the darkness of her own being, repelled at the site. It was dangerous, a place of death and final torment. It was a sacred place, and she a profane being, and yet, as Anatole worked his way steadily closer to the huge edifice, she followed close behind.

The monk did not seem disturbed by what was to come. He moved with consummate grace, seeming to glide, rather than to run. More than once they came close to detection, but each time, before they came into plain view of Alexander's men, Anatole stopped. He seemed to see them before they arrived, to hear them before there was any sound to hear. Zoë felt clumsy, stumbling in his wake and unable to rid herself of the growing terror of ascending the cathedral steps. She knew she would have been caught easily without him, and knew as well that if he had not been with her, she would not have had the courage or the strength to make the journey at all.

There was a danger that they would be spotted as they crossed the large, open area before the cathedral's huge west-facing doors. Anatole didn't hesitate. He crossed the courtyard without a sideward glance, and mounted the great steps. Zoë hesitated at the bottom. She took the first step easily enough, but each progressive lift and fall of her feet was more difficult. Her mind and heart raged against it, as though she were stepping into a field of bright sunlight. As though she'd been offered a goblet of holy water by the pale, blessed hand of a priest. She felt unclean. Soiled beyond comprehension, and slowly forcing her way up the stairs in Anatole's wake, the weight of her sin pressed down on her shoulders. She shivered in sudden pain, fright, and memories of the inquisitor Isidro who had destroyed her sire. He had wielded power from the same source, but here it felt purer. There was no hated man on whom she could focus her anger—here it was just her and the weight of her ever-accumulating sin.

Anatole had reached the top of the stairs. He turned back to her. The pain shivered through him as well, Zoë sensed it. He did not fight it, he embraced it. His face was a mask of deep joy and dark dread. He did not speak to her. He did not admonish her for her lack of faith, or cajole her into continuing her climb. He stood, an example in the dead, undying flesh of his own faith, and he waited.

Zoë locked her gaze to his, and took another step, and then another. If her faith could not get her to the top of those steps, perhaps his could. Perhaps, after all the roads she'd followed him down, and all the times he'd lifted her up when she felt ready to topple back into darkness and despair, he would be the rock against which she could anchor herself for this last test. She knew that time was important to them. Alexander's patrols would come this way eventually, and if they were caught on the steps, though Olivier could not—or likely would not, in any case—follow them where they now went, there were others who could. Men could mount these steps with none of the fear or the pain, and would do so if commanded. She had to move.

The climb took what was likely no more than a couple of moments, but seemed to Zoë more than sufficient time to replay every dark deed of her existence, every torn throat and drop of blood—every lost soul imprinted with her dark touch. Her feet, which had tingled at the first touch of the stone steps, were burning. It was not the consuming fire, but it was burning all the same, the excruciating pain inching its way up her legs stroking the nerves of her being with each step. She could sense her own destruction with each passing moment, could catch the whiff of the final burning in the air about her. She could see eternity in the depths of Anatole's unblinking, rapturous gaze.

And now, standing at his side, her limbs stiffened and locked. She could not take another step, though Anatole held out his hand to her. She shook like a leaf in the breeze, the pain searing her. But, it wasn't the pain, she knew, that was stopping her. She had endured pain, and would do so again. She could not enter this place. She was not worthy, not ready, and she feared it. She feared redemption as much as damnation, though she was much more intimately familiar with the latter. She would be a blemish on holy ground, and she could not continue.

Anatole read it in her eyes. He took a half step toward her, reaching out, but before they touched, he checked his motion. Slowly, he drew back his hand, and stood for a moment longer, meeting her gaze.

"There will come a time," he told her, "when you will not feel the fear. There is no easy step on the road to redemption."

Zoë nodded, or believed that she did, but she could do nothing more. Anatole glanced to the streets, but they remained empty. Zoë stood near the side of the center portal of the cathedral, and she would not be immediately visible if any approached. The door still stood slightly ajar.

"Wait for me," he said softly. Then he was gone. Where he stood was now only the shadowy crack of the doorway and absolute silence. In that silence, with nothing left to sustain her, Zoë closed her eyes. She lowered her chin to her breast and in a soft voice, as the pain flickered and teased through her, she prayed.

* * *

Anatole entered the huge cathedral slowly and reverently. It had been a long time since he'd braved holy ground, and the beauty and sheer enormity of the grand temple was staggering. There was a huge window of stained glass that filtered the comet's light into odd, muted hues. There were halls and stairs leading up to the two towers, and there was scaffolding and the evidence of artisans on all sides, the bits and pieces of the world that would become the final monument: the temple.

Anatole spared little attention to each detail, allowing the enormity of the place to swallow him as the whale had taken Jonah. His entire being was on fire—his sin burning away, his mind and heart stretching out, fingers grasping, embracing the cleansing heat. Despite this, he moved quickly. The great altar beckoned, and it was there he knew that he would find what he sought. It was there that St. Lys would face the heart of Christendom—the last fortress of his sworn enemy.

As Anatole came in sight of the altar, he saw that there were four figures gathered around it. St. Lys stood behind the altar, his eyes raised to the great stained glass portal looming above. Sister Takhoui stood at one end of the altar, and one of the bishop's acolytes stood at the other. In front, one last figure knelt, as if bowed under the weight of the burning, inner fire.

St. Lys dropped his gaze, and as Anatole approached slowly, his face stoic in the immensity of his pain, their gazes locked. The bishop seemed illuminated from within. His eyes were wild, distant and half-mad with the warring sensations—his faith, the pain, the incredible heat and the energy that pulsed and radiated from the great altar.

"Have you come to await his coming at my side, old friend?" the bishop crooned. "Have you come to admit this night that the time is upon us to rise up and take our destinies, and our redemption, into our own hands? Have you come," he hesitated for just a second, then said, "to meet Caine?"

"You know I do not," Anatole said. His voice wavered, just for a second, as he accustomed himself to speaking through the pain. He continued to move slowly forward. The motion seemed to help to spread the heat, or at least to vary the degree of agony, and this helped him to focus.

"It is a shame," St. Lys sighed in mock pity. "I had hoped you might have come around to the truth in the end, perhaps even in time for a taste of what is to come. Perhaps he will take pity on you, monk. There may be a place for you in Caine's blessing, but your chance is sliding away. The comet fills the firmament, and when its spirit overflows the Demiurge's base creation, all clocks will have wound down without a key to rewind them."

Anatole didn't answer immediately. He glanced at Sister Takhoui, still muttering her own prayers under her breath. She pretended to be watching the floor, but Anatole felt her gaze upon him more than once. The other two stood much as Zoë had when he had last seen her, on the threshold of the temple's vast doors. They held their ground, but it was by force of will alone. Their senses were not theirs to control, and they waited, held by St. Lys' faith, and his conviction that Caine would come to them and drive away the pain.

"You should hear yourself, Bishop," Anatole said at last. "You should listen to your own words through the ears of another, and hear the self-aggrandizing, ridiculous claims you make against a backdrop of reason and true faith.

"The world is not aligned so that you can walk through it, reaching to the right and left and freely plucking everything you believe should be yours. If it is easier for you to believe that Caine will come for you in person, offer you his powerful, shining blood, and drive away all that would punish you for the sins of your long existence, that does not make it a truth, it only makes it a selfish dream. That is what your beliefs have become. Your belief is a belief that nothing bad can come of you, or to you, and that you can flaunt your sin in the face of God with impunity."

"You speak with the naïveté of a child," St. Lys replied, his face contorting into a sneer. "We are Caine's chosen, and if we lack the strength to take up that destiny, we deserve the flame that will consume the unworthy."

"You are damned," Anatole stated. His voice was louder now, and he was drawing strength from the pain. "You follow a faith that justifies whatever dark whim you are pleased with at the moment, but you have no faith in Caine nor in God. Faith is a matter of sacrifice, a path of pain and personal growth. You have been cursed, but you have also been given the gift of near- immortality to follow a road of redemption, and to answer for all the sin of your long days, and yet you refuse that gift. You throw that in the face of God, and stand on his very altar, crying out that the world should give you what you want."

Takhoui's swaying had become more pronounced. Her eyes darted from St. Lys, whose features had taken on the expression of a madman, to Anatole, calm and strong. He was glowing in the light from the huge stained-glass portal far above, as if caught in the light of God himself. Then, Takhoui broke. Stumbling, falling to her knees and rising with great effort, she staggered away from the altar. She was still whispering to herself, but her eyes had grown bright and fearful. She turned her head to one side, then the other, as if accosted by a host of inner voices, but when she fell at last to her knees on the cathedral floor, the eyes she raised to Anatole were lucid.

"I have lost sight of the Lord," she whispered. "I have taken the wrong path, been led into the very darkness I have warned so many others of. "

Smoke rose from where her knees brushed the stone floor, but she ignored the heat and Anatole reached out to her.

"Rise up, sister," he said softly. "Redemption is not lost, but as ever, hangs before you. You have but to take that road, and to allow the fire, the pain and the infinite love to burn the sin away. You may always return to him."

St. Lys had raised his hands overhead, and he cried out, his voice like thunder. "You will be lost! You will be a base creature, no more than he," the bishop pointed at Anatole, his hand shaking, barely able to support the finger that drew arcane characters in the air. "Caine will turn away from you, and there will be no coming back."

Anatole turned back to St. Lys. "The sun will rise very soon, Bishop, and I see no sign of our Dark Father's arrival. The comet is waning, the time for great miracles is passing, and you stand on the altar of my God, arrogant and full of the pride that will be your downfall."

St. Lys threw back his head at this, eyes wide, and began to laugh. The laughter echoed like thunder through the cathedral, booming off the massive walls and vaulted ceilings. His acolytes stepped back in consternation and fright, and the one who knelt at the foot of the altar glanced up at his lord in dismay.

Raising his hands to either side, St. Lys continued to laugh, but the sound was broken now and then by a crackling sound. He lowered his gaze a final time, and ignoring Anatole, glared down at Takhoui, who had risen to stand, bent and wracked with pain, at the monk's side.

"I believed in your vision," he called to her, taunting. "I can hear him, even now, coming for me."

"Then may God forgive me for leading you astray," Takhoui whispered, lowering her gaze. "My vision was unclear. May He forgive us all."

"What?" The doubt and mad confusion that had been building in St. Lys' voice burst forth onto his face for just a second.

In the next second all other sound ceased to matter as St. Lys screamed. The sound rose with the intensity of a banshee's wail, rising from deep within his being and filtering out through the cracks now showing in his skin. He did not burn in seconds, but by degrees. Great fissures tore up the length of his flesh, glowing flames licking up from within, winding about him and flickering madly, caught in a breeze that did not exist, dancing up to engulf his face in brilliant heat.

Takhoui took a step forward. She whispered "No," but it was too late. Anatole stopped her with a firm hand on her shoulder, and held her in place. St. Lys spun around slowly, staggering back away from the altar, far too late to save himself, and as he moved, his flesh gave up its hold, falling away in clumps and disintegrating to dust. There was a final flash, so brilliant and bright that it robbed their sight for what seemed an eternity, blending that brilliance with the heat coursing through their own bodies and bringing the fear of destruction to their hearts for a quick, lingering kiss, before it fell away to darkness and to silence.

Anatole stared at the altar for a long moment, then withdrew his hand from Takhoui.

"We must go," he said. "It is not long before the dawn, and we must be away from here."

He did not wait to see if she followed, but walked slowly away, the heat of the bishop's passing still warming his back and searing his mind.

He did not look back.

Epilogue:

The Sacraments

Stephanos was with Lasthenia when Anatole and Zoë found them, the Brujah girl lain quietly across one of the standing stones near the caves where the refugees had found shelter before all this madness had begun. The Nosferatu was one of the few of that blood who had chosen to remain in the Bière Forest instead of following Malachite east. Stephanos was a believer in Brother Anatole's teaching before any business of the Dracon or Dream.

"Is she in torpor?" Zoë remembered well the deathlike slumber that had taken Anatole a few years before. Lasthenia, laying in quiet repose with her arms folded over her chest as if she were awaiting the grave, had that same look abut her.

"You never know with this one," Stephanos responded. "Malachite tasked me with watching over her and following her instructions on a situation like this."

Anatole arched an eyebrow. "What were those instructions?"

"To lay her out for the sun, if she were to fall into slumber at night," Stephanos said. "St. Lys wounded her in the last debate and she was caught in the crowd after that. Every night since, she has been becoming weaker and this night she did not wake at all. This has happened before when she traveled with Malachite, apparently. He called it an old game between them."

Zoë looked to the eastern sky, already just a touch more purple than black. "This is no game, Stephanos."

"No," Anatole agreed, "it is not. It is faith."

"Malachite called her a prodigal, Brother," Stephanos said. "He said her beliefs were in philosophies, in theories, not in God."

"But she was—" Zoë caught herself—"is Jewish. She recognized God."

"We all walk our own roads," Anatole said. "You of all people should know this, Zoë. Her life in a Jewish family is as far behind her as yours as an apprentice metalsmith. Further, even."

Zoë's hackles rose. *Apprentice metalsmith?* She'd been the student of Gregory Lakeritos, whose work caused wonderment across the Empire and far beyond! To dismiss what she'd been as a simple apprentice... The lesson sunk in.

"She made choices since her becoming," Zoë said, "just as I have. Her beliefs have changed."

"Indeed. Even more than Veronique, I expect she believed in a world made by man's hands and governed by man's laws—and his crimes."

"But you said she was faithful, Brother," Stephanos said.

"Indeed," Anatole answered, "simply because we refuse to acknowledge God does not mean He is absent. Perhaps she called it destiny or chance, but to ask to be left for the sun like this—it is a call for God's hand."

"Abandoned by man," Zoë said, "she commits herself to God, to take or spare as He sees fit."

Anatole smiled. "The mind may deny God, but the soul does not."

"But we have not abandoned her," Zoë said. "There is still time to get her into the caves where she can mend. Let her find God some other time, when it won't destroy her."

"Would you rob her of her one concession to God?"

Ellen Porter Kiley   247

Zoë hesitated. She could just take Lasthenia and argue the point with Anatole at another time. "No," she said at last. "No, I won't."

They turned and headed for the caves, leaving Lasthenia in hands better than their own. When they returned the next dusk, she was gone, leaving neither ash nor a trail behind.

* * *

The Bishop de Navarre let the last of St. Lys' letters slip into the brazier and suppressed a flinch as it flared before being consumed. The letters had been layer upon layer of apocalyptic foolishness and regurgitated apocrypha. The worst brand of self-aggrandizing tripe. "I will kiss the lips of the Third Caine," de Navarre said, quoting his predecessor with open derision and pacing the room. "The Demiurge will fall and the perfect world of spirit will take us. Bah!"

De Navarre turned to face the brazier—now across the room from him—and clenched his fist. The shadows that had been dancing across the stone floor leaped to his call and closed around the large dish, crushing the life and fire from it. It's torn metal bulk fell through shadow and into the dark abyss that was the real truth.

De Navarre was now the ranking bishop in a heresy that he knew to be laughably flawed in its precepts. The instruments of the "True Church of Caine" were useful, but the faithful were nothing but sheep. The physical world was a patina over the truth, yes, but that truth was no shining world of spiritual perfection. The truth was the absolute nothingness of the Abyss, of the oblivion of Ahriman itself. De Navarre had spent an eternity parsing the mysteries of this truth, positioning himself to be among the elect of darkness when the time came.

Looking out the single window at the rising spires of Notre Dame Cathedral across the way, he allowed himself to imagine that glorious night of nights. Sun, moon and planets would cease their rotations. The stars would wink out and the sky would become unsullied blackness so complete no comet would dare streak across it. Finally the firmament would shatter like black glass and oblivion would swallow all. He felt the cold thrill of excitement at that glorious future, and without his conscious thought, shadows across the Ile de la Cité slithered across paving stones and up walls.

"Congratulations on your elevation, my bishop." The voice was chilling and beautiful, like a layer of ice stilling a river at midwinter. "I wonder what Archbishop Nikita would think of your faithfulness to the church you lead?"

De Navarre turned around and gazed at the Countess Saviarre, who stood just inside the doorway leading from the underground chambers to the offices. Her seeming was as dagger-sharp as her voice and she was resplendent in the fine robes—spattered just slightly with the blood of some unfortunate—she'd chosen for the evening. "His Grace is welcome to walk into the wilds of Germany and never return."

"Well said, my bishop."

De Navarre looked at her anew and saw beyond the patina of undead flesh. To his eyes, she was a woman-shaped maw into the Abyss itself. Not for the first time, he felt as if his soul might tip and fall into her and to the oblivion it longed for. She was no Lasombra and left the shadow magics to him, but de Navarre had known from the first instant he met the Countess Saviarre that she was an avatar of Ahriman. Her soul was cold, empty and hungry and he was quite sure it would, one glorious night, consume the world as it had already consumed him. Overcome by the glory of it all, the bishop fell to his knees, red-black tears of blood streaming down his cheeks.

"There, there, my bishop," Saviarre said as she cupped his face in her hands. "All will be well now."

He knew it would.

Enjoy the following preview of **Dark Ages: Brujah™**, the eigth Dark Ages Clan Novel, available in November of 2003.

Dark ages
BRUJAH™

MYRANDA KALIS

Dark ages
VAMPIRE

ISBN 1-58846-832-1

WW11212

Paris, Kingdom of France

January, 1223

Veronique d'Orleans woke quickly, as was her wont, sat up in her narrow cupboard bed, and listened for a moment to the sounds of the world beyond the locked door of her daytime sanctuary in Paris's Latin Quarter. Music filtered down through the floorboards, a rousing Provençal tune that made Veronique's toes itch to touch the floor, partially disguised by a rhythmic thumping that suggested few of the house's patrons were denying the music's call. Laughter—Yvonnet's trilling, distinctive laugh, the answering chuckle of whatever customer she was attending—and their voices, too muffled for Veronique to make out specific words through all the layers of wood and stone and plaster. Water splashing, quite nearby, and two female voices, engaged in a low-voiced but fierce disagreement. Alainne and Girauda.

She reached up and undid the interior locks of the solidly lightproof cabinet door. Someone had come in while she slept to place a fat tallow candle in the sconce and light a brazier in the farthest corner of the chamber from her bed, but the floor was still unpleasantly cold underfoot. It was the middle of January, and so far the winter of 1223 was proving itself especially harsh. A stack of freshly arrived correspondence sat on her writing desk, seals intact; she stood on the very tips of her toes to examine it, her feet refusing to spend more time on the icy stone than they absolutely had to. Several brief notes from her various agents and spies, a handful of invitations to this or that midwinter fête, and a slightly thicker package wrapped in oilskin and tied in ribbons, sealed in black wax and stamped with arms she hadn't seen in more than a decade. She couldn't tell whether her hands were trembling in excitement or because her blood was about to freeze in her veins. Someone had also moved her shoes and taken away her chemise, and she could just imagine who *that* was. With an irritated growl, she flung open the door separating the two chambers of her suite and snapped, "Bring them here *right now.*"

The low-voiced argument taking place in the next room abruptly ceased. Then, "Your bath is ready, Vero."

Veronique closed her eyes in despair. "Girauda, I'm *freezing.* At least give me the chemise until I'm finished reading my letters."

"Bath. Then letters. The water won't stay warm forever, you know."

Veronique was forced to concede the logic. She laid the oilskin package back down with a sigh, squared her shoulders, and went forth to do battle with Girauda and Alainne, both of whom were prepared for her. The wooden bathing trough was steaming gently, lined with towels and scented with herbs—Veronique caught a hint of rose and lavender—and Girauda was standing next to it, a scrub brush and cake of soap in hand. Girauda, her dark hair threaded with iron gray and pulled back in a tight bun, her dark Occitan gaze completely devoid of nonsense, smiled at her as Veronique came into the room on tiptoes. A low fire was burning in the grate and candles cast a golden circle of light around the chair that Alainne had set up, likewise draped in towels, next to a low table containing a vast assortment of vials and bottles, pots and crocks, and more varieties of tiny scissors than Veronique even knew existed. Alainne was fussily adjusting the angle of the mirror she had brought downstairs for the evening's entertainment. Alainne, sunnily fair everywhere that Girauda was dark, youthful and slender as an aspen tree where Girauda was fully rounded and matronly, also turned to smile at her, clearly anticipating the use of a canvas she was rarely permitted to embellish. A fresh, snowy white chemise, discreetly embroidered with fine needlework at neck and hem, her long-sleeved kirtle, and a blue brocade surcoat that she had never seen before hung next to the fire, warming.

"I see you planned this in advance," Veronique muttered and allowed herself to be guided into the bath, which was, she had to admit, quite a bit warmer than the floor. "I'm not attending court, you realize—"

"Of course we realize." Girauda dipped the brush in the bath, soaped it, and applied it vigorously to Veronique's milk-white shoulders, releasing the scent of even more herbs. "Red is for court. Blue is for business meetings."

"Oh, for heaven's sake." She couldn't help but laugh, and lean back into Girauda's scrubbing. "There… right there… ah, good. What's passed today?"

"It's bitter outside," Alainne chose that moment to chime in, coming over to join them and set to work with soft cloths on Veronique's face and limbs.

"No snow, I hope?"

"Oh, no, none. But the wind's keen and they're saying that the river might freeze through if it keeps this cold much longer." Alainne cheerfully dumped a dipper of warm water over Veronique's irregularly cropped hair, then another. "The roads are still clear at any rate, if a little icy."

"Thierry—"

"Thierry is upstairs seeing to the carriage." Girauda passed Alainne the soap and it promptly found its way into Veronique's hair. "We packed your traveling case earlier."

"I'm only going to be gone a night or three. Four, at most." Further commentary was briefly prevented by several dippers of water rinsing her hair.

"And on each of those nights you shall be attired as befits a woman of your quality," Girauda replied, sternly. "We also packed your traveling desk, and anything you might need to correspond. You have but one thing left to do."

"Besides submit to your tender ministrations?" Veronique asked wryly, lifting her dripping bangs out of her eyes.

"Yes. Thierry and Sandrin will accompany you for safety's sake, of course, but you will likely need a lady's maid, as well…."

"Girauda should stay here to oversee the house," Alainne opined, earning herself a glare. "I can more easily accompany you the short distance you travel this time and—"

"Alainne, if I have said it once I have said it a dozen times, *you* are more needed *here*. The younger girls require *your* assistance more often than mine—"

"I am going to be gone *four nights* at most." Veronique's voice cut across the incipient argument. "And I am more than capable of dressing myself and even applying paint and scent if I have to. You are *both* staying here." Silence fell as she rose dripping from the bath, stepped out onto the towels set on the floor for her, and allowed Girauda and Alainne to pat her dry. Alainne guided her to the chair, somewhat sullenly, and sat her down. Veronique submitted to a manicure and a hair trim, lavender-scented oil massaged into her shoulders and breasts, and a bit of tasteful embellishment of her natural charms with the paints Alainne was so expert in applying. Even Veronique, who had witnessed the art she was capable of performing on the faces of even the plainest girls, was impressed with the overall effect.

While they were engaged in lacing up her kirtle, she said quietly, "I'm not angry with you for wanting to go. I'm sure it seems better than staying here, some greater adventure, but this is where I need you both to be. You're my eyes and my ears in this place, and my hands." She caught their eyes as they looked up at her. "If I didn't trust you, I wouldn't rely on you, even if I don't take you with me everywhere I go. Do you understand?"

Girauda's expression softened perceptibly. "Ah, Vero. I understand. Forgive an old and stubborn woman her vanity. I wanted to take the measure of this woman you're to meet and work with."

Alainne glanced away, and then back. "I... You know me too well. I wanted the adventure of going on this journey with you... I should have thought."

"Believe me," Veronique replied, as the surcoat went over her head, "when I say that I think you'll both have your wishes before all is said and done. Now, bring me my letters."

* * *

The reports were all written in Thierry's careful, Cathedral-school-trained hand, and encompassed a variety of topics, none of which were of any immediate import. Or, rather, none of which were important enough to cause a rearrangement of her plans for the next few nights. The invitations all pertained, as she had expected, to various social gatherings intended to take the edge off the midwinter doldrums. After the excitement of the comet, which had hung ominously over the Parisian sky, sparking the debates between Anatole and St. Lys, and then outright civil unrest, the winter had settled in hard and fierce, with heavy snow and bone-gnawing cold. Voluntarily or otherwise, most of the Cainites in Paris and its outlying regions had found themselves haven-bound since shortly before Christ-Mass; only now were the roads beginning to clear enough to allow for even short-distance travel. Lord Navarre was planning a winter garden party, and Veronique could feel her blood icing over at the mere thought, not only from the concept but the myriad unpleasant possibilities when it came to execution. Navarre was many things, but exceptionally humane was not one of them.

Veronique broke the seals on the oilskin package. Within were three letters, two thick, one thin, each with its own wax and ribbon seal intact. The first was sealed with the arms of Queen Esclarmonde the Black, her sire's longtime friend and confidante, who had, in Veronique's youth, given them both a home in her court at Carcassonne. Veronique was slightly surprised that a response to her own letter had come so quickly from Esclarmonde's court, relocated to mountainous Foix in the wake of the crusade against it, but at least the surprise was a pleasant one. She broke the seal and quickly scanned the first of the four pages, pale eyes tracking across the close-written lines, searching for the pattern of the cipher she had been taught all those years ago. She found it, and smiled as she picked out the first line of Esclarmonde's true message, hidden amidst a sea of courtly pleasantries: *Vero, you take a great risk writing to us this way, but I am grateful to hear from you, nonetheless.* Then she refolded the heavy parchment and set it aside for greater consideration when she returned, retying the ribbon around it.

The second thick letter was from Aimeric de Cabaret, Esclarmonde's grandchilde, and it took Veronique a moment to discipline herself enough to read his message calmly. She had learned, the summer before, that he had failed to return from a diplomatic mission to Montpellier. Hot on the heels of that, the word had come that he'd been captured by the Prince of Béziers, a northerner installed after the slaughter of the Albigensian Crusade. It had been a subject of considerable gloating and obnoxious satisfaction among no small number of his Parisian clanmates; it had tested all the self-control Veronique possessed not to kill someone and arrange for his ashes never to be found. She had been closest to Aimeric of all of Esclarmonde's kin, childer and grandchilder, during her time in the Languedoc; they were of an age and closer in temperament than most, and she had missed him fiercely when she and Portia finally moved north to the court of Julia Antasia. The slurs slung at him had been difficult to listen to with even feigned indifference, for she knew the man, and considered him more than the equal of any of his northern brethren. A part of her had mourned him as already dead, and refused to nourish false hope that he might survive the fate that had befallen him; Béziers's prince was not noted for his mercy or his tolerance, and if an example of the follies of continued resistance was to be made, Aimeric was a perfect prize in that regard. It had shocked Paris for weeks afterwards when no example was made and, in fact, diplomatic ties were opened between the courts of Foix and Béziers. It drove Saviarre to a public, frothing display of outrage to learn that Eon de l'Etoile, the northern Prince of Béziers, theoretically a vassal directly beholden to Alexander of Paris himself, had concluded a separate peace with Queen Esclarmonde the Black, in blunt defiance of his liege lord's intent that she be dragged from Foix in chains and likely marched through the streets of Paris in disgrace. It drove half the Toreador in Paris insane with rage, when copies of the peace treaty had arrived for the delectation of the Grand Court, that Aimeric de Cabaret had been intimately involved in the negotiation of that treaty. A chill had definitely settled into the air between Paris and Béziers, though no official sanction had yet been levied against its prince, and most believed that sanction was only waiting for the spring to come.

Aimeric's letter was actually somewhat thicker than Esclarmonde's, and likewise encrypted. This one, Veronique sat to read all the way through. Aimeric never *could* resist the temptation to tell a story, particularly not a story in which he was personally involved, but she supposed she could forgive him that, especially since his version of events was actually entertaining rather than suffused with righteous outrage. And his opinions concerning the character of Eon de l'Etoile were, she suspected, a trifle more accurate than those of anyone currently dwelling in Paris. It helped somewhat that the first line of his coded message was, *Don't you wish you were here now?*

Oh, my friend. I do wish. Perhaps, when this is all over, we will meet again. She refolded the letter, resisted the urge to slide it into the traveling bag sitting strapped shut at her feet, and opened the third, sealed with unfamiliar arms. And discovered that Aimeric had, even *in absentia*, served her far better than she knew and probably better than she deserved. The letter was from Eon de l'Etoile, and it was a brief, diplomatically pithy request for her assistance. Apparently it wasn't only the opinion of Paris's Cainites that swift and unpleasant retribution was in the offing for Eon once the spring thaws came. She retied that message, as well, and added it to her mental list of options to consider and review, then locked all three letters in her desk.

Girauda fetched a freshly warmed cloak, and then Veronique hefted her bag to her shoulder in an unladylike display that brought a scowl to her maid's face. Veronique couldn't help smiling at it. "I shall return. If Jean-Battiste turns up sniffing after me, tell him you don't know where I've gone, but that I'll be back shortly. And don't let the little viper in the house if you don't have to."

"Of course not, he stole two girls the last time he was here...."

The cold outside of Veronique's lower-story haven was, as Alainne had warned her, bitter; the wind cut through her clothing and stole any remaining residual warmth before she'd gone two steps. Fortunately, she didn't have far to go. Thierry stood at the end of the alley, lamp in hand, breath escaping him in explosive puffs of frost, huddled inside a hand-me-down wrapping that made him look even smaller than he actually was. Behind him, Sandrin and the driver were making certain that all was in readiness to depart with her cart.

"Thierry, why in the name of God are you standing *outside?*" Veronique demanded, shooing him in the direction of the cart's open entrance flap, tied back to allow their entry. "Get in before you catch your death."

Thierry's rapidly chattering teeth nearly amputated the tip of his tongue as he replied, "I didn't want you to fall in a snowdrift and be lost until spring."

"Thank you for the concern," she replied, wryly, "but I'm afraid that, if your fingers freeze off, you're of no further use to me, and I'll have to replace you with someone even younger. Get in. And take this." She exchanged her bag for his shaded lamp, and crossed around to the front of the cart, where the driver and her bodyguard were conversing. The driver was muffled to the eyes in layers of thick wool, clearly none too pleased to be taking to the road on such a raw night, but accustomed to his employer's unpredictable travel needs. Sandrin chimed gently as he moved, indicating that he was hiding a layer of chain underneath his heavy winter clothing. "I trust that everything is in order for our departure?"

"Yes, lady." Sandrin was, unlike most of Veronique's other companions, *unfailingly* polite. His mother had beaten such good manners into him that not even a decade making his fortune in the mercenary trade could completely break him of them. "I took the liberty of riding out ahead to scout the way earlier. The road is clear."

"Good. Have a care, Sandrin—if it gets too cold to ride, tether your horse and come on the cart." The lamp went to the driver's hands, to be clamped to the front of the cart to illuminate their way, and Sandrin helped her up the steps and inside, lacing the door flap closed behind her.

Thierry had stowed her bag in the long, lightproofed box she used for safe, if not particularly comfortable, daylight travel, and had retreated beneath a pile of lap rugs and embroidered cushions to conserve heat. Veronique smiled down at the top of his head, the only visible part of his body, and squirreled beneath the blankets with him. "Well, Thierry, if you ever wanted the chance to complain about my cold feet, now would be the ideal time…. "

* * *

Rosamund d'Islington sat at her desk in the embassy's sole oriel room, her *vade mecum* open before her, a candle burning at the corner behind a shade of painted parchment, ink and pens at the ready. Behind her, a fire burned cheerily and, next to it, her maids Margery and Blanche sat gossiping quietly as they worked together at a bit of sewing. The oriel's unglazed window, situated to the right of her desk, was shuttered firmly and curtained with a thick wool hanging; even so, an occasional breath of stinging cold made it through to stir the relatively warm air in the chamber with a hint of the winter outside. She needed no gifts of the blood to hear the wind whistling shrilly through the house's eaves and roaring through the forest like a bloodthirsty beast on the prowl, thick though the stone walls were. A little shiver, having nothing to do with any response to the cold, traveled through her at the images that her active imagination painted with that thought. Silently, Margery brought a warmed lap robe to lay across her legs. Rosamund smiled her thanks at her maidservant.

She knew that she should be thinking of other things, doing other things, rather than staring blankly at a piece of parchment and indulging in the idle fancies of a dark winter night. She had letters to write: to her sire, Isouda; to Isouda's liege, Queen Salianna, by whose graciousness she was presently housed and employed; to Alexander, Prince of Paris, on whose pleasure and sufferance she was currently obliged to wait. Rosamund picked up her pen, inked it, held it poised to write, and put it back down again. What she *really* wanted to be doing was pacing from one end of the great hall to the other in an effort to release all the nervous tension that had been accumulating in her for the better part of the last fortnight. That, and chewing her brother Josselin's ear about the Brujah emissary due to visit them sometime in the next night or so.

A fortnight ago, Rosamund had arrived in the near vicinity of Paris with her retinue, armed with letters of introduction, two banners (one bearing the arms of her sire, the Queen of Blois, Isouda de Blaise, the other the traditional Toreador ambassadorial arms to which she was personally entitled), and instructions on whom she was to contact first and how she was to go about it. Before she had departed Chartres, she had received extremely explicit instructions from both her sire and Queen Salianna regarding the customs that prevailed in formal diplomatic relations between the Grand Court of Paris and the Courts of Love. It was, in the currently cool but nominally friendly climate, customary for a Toreador diplomat arriving from the Courts of Love to refrain from entering Paris without explicit permission from Prince Alexander. As a result, several secondary "embassies" had been obtained for the use of the Courts of Love. It was to one of those embassies, a fortified manor house lying just off the road connecting Paris and Chartres, that Rosamund had come.

One of her letters of introduction had gone to the lord and lady of the manor, securing their cooperation and assistance for the duration of her stay. The lord and lady were Queen Salianna's ghouls and had been for nearly as long as Rosamund had been undead; they were unshakably loyal and accustomed to answering nearly every demand made on their resources and abilities with grace and efficiency. They made Rosamund and her sole Cainite companion, her brother-in-blood Sir Josselin, as comfortable as it was possible to be, far from home and in a potentially dangerous position.

The second of her letters of introduction went to the Grand Court itself, to be laid only in the hands of Prince Alexander himself, and the third to another resident of Paris, one Veronique d'Orleans, a Brujah described to Rosamund as another diplomat. Rosamund chose to overlook the contradiction in terms that came of using the words "Brujah" and "diplomat" in the same sentence and took that at face value. Her letter of introduction to Prince Alexander formally requested his permission to enter Paris and take up the currently vacant position of ambassador to the Grand Court. It was signed and sealed by both her sire and Queen Salianna, who provided their personal assurances of her status as both a diplomat and a courier. The letter to the Brujah, Veronique, had been written by Queen Salianna and sealed by her alone; Rosamund had no idea precisely what it contained.

With all three letters sent, Rosamund had settled in to wait for the responses that she knew must come, and to her not inconsiderable surprise, Veronique d'Orleans had replied first. The Brujah's letter had been brief and to the point, acknowledging the receipt of Rosamund's letter of introduction and informing her that they would communicate again soon. And, then, Rosamund had waited. She had waited anxiously for more than a week, expecting Alexander's letter of acceptance of her request to arrive any night. A second letter from Veronique had arrived instead. There was, apparently, some sort of difficulty with regard to Rosamund's entrance into Parisian society; Veronique had not gone into specifics as to what that problem might be, but had expressed her intention to visit Rosamund's temporary embassy to discuss the issue privately. A second, shorter missive had arrived from Veronique a week later, stipulating her intended date of arrival, along with a possible need for accommodations for at least three: herself and two retainers. Rosamund had made the necessary arrangements with her host, and now she waited on tenterhooks for the Brujah to arrive.

With a sudden burst of nervous energy that surprised both her maids, Rosamund came to her feet, draped the lap robe over the back of her chair, and stalked out of the oriel room into the main hall. The hall itself was mostly abandoned save for those few members of her own staff on duty that night, the rest of the household having retired some hours before in order to avoid intruding on their illustrious guest's business. The fire in the main hearth was tamped down and the trestle tables all cleared away, leaving a pleasantly wide and open rush-strewn space in which she could express her frustration and excess energy without stubbing her toes against a wall every four strides. She paused on the dais before the fireplace, took a deep, unnecessary breath and expelled it, trying to force serenity on herself. Raising her hands, she clapped out a rhythm and stepped down into the rushes, executing with flawless grace and inimitable style the opening steps of a dance currently popular in Blois. With something to concentrate on besides the seething frustration clawing away at her breast, she attained a bit of calm, until her servants came out to make the last of the preparations for the ambassador's arrival. Their presence obliged her to stop being silly. She stood to one side as they placed fresh tallow candles in several of the sconces and set up one of the smaller trestle tables, spreading it with fresh linen and setting a fat beeswax candle in a pewter holder in the very center. Rosamund watched these preparations in silence and nodded her approval; as soon as her servants cleared the room, she exploded. "Where the devil *is* she, it's nearly *dawn*!"

"The road from Paris is almost as bad as the road from Chartres, *ma petite fleur*." Rosamund jumped slightly, realizing that she wasn't as alone as she'd thought. Josselin had crept in while her back was turned, and now sat on the small dais before the fireplace, his back to the flaring embers. "And it is still more than a few hours before dawn, in any case. Be patient. I'm sure she's on the way."

Rosamund huffed out the breath she'd taken in an irritated little sigh, and came to join him on the dais. He'd brought an embroidered pillow for her, so she made use of it, tucking her feet underneath her to restrain any further outbursts of motion. She knew they looked a pair, seated together that way, he with his fine blonde hair and laughing blue eyes, dressed in the best of the clothing he'd brought with him to greet the mysterious woman Queen Salianna had placed such trust in, she with hair the color of a new copper obol confined by a fillet and a new cotte of forest green that drew out the color in her own eyes. "I just wish we knew more about her, Josselin. This whole situation is just so... so..."

"Political?" he asked wryly.

"*Irregular*, is the word I was considering," Rosamund replied tartly, and rewarded his wit with a poke in the ribs. "Political, I have seen before. Political, I can navigate my way through without the help of some... some..."

"Now, *petite*, give the lady a chance," Josselin chided her gently. "We know nothing about her, except the fact that Queen Salianna places some faith in her, which, in itself, says much. The queen trusts *you* in such a way, as well. Pass no judgments until you meet her."

"I'm trying not to." Rosamund realized she was chewing her lower lip, a habit her sire had always deplored, and stopped. "It's... It's silly, I know, but..."

"But?"

"I keep having these horrible visions." Rosamund's voice dropped to the barest whisper. "I keep seeing her walking through that door, dressed as a man, covered in mud and dust to midthigh, with a face like... like... I lack the words to describe it...."

"*Petite*," Josselin drawled easily, "I think you've been reading too many *lais* in which the she finds out her he is more than he seems, and vice versa."

"You aren't helping, you know."

"I do my best, *petite*."

* * *

The road to the Toreador ambassador's residence was, in the loosest technical definition of the term, clear. It hadn't snowed in any significant amount in more than a week and, while it was windy, the snow itself was covered in a thick rime of ice, preventing the formation of road-blocking drifts. The road itself was a mess of deep ruts and gullies, but at least it was frozen solid and not a soupy quagmire. They made, in Veronique's opinion, decent enough time until they reached the winding side lane that led to the temporary embassy. There things became slightly more difficult: Progress was hampered by numerous obstacles, not the least of which were frost-covered tree limbs cracking in the high wind and falling across their path, or else discharging their catapult-weighted coverings of ice on the cart's canvas roof, the backs of the horses, and the driver. Sandrin spent much of his time keeping warm by clearing debris from their path. Thierry spent much of that same time making dire predictions concerning their high likelihood of being devoured by wolves, or telling dark stories from his grandmother's day about why one should never set foot outside the city limits in the dead of winter. Veronique, for her part, patiently refrained from reminding her excitable clerk that she was at least as old as his grandmother and knew all those stories as well, but instead suggested that, if they were attacked by wolves, he'd survive, being too skinny to make much of a meal. Strangely enough, that seemed to calm him a bit, and he spent the rest of the trip confining his commentary to complaints about the drafty roof and the jouncing of the cart as it wallowed down the road. Veronique could only agree, and hold on.

After a particularly bone-rattling interval of supreme discomfort, Sandrin's somewhat muffled voice sounded, just outside the entrance flap. "I believe we've arrived, milady."

Veronique extracted herself from the mass of coverlets in which she and Thierry were entangled and, miraculously, managed to slide across to the door flap without losing her veil or tearing the hem out of her new surcoat. The lacing was a bit difficult to undo with her cold-stiffened and gloved fingers, but eventually she managed to open enough of a gap that she could peer out at their destination.

The temporary embassy had been described to her as a "hunting lodge," a designation that she rather doubted. She lacked the imagination necessary to envision the new Toreador ambassador to the Grand Court voluntarily spending a delay of unknown duration in a glorified wattle-and-daub shack, stinking of smoke and blood and surrounded by skinning yards and trappers' tents. Her first impulse, as it turned out, was correct. The "hunting lodge" loomed out of the gloom, lit by a pair of lamps bracketed next to the main doors and the light of the gibbous moon overhead. The precise dimensions of the "lodge" were difficult to discern, but to Veronique's eye it was more a fortified manor than anything else, with walls of stone and a shingled roof. Irregular shadows hinted at the presence of outbuildings, and possibly a squat tower as well.

Veronique nodded to Sandrin. "Tell the driver to pull us in. Then go to the door and knock—there should be someone on duty there—and ask that our presence be announced."

Sandrin's hood nodded, and Veronique pulled her head back through the door flap, tucking the sides together but leaving them otherwise unlaced. Behind her, Thierry put the inside of the cart back in order, roughly folding the lap blankets and stowing them in Veronique's daylight box, then retrieving her courier's case from among the rest of the baggage. The last stretch of the driveway was considerably smoother than the first, and Veronique took the opportunity to pull herself upright, brush out her heavy, ankle-length skirts and straighten her veil, bracing herself on leather straps provided for that purpose. The cart came to a shuddering stop, and over the sound of the horses stomping and blowing and their harness jingling, Veronique heard a door opening and low-voiced conversation. She refrained from doing anything that might damage her reception and waited for Sandrin to come open the door flap and help her down. Thierry scrambled down behind her, carrying the courier's pouch over one shoulder and his mistress's traveling bag in the other.

A sleepy-looking page took the driver and the cart in hand. A young man, possibly a knight in service to Lady Rosamund, was standing close by the door, clearly awaiting her attention. She approached him, and gave him a courtesy. "I am Veronique d'Orleans, Ambassador to the Grand Court of Paris, and I have come to speak to your mistress, whose name is given me as Lady Rosamund d'Islington."

The servant bowed low, and rose to hold the door.

* * *

"Lady Rosamund!" Peter came into the great hall at a trot, and barely managed to stop on the fresh rushes. "Lady Rosamund, Raoul commands me to tell you that the ambassador's cart approaches."

Rosamund's heart gave a little lurch and cartwheel of cheer, and Josselin chuckled in her ear. With all the dignity she could muster, Rosamund rose and smoothed her heavy skirts in a single, practiced motion. "Peter, inform Raoul that the ambassador is to be admitted with all haste. Rouse a page and ask him to guide her driver and team to the barns."

Peter bobbed his head in response to these commands, and scurried off to see that they were carried out. Rosamund stood, inhaling calm and serenity and exhaling the desire to rush outside and greet the ambassador—the first official notice she had received from anyone with standing in Paris—on the doorstep. She looked up at the two banners hanging above the table where they would shortly be sitting and tried to extract more confidence than she really felt from them. Her sire's arms and her own, a simple dark green length of silk marked with a single white rose, the traditional symbol borne by all Toreador diplomats.

The sound of the great hall door opening echoed to her ears, and she released the last of her tension with a quiet sigh, letting her hands fall modestly folded before her. Behind her, Josselin rose and stood a pace or two back, and off to one side, a guardian both practical and ceremonial. He wore the sword he was, as a knight, entitled to bear in the presence of all Cainites but princes. Peter returned as well, and took up station opposite Josselin.

Raoul preceded the Brujah ambassador into the hall and announced her with all the ceremony he had in him. "The Lady Veronique d'Orleans, Ambassador to the Grand Court of Paris, craves Milady Rosamund d'Islington's permission to approach and be acknowledged."

Rosamund wet her tongue and replied in a clear and ringing voice, "My permission is granted to Lady Veronique d'Orleans, to approach and be named friend."

Veronique d'Orleans emerged from the short corridor linking the main hall to its doors. Rosamund forcibly restrained a start of surprise. The Brujah ambassador was a very tall woman—she had more than a head on Rosamund herself, and was actually closer in height to Josselin. She was also not, as Rosamund had feared so vividly, dressed as a man. Veronique d'Orleans's hair was modestly covered by a fine white veil bound with a simple circlet, and she was dressed in what Rosamund knew must be the height of current fashion in Paris, in shades of green and blue, a long-sleeved sea-green kirtle and a blue damask surcoat that suited her shape and coloring admirably. There was a faint blush of life about her lips and ivory cheeks. She had done something to make her nicely shaped ice-blue eyes seem even brighter in the candlelight. Very deliberately, the Brujah woman spread her voluminous skirts, lowered her head, and offered an appropriately deep courtesy, which she held. Her servants, who had entered unremarked at her back, offered their own deep bows.

"You may rise, Lady Veronique d'Orleans, as may your companions," Rosamund kept her voice clear and strong, "and approach."

Veronique rose, and stretched a hand out to one of her servants. He was as small and brown as a mouse, with hands that looked quick and deft even in the brief motion he accorded them. He placed a sealed and ribboned document in his mistress's hand; then both he and Veronique's armed protector held their places as she crossed the hall. Rosamund watched her move, careful to avoid becoming entranced by the play of candlelight across fine blue damask or the grace of the taller woman's movements; she was *very* graceful, and Rosamund knew she would be a fine dancer. Josselin came forward to greet her, and Veronique offered him a second, shallower courtesy, and handed him the letter. He broke its seals and scanned it quickly, his fair eyebrows arching toward his hairline in mild surprise as he reached the seals at the bottom of the document, then handed it to Rosamund.

It was the Brujah ambassador's own letter of accredit, and Rosamund scanned it quickly, as well—and stopped short when she reached the name of Veronique d'Orleans's sponsor. No less a Cainite stood surety for her than Julia Antasia, the Prince of Hamburg, and one of the oldest and most powerful Roman Cainites still awake and ruling her own dominions. That explained much: Julia Antasia shared age and influence and possibly origin with Prince Alexander, and any diplomat who operated under her aegis might very well have an easier time obtaining his indulgence, or at least his tolerance. Rosamund glanced up at the patiently waiting Brujah, who smiled kindly at her.

"Lady Rosamund," Veronique said, "I believe that we have much to discuss."

* * *

Veronique permitted Sandrin and Thierry to accompany Rosamund's servant to the kitchens to warm themselves and take a bit of hot soup and mulled cider. She waited until the last echo of their footsteps faded before she spoke again. "I fear, Lady Rosamund, that I do not bear any good tidings tonight. I had hoped to have better news for you, but events have conspired against me in that regard."

If the Toreador girl—*not a girl*, Veronique was forced to remind herself, *not a girl any longer, no matter how young she was when Embraced*—was disappointed by this, she did not permit much of that disappointment to show on her face. "I admit that I suspected as much, Lady Veronique. Please, let us sit and talk." She gestured to the table, clearly set solely for their use. "May I offer you refreshment, as well?"

"I am well for the moment."

Sir Josselin drew the chairs out for both women, and then settled to a position a few feet away, on guard at Rosamund's back. Once they were both sitting, Veronique asked, "I assume that you are familiar with the situation in Paris as it currently exists?"

"I have been kept abreast of events, yes," Rosamund replied guardedly. "There is little—fact or rumor—that originates in Paris that does not eventually reach the Courts of Love, as you may well guess."

"I had assumed as much. The difficulty that arises here is primarily the result of recent years' excitement." Veronique undid the straps on her courier's case laying on the table before her and extracted a handful of wax-sealed reports, depositions taken by Thierry from her various eyes and ears about the city, carefully shorn of any incriminating details of identity, and passed them across the table to Rosamund. "The Countess Saviarre, I fear, is feeling a trifle insecure this season. She has been tightening her grip on the city, and strictly limiting the amount of diplomatic and social congress that takes place under the prince's aegis—not that there has been much in the way of it this winter. She has, it appears, been turning back emissaries since late last autumn. Had my opinion been solicited, I would have advised that you wait until spring to come to Paris."

Rosamund's shoulders stiffened slightly, and she looked up from the papers. "I am certain that my Lady Isouda and my Lady Salianna had their reasons for pursuing this course at this time."

"That was no slur, Lady Rosamund," Veronique said evenly, "merely an observation. As it is, we must deal with the situation as it presently unfolds. I do not think your letter of introduction, and any requests you sent with it, actually reached Prince Alexander. If it did, he has been convinced or compelled not to act on it. We must find some means of dissipating that interference."

"Can *you* not accomplish that task?" Rosamund's coppery brow rose in a delicate, questioning arch. "You are far better established than any other assistance I might call upon at the Grand Court."

Veronique shook her head slightly. "Not yet. My position at court is not precisely tenuous, but it is also not as strong as it could be—not strong enough to successfully maneuver around Saviarre on the issue of your embassy, at any rate. I do, however, enjoy a good working relationship with Lord Valerian, the prince's most capable diplomatic envoy. We may be able to enlist his assistance in this matter. He is one of the few Cainites in Paris who can approach Alexander directly, without Saviarre's interference."

"What will you need me to do?" Rosamund leaned forward slightly.

"Do you have another copy of your letters of accreditation from Queen Salianna and Queen Isouda?"

"Three, actually, and another copy of the letter of introduction."

"I will need one copy of each of those documents, as well."

"That can be done. What else?"

"I will need you to be patient, and to lend me your trust. We are engaged in the same enterprise, you and I. The risks we take are the same, the dangers we face are the same, and the rewards we reap will be the same. But we cannot gain anything by acting hastily or working at cross-purposes. Are we agreed?" Veronique, very deliberately, met Rosamund's eyes. And she did have lovely eyes, a bewitching green-hazel that Veronique could easily imagine men willing to kill and die for.

Rosamund, after a moment of silent consideration, finally murmured, "Yes," and dropped her eyes modestly. "Patience, I think you will find, is my cardinal virtue."

* * *

The night waned, and the three Cainites retired to their daytime chambers, slightly rearranged to accommodate the presence of the Brujah ambassador. Rosamund politely yielded her room to Veronique. Josselin's bed became Rosamund's and he moved, with his squire Fabien, to a pallet in that same chamber. A wooden screen had been set up to partition the room and give them both a bit more privacy as they disrobed and slept, but it did not impede their conversation as they prepared for their rest.

Rosamund's serving women were well trained and accustomed to their mistress's quirks. They assisted her in disrobing, Blanche brushing out the cotte and hanging it up to air, Margery fetching warmed water to bathe Rosamund's face and neck, both assisting in brushing out and braiding her long hair for the day. On the other side of the partition, they could hear Josselin's servant aiding him in much the same way. "What did you think, Josselin?"

"I think it's a little too early to be making any real judgments, *petite*," Josselin said.

Rosamund resisted the urge to throw a comb over the top of the screen in a (probably vain) effort to hit him. "I'm not asking you to *pass judgment*, Josselin—what did you think of *her*?"

He was silent for a long moment. "She... seems forthright enough. I do not think she was trying to deceive or mislead you; she was too direct for that. Whatever else she might believe, she genuinely holds that Countess Saviarre is set against you and must be worked around—but, since our Lady Isouda and Lady Salianna believed that already, it merely confirms suspicions. That may be why Lady Salianna recommended that you work together."

"Evading Saviarre, you mean?"

"Yes. I think—and this is only groundless supposition based on wild speculation, mind you—that there may be something more than simple politics to her interest in aiding you against Saviarre." Another pause, somewhat longer, punctuated by a few low-voiced commands to Fabien. "I was watching her colors. There was nothing I could name solidly, but there was a hint about her that suggested that her interest is less than completely neutral. She comes from Orleans—I could harass Oderic to see if he knows her and inform you of my results. There may be some sort of history between our lady ambassador and Countess Saviarre, though it begs the question that, if there is, why was she accepted in Paris no matter *who* spoke for her?"

"That would be excellent. And, yes, there are more questions lacking answers now than there were before." Rosamund rose, and let her maids remove her chemise. "But at least we can be relatively certain that, on the issue of Saviarre, Lady Veronique and I are not, in fact, working at cross-purposes. The countess's influence on Prince Alexander must be broken if I am to have even the smallest chance of repairing the rift between the Grand Court and the Courts of Love."

"The question then becomes," Josselin said, "what precisely does Lady Veronique stand to gain from aiding in *that* mission—the effort to heal the wounds of the past, and bring the two courts into closer alliance again? Or, rather, what does her patron stand to gain? From what I've heard of her, Julia Antasia rarely meddles in the affairs of other domains, though I suppose she might be moved to take action if the need, or the reward for doing so, were great enough."

"Now, that *would* be wild speculation based on nothing but our own best guesses," Rosamund said. Blanche turned down the covers on the bed, and both of Rosamund's maids set about preparing themselves for rest, one to sleep on the pallet at the foot of her bed, and the other to share the sheets with their mistress, to keep her warm through the chilly winter day. Rosamund herself slipped beneath the embroidered, fur-lined coverlet and linen sheet, attempting to make herself comfortable, even as her thoughts raced speedily enough to banish the beginning tug of daylight fatigue. "Yes... I think you should speak to Oderic... and I will keep you apprised of events in Paris... when we actually get to Paris...."

"As you wish, *petite*. Sleep now. We'll have more than enough to do when we rise this evening...."

"Yes... we will. A good rest to you, Josselin."

"And to you, *petite*. Sleep well."

* * *

The room that Veronique was escorted to showed signs of a recent, thorough cleaning: The floor had been swept, the mattress on the bed turned and fluffed, the linen and coverings all smelled of fresh closet herbs. Even the pallet set at its foot was freshly made up. Sandrin pronounced the door stout as well as lockable from the inside, and the room itself, constructed in the space beneath the upstairs solar, was without windows and completely sealed against light. A chest had been provided for storage, along with the usual assortment of pegs for hanging garments. Rosamund's man Raoul helped Thierry fetch a basin of water and a cloth for Veronique to wash the paint off her face. Sandrin stood guard outside.

As Veronique awaited their return, she went about the soothing evening rituals of her own toilette, and considered the exchange she had just had with the Grand Court's newest would-be diplomat. The brevity of that conversation allowed her little ground on which to base a reasonable opinion, but in that time, Rosamund had nevertheless demonstrated an admirable degree of intelligence and a willingness to act where action appeared to be necessary. Salianna had apparently not been lying when she wrote Veronique and informed her that Rosamund had been sent to Paris deliberately ignorant of all her elders' objectives, of their motives in choosing this time, and her person, as ideal for attempting diplomatic rapprochement with the Grand Court. Veronique chewed that thought over with considerable distaste, then laid it aside for the day. There was nothing she could do about it now, at any rate, and there was always the possibility that Rosamund was a much more skillful dissembler than she seemed. One did not necessarily earn the white rose through the expression of supreme moral rectitude and personal probity, after all, though in the case of Rosamund, Veronique was inclined to grant the benefit of the doubt.

News of one of Rosamund's exploits had come to Veronique some years before, in a letter from her sire Portia, dwelling at the court of Julia Antasia in Hamburg. Portia had not mentioned Rosamund by name—referring to her only as "one of Salianna's pets"—but had described the events as best she knew them: a near-disastrous embassy to the court of Jürgen of Magdeburg, a tangled web of intrigue and treachery, in which the Toreador ambassador came out smelling the best of all the participants, after Jürgen himself. Rumor circulating among the Cainites of Paris had provided Rosamund's name, and more detail: treachery in the ranks of the Toreador embassy, though not apparently at the order or with the knowledge of the ambassador herself, aided and abetted by parties interested in thwarting more congenial relations between the Black Cross Fiefs (the domains of Jürgen's sire and liege, Lord Hardestadt) and the Courts of Love. Rosamund had apparently handled the situation with considerable tact and skill, salvaging what could have been a total disaster, making assurances to Jürgen and his sire that the Toreador malefactor's treason would be punished, and generally rising to the challenge. Veronique rather hoped she would be able to manage a repeat performance in Paris, where both the pressure and the stakes would be higher.

Thierry returned, bearing a wooden pitcher of warmed water, a towel and a facecloth over one arm, all of which Veronique made use of, thinking all the while. It had been in her mind when she departed

Paris to make two stops this trip, one to visit Rosamund and enlist her active participation in the effort to bring her into the society of the Grand Court, and one to pay a visit to her old colleagues Anatole and Zoë, to inquire if there was anything they needed of her, or required at their new haven. They and their followers—mostly Cainite "refugees" from the east, along with a handful of local converts to Anatole's particular brand of worship—continued to dwell outside the city, only barely acknowledged and actively unwanted, a constant irritant to Saviarre and no small number of Cainite Heretics with whom they had clashed off and on for years. Anatole had permission to enter the city walls and haven there, but not with his flock. They were, for the most part, capable of taking care of themselves when it came down to it, but Veronique nourished a concern for them, anyway. Anatole wasn't the most mentally focused man ever to find himself leading a religious crusade and his chief disciple and adopted daughter, Zoë, was herself little more than a child. Veronique looked after them as best she could, and had, in the process, benefited from their endeavors over the years. Now, however, it seemed somewhat more urgent to return to Paris as quickly as possible and recruit Lord Valerian's efforts on Rosamund's behalf. The kernel of an idea was forming in the back of her mind, vague in its precise details as yet, but sure in one thing— she would need all the skill she could muster to bring her thought to pass.

* * *

Jean-Battiste de Montrond did a very good impression of being beside himself with frustration. "What do you *mean* she's not here?"

Alainne looked up from the face of the girl she was expertly rouging, and gave him a narrow-eyed look. "Lady Veronique is not in Paris at the moment.

She will return shortly. And what are you doing in here?!"

That last was fired past his shoulder, at the young woman standing in the doorframe, looking halfway between silently lust-struck and mortally embarrassed at her inability to do her duty. She did not answer, and only took a tentative step away, more seeking the shelter of the doorframe than actually leaving Alainne and Jean-Battiste's presence.

"Go on!" Alainne ordered. "I'm sure there's a student upstairs with your name on his lips." The girl scurried out, chemise fluttering, and Alainne turned the full force of her considerable personality back upon her mistress's guest.

"My dear Lady Alainne," he began.

"Don't you 'my dear' or 'my lady' *me*." Alainne stood and wiped her hands on a damp towel. "You heard me. Lady Veronique isn't here right now. If you've a message for her, you may leave it with me. Otherwise, you are—"

Jean-Battiste slid an arm around Alainne's waist and pulled her close, offering her his most heartfelt smile, along with a dosage of the sincere blue eyes that had won him passage beneath girls' skirts from Brittany to Sicily. "Alainne, you aren't still angry with me over those two little chits, are you? Truly, you cannot possibly be—those girls were flighty! Untrustworthy! They would have run off with the first drover to whisper sweet nothings in their ears and you would have had to replace them anyway…."

Alainne, unfortunately for him, didn't lift her skirts for any man who didn't pay up front in *deniers de provins*. "Yes, I *am* still angry with you about that, so you can scrub the honey off your tongue, take your hand off my bottom, and give me the message if you have one. If not, I'll scream for Philippe and we'll see how high you bounce when you hit the cobbles."

"You're a hard, hard, uncompassionate woman, Alainne." Jean-Battiste sighed, reached into his tunic, and withdrew a note, compactly folded and sealed in wax. "But I'll forgive you. One night, you'll be happy to see me...."

Alainne snatched the note and spun out of his loosened grip, giving him a bump with one nicely curved hip in passing. "Yes, and that night will be shortly after the Last Trump. Don't you have a business of your own to tend to?"

"Is it *my* fault all the best-looking girls want to work for *you*, and so I must seek outside my own establishment when I desire to drown myself in feminine charms?"

"You're so full of dung your ears stink."

"They do not. I washed them just tonight."

Alainne couldn't help but laugh as she went about straightening up her worktable, carefully packing away her store of cosmetic ointments and perfumes. "Oh... all right. I'm fairly certain that Veronique doesn't want you corrupting the girls, but since I'm already corrupt, you can sit and drown in *my* feminine charms."

Jean-Battiste captured her hand and deposited a kiss on her knuckles with a courtly flourish. "You are, indeed, a goddess, and I shall worship forever at the altar of your kindness."

"Oh, stop." She snatched back her hand and swatted him with a damp towel.

Jean-Battiste smiled easily and settled himself on one of the cushioned benches scattered about the room. Alainne fed up the nearest brazier a bit, fetched her basket of dried herbs, and sat down to her idle evening work of making bath sachets. In truth, they'd passed many a night this way in the last several years, since Veronique and Jean-Battiste had made their little "arrangement," exchanging gossip and rumor, idly flirting back and forth, and simply enjoying one another's company. Alainne didn't trust him as far as Philippe or Veronique could throw him, but he was better company than any of the debauched students that made up the majority of their clientele, and had a better ear for gossip than most men could claim. "Has the furor finally died down?"

Jean-Battiste's lips quirked slightly. "That depends entirely upon how you define 'died down.' If you mean, are people over on the isle still frothing at the mouth and proclaiming the imminent second coming, the answer is 'no.' If you mean, has everyone completely forgotten about it… well, the answer is also 'no.' For myself, I'm rather sorry the pitch has died down—the whole affair was good for business, to be honest."

"You noticed that, too? Nothing apparently induces honest tradesmen to drop their coin on wine and whores like the conviction that the world might end tomorrow." Alainne snorted with amusement. "If it'd kept up another five months, I might have been tempted to ask Veronique for my share and retire to some hospitable convent somewhere."

"Alainne, you know such thoughts strike me to the soul—you would be *utterly wasted* on the cloister. Except mine. Mine would have you in a moment." He offered another winning smile, which she ignored. "Hard-hearted. You know, part of this game involves you granting me at least the illusion of hope…."

Alainne shook the pestle she was using to grind bath herbs at him. "If I give *you* an inch, you'll take a foot. And part of this game involves *you* paying for the pleasure of my companionship, which you've not yet done. You have no idea how boring it's been here lately—if I wanted to listen to poetry in a language I don't even speak, I'd move to Narbonne, not spend my time rousting out unruly Latin scholars."

"Ah, my lady craves news. Well, I think you'll find that everyone else is finding this winter to be less than satisfactory on the lurid innuendo front, as well—and you've no doubt heard the results of St. Lys's little follies from Veronique already."

"Losing his head, you mean? Yes, I'd heard. Pity, that. He wasn't a bad sort as far as serpent-tongued heretics go—at least he wasn't the sort of heretic who thinks everyone should be dead from the waist down, or else your only possible destination is Hell." Alainne snorted and shook her head. "I know Veronique tends to favor that Anatole creature, but I can't imagine why—the last time he was here he took the opportunity to remonstrate with the girls about the evils of the flesh and exhorted them to marry for the sake of their souls. Or take up a profession of faith, even if they didn't go into the cloister! Can you imagine Nicolette as a *beguine*? Neither can I."

"Anatole," Jean-Battiste replied, not without irony, "has a more useful stink of piety about him."

"Perhaps, perhaps not. I just wish Veronique would let us accidentally push him into a vat of hot, soapy water every now and again. I'm sure Zoë would thank us. Have you heard from her lately?"

"Zoë? No. They're squirreled away out there in the woods, keeping their heads down, the last I heard. What was left of St. Lys's men and those red friars were both hunting them before the snows started—" He held up a hand to forestall her worried question. "If they'd been caught, we'd have heard something by now, I assure you."

"Ah, good. I'd be lying if I said I didn't fear for that girl, sometimes. I had hoped Veronique could convince Anatole to let her winter here in the city with us—a filthy little refugee camp in the woods is no place for a girl her age!"

"You think a *whorehouse* is a better place for a girl her age?" Jean-Battiste asked, honestly amused on numerous levels by that statement.

"Mind your tongue, snake—this is a whorehouse where she could bathe regularly and learn how to read and write doggerel in Latin."

Further banter was interrupted by the sound of wooden wheels rattling on the cobbles outside. Alainne half-rose in surprise. "That has to be Veronique's cart—she's home *early!*"

"And I fear that must be my signal to climb down a drain and escape before her wrath finds me here," Jean-Battiste rose, and captured Alainne's hand for another kiss. "Can you tell her one thing for me, my heartless beauty?"

"Oh, I suppose… what might that be?"

"The good Bishop de Navarre's party. She'll want to attend it, no matter how personally distasteful she may find the man." A quick smile. "If for no other reason than because I'm providing the party favors."

"I'll let her know. Go, now."

He went.

* * *

Veronique spent the next several nights engaging in the lifeblood of her profession, namely, writing letters. She decided, after much interior agonizing, to accept the invitation to Bishop de Navarre's winter fête. She had, she felt, kept her head down quite long enough. A good part of the responsibility for instigating the religious debates of a few years past—and the ensuing civil unrest—could be legitimately laid at her door; she would have to face any socially unpleasant accusations arising therefrom sooner or later. On the whole, she preferred sooner. Ideally, before she began executing any further noticeable political moves. If nothing else, de Navarre's party would offer an opportunity for anyone cherishing a grudge to make that bias known, as well as granting her the opportunity to read the relative social climate of the court. All things being equal, she doubted the winter doldrums had permitted much tension to dissipate yet. To de Navarre, she sent a politely worded note.

To Lord Valerian, she wrote an even more politely worded letter, in which she briefly outlined the situation surrounding Lady Rosamund's embassy and cordially requested a meeting to discuss some means of resolving that situation. Valerian, she knew, was the truest elder statesman of the Grand Court, an experienced and canny politician, the instigator and survivor of countless intrigues and diplomacies. He had, until the last handful of years, been in service to the Grand Court primarily as Prince Alexander's chief envoy, plying his trade as far east as Byzantium and as far north as Scotland. His face and his manner were well known throughout most of the more civilized Cainite courts in Christendom. When he'd returned from his last visit to Constantinople, instead of dispatching him back to the field, either Alexander or Saviarre had elected to keep him close to home. Veronique rather suspected that wise decision to have been Alexander's; she had observed, as best she could, the public interactions between Valerian and Saviarre, and was inclined to characterize their relationship as coolly professional. They seemed to be allies of necessity, more so even than convenience. She doubted there was much personal loyalty involved in any of the political bonds between them. Veronique had no illusions regarding her ability to deceive or manipulate Valerian. With him, she thought it much safer altogether to err on the side of honest political self-interest. .

Dame Mnemach was another little-seen elder power of the Grand Court, and another potential ally whom Veronique acknowledged would have to be handled quite delicately. The Nosferatu warren of Paris enjoyed little palpable power in the Ventrue- and Toreador-dominated Grand Court, where the high-blooded Cainites showered their derision on the "pretensions" of their "lesser kin." Nonetheless, the Nosferatu wielded a subtle influence Veronique had learned to respect. Posture though they might, there were few among the high-blooded who had never found a use for the talents of the Nosferatu, and some favors were not paid for in coin alone. Dame Mnemach, the matriarch of the Nosferatu, was rumored to be older than the city itself, to have dwelt on Île de la Cité from before the time of the Romans and to have a stronger claim by law and custom to territory there than any Cainite but the prince himself. Those claims were naturally less than respected by the more arrogant members of the Grand Court. There had been, over the years, nearly open bloodshed between Mnemach's kin and Bishop de Navarre over conflicts arising from his violation of her domain. Alexander had made the minimum gestures necessary to smooth the matter over, neither explicitly reprimanding the Lasombra for his actions nor reaffirming Mnemach's sovereign claim of domain, and left it to simmer quietly, flaring up every now and then as new provocations occurred. Veronique had watched the situation with interest, and kept her ear to the ground in an attempt to determine how deeply Countess Saviarre was involved in fueling or perpetuating the conflict. It seemed very much to fit with the countess's past history of playing opponents against each other, then sweeping in to clean up the mess and collect the credit for doing so. Veronique had thus far obtained no hard evidence of any such maneuvering on Saviarre's part, though that hardly proved anything.

A lack of evidence regarding Saviarre's specific malice had also hardly prevented Dame Mnemach from taking an instantaneous dislike to the countess—or, more likely, Mnemach had sources of intelligence that Veronique could only guess at and had all the evidence she needed. The Nosferatu matriarch was not known for her unannounced appearances at court, but when she *did* bother to attend functions or respond to her prince's requests for her counsel, her withering disdain for the prince's chief advisor could hardly be overlooked. She apparently did not believe that subtlety was the best weapon in all cases, though, to be just, Saviarre returned the contempt with interest, and didn't overly trouble to hide it, either. Veronique had been attempting to make direct contact with Mnemach for more than a year, in between various other activities, and her efforts had, in the form of the note delivered by Jean-Battiste, finally borne fruit. Mnemach was willing to meet with her, face-to-face, to discuss the possibilities of an alliance of mutual benefit. Veronique wrote her a short note indicating her understanding of and agreement to the terms required, which she left precisely where she was instructed to, no more and no less.